My Heart Belongs

in

Glenwood Springs,

COLORADO

1°

My Heart Belongs

in
Glenwood Springs,
COLORADO

Millie's
Resolve

REBECCA JEPSON

BARBOUR BOOKS
An Imprint of Barbour Publishing, Inc.

© 2018 by Rebecca Jepson

ISBN 978-1-68322-603-1

Adobe Digital Edition (.epub) 978-1-68322-605-5
Kindle and MobiPocket Edition (.prc) 978-1-68322-604-8

All scripture quotations are taken from the King James Version of the Bible.

This book is a work of fiction. Names, characters, places, and incidents are either products of the author's imagination or used fictitiously. Any similarity to actual people, organizations, and/or events is purely coincidental.

Series Design: Kirk DouPonce, DogEared Design
Model Photo: Ilina Simeonova/ Trevillion Images

Published by Barbour Books, an imprint of Barbour Publishing, Inc., 1810 Barbour Drive, Uhrichsville, OH 44683, www.barbourbooks.com

Our mission is to inspire the world with the life-changing message of the Bible.

ecpa Member of the
Evangelical Christian
Publishers Association

Printed in the United States of America.

Chapter One

Glenwood Springs, Colorado
September 1888

$\mathscr{I}$t was his voice.

The troublesome knot that had formed in Millie Cooper's stomach was there because of his voice. The rich timbre fluttered about the edges of her memory, just out of reach. How could a voice be so familiar, yet so forgotten? And how could her pulse leap at the sound, while at the same time her veins filled with spreading apprehension?

She peered around the corner of the stairwell at the man, who was talking to Dr. Murphy in the office across the entrance hall. He stood against a backdrop of towering golden cliffs and forested green mountains, visible through the office window. His back was to her. He wore no hat, so she could see his russet-brown hair. The straightness in his posture, the neatness in the cut of his waistcoat, marked him an easterner. *That's no reason for me to be so upset.* Yet the clenching in her middle only tightened.

She circled her waist with her hand and smoothed the folds of her starched white apron, as if to soothe away her worries. A strand of sandy-brown hair escaped her coiled braids, temporarily blocking her view. But there was nothing wrong with her hearing.

"No doubt we'll require the services of a midwife before long as well," the man said.

The doctor, usually so unflappable, sounded startled. "Your mother is expecting a baby?"

"No, my brother's wife is. Unless I'm mistaken."

Realizing she was eavesdropping on a private conversation, Millie descended the last two steps and crossed the entrance hall. There were no patients seated in the cramped alcove, where the wooden bench and two threadbare red armchairs formed a waiting room.

The uneven floorboards creaked under her feet as she passed the office and entered the room beside it. She began wiping down the examination table, a frail-looking piece of equipment. Dr. Murphy had taught her to work "antiseptically," a newfangled method touted by British surgeon Joseph Lister. Millie was instructed to clean the equipment whenever she had time.

Once finished with the table, she turned her attention to the medicine counter and started scrubbing the assortment of doctors' tools, scalpels, speculums, syringes, and the like. The maple counter shared a parchment-thin wall with the office, making it difficult to shut out the conversation on the other side. She managed to focus on her task—until she heard the doctor say her name.

"Couldn't do better than Millie, I assure you. She's the equal of any doctor, even if she's never been to medical school. I've taught her all I could these past five years. The only procedure she hasn't undertaken is performing surgery."

Millie knew of course that Dr. Murphy respected her. He wouldn't have asked her to come with him and his grown daughter to Glenwood Springs if he hadn't.

What a day that had been. She'd never forget her first glimpse of the breathtaking valley, dotted with canvas tents and log huts, all tucked in the heart of the Rocky Mountains. The Grand River and Roaring Fork merged on the valley floor, the flowing waterways sparkling in the pale November sun. Smoke curled up from chimneys and steam rose from the hot springs, melting the early frost that blanketed the evergreen trees. Millie recalled feeling set free, like something inside her had loosened upon arrival.

Though delighted that Dr. Murphy had brought her along, she always wondered if he'd done so partly out of pity. She hadn't realized until today how highly he valued her nursing skills. *A poor fisherman's daughter. . .the equal of any doctor.* She felt her chest expand and her lips curve upward.

Then her smile faded. *Just what position is he recommending me for?*

The man spoke again. "My mother's condition wouldn't involve surgery, at least it hasn't yet. She's had these attacks of the lungs, as I mentioned. The severity and frequency of the episodes requires the promptest of attention."

Millie's limbs went cold. *Does the woman have asthma—or consumption?* She had little experience with the former. The latter was another matter. She suppressed a shiver. Sufferers of the disease rarely survived, even surrounded by the famed Colorado mountain air and soothing hot springs that beckoned the afflicted masses.

There was a momentary silence.

"Millie hasn't dealt with asthma much, I'll admit," Dr. Murphy said. *At least it's not consumption.*

"But I've educated her on the subject, and she's proved herself efficient in any crisis. Still, perhaps you'd like to locate a nurse who's more familiar with the malady before approaching Millie?"

"There isn't time. My mother must not be left unattended, even for a few days."

Something in the man's decisive tone struck Millie. *I know him, I know I do.* A fact that couldn't explain the uneasy churning in her breast.

She reached for the nearby microscope and began cleaning its brass tube and various lenses and knobs. As she worked, she attempted to force her mind elsewhere. *Any minute now, that man is going to come through the door and offer me a position.* She wondered what it would be like to have the luxury of tending only one patient. *Well, two.* There was the expectant sister-in-law as well. But two patients seemed an easy task compared to her work with Dr. Murphy. In addition to caring for the ailing visitors that flooded his office, Millie accompanied him on house calls, often trekking to remote homesteads or faraway mines. Nearer at hand but equally trying were their trips to the red-light district, where unmentionable female illnesses abounded. By the end of the day, her heart would be as heavy as her throbbing feet. But even during those times, she knew she wouldn't trade her work for anything.

"Ahem."

Millie whirled, her cleaning rag still in her hand. Her gaze flew to the doorway, where, framed by the peeling white trim, stood the man with the familiar voice.

Millie's breath came to a halt in her throat. The rag fell from her hand to the floor with a soft plop.

It wasn't his aristocratic demeanor or lean good looks that had such an effect on her.

It was the recognition that welled in her consciousness. Oh, she knew him, all right. He was the very man who'd caused her heart to break six years ago, when he'd kept her from marrying his younger brother.

❤

The sight of John Drexel took Millie on a slippery journey, a downward spiral she had no control over. In a matter of seconds, she went from a confident nurse in the Rocky Mountains to a trembling girl on the Nantucket shoreline. The one who was deemed unworthy of a man's love and devotion. *How can I look at him and not be angry?* Worse, how could she look at him and not think of Stephen?

Try as she might, she couldn't.

Her thoughts went back to that terrible day. Her senses well remembered the rapid beats of her heart when the hour finally arrived. Her childhood friend turned sweetheart had promised to meet her in their special spot at dusk. To take her away to a world in which she was someone's cherished wife.

She recalled hurrying along the misty autumn lane, the fallen leaves crunching beneath her scuffed leather shoes. She rounded the corner, the tangy smell of the sea rising to greet her. And there, in the clearing in the woods, waiting between the black iron lampposts, next to the perfect-for-two bench was. . .John.

Not Stephen, John.

Instead of her beloved, she beheld his strictly business, to-himself older brother, who'd never had time to play.

Somehow she knew at once that he was on a mission, that his unbending aim was to keep her and Stephen apart. He'd succeeded too, because she hadn't found the courage to defy him—and because, deep down, she believed his unspoken implication that she wasn't good enough for his brother.

And now, six years later, here he was again. Shattering her confidence, causing an aching swell of memory. . .and, contrarily, speeding her pulse.

Does he even recognize me?

She didn't think so. The relaxed way in which he stood, hands in his trouser pockets, short ruddy curls tilted to the side, indicated he had no idea who she was.

Then there was a flicker in those distinctly blue eyes. *A family trait, that light shade of blue.* But Stephen's sometimes appeared green. *Like the depths of the ocean.*

She swallowed down a knot of pain.

John's gaze slid from hers, and he gnawed on his lower lip.

He knows exactly who I am. The realization that he was caught off guard somehow brought Millie a wave of strength. On its heels came the bracing awareness that she was no longer a timid girl from the fishing quarter of Nantucket. She was a trained nurse, able to bring wellness to the ill. She'd delivered babies, sutured wounds, coaxed fevers to subside.

She lifted her chin. "How can I help you, Mr. Drexel?"

He expelled his breath as if he'd held it in for some time. "Millie Cooper. You've grown."

Hardly flattering, since she was eighteen the last time she saw him. "Thank you. . .I suppose."

A flush crept up his neck. The silence ran on. "I trust you've been well?" he asked finally.

Yes, little thanks to you. "I've managed."

"And your father? Is he—"

"He passed away, shortly after I left Nantucket. An accident at sea."

"I'm terribly sorry," John murmured. After an awkward pause, he added, "The doctor tells me you're quite an able nurse."

"There are many things I might have been 'quite able' at, if I'd been permitted to try." She couldn't believe she'd said it. Her extremities turned numb as she awaited his reply.

He gave her a wary glance. "We're discussing the past, are we?"

"If you want my help, I think we must."

He leaned against the doorframe. "It was a long time ago."

It was yesterday, her heart cried.

He studied her a moment then sighed. "What do you want to know?"

Is Stephen happy?

His wife was expecting a baby, that much she knew. John had no other brothers, only their sister, Rena, so there could be no other expectant sister-in-law. *Stephen probably has several children by now.*

Unable to voice the somehow dismaying thought, Millie searched her mind for something else to say. "Do you still visit the cottage?"

A ridiculous question, since he'd rarely visited his family's summerhouse even when he was young. She'd never understood how he stayed away. She could still picture the quaint cottage, overgrown with pink climbing roses. It was a charming place, perfectly suited to the New England seashore.

He shrugged. "When I have the time."

It was her turn to scrutinize him. "And when would that be, Mr. Drexel?"

He shifted his weight, gaze darting away from hers once more. When it returned, he appeared resolved, his jaw set. "I know your view of my family isn't a favorable one, but I have some very pressing concerns just now. My mother's condition is grave."

She fought an inward battle then nodded.

"Her illness began a little over a year ago, the onslaught brought on by an unknown cause. We consulted with the best doctors in Philadelphia. I even traveled to New York on a number of occasions to seek the counsel of respected physicians there. In the end, it was our trusted family doctor whose opinion I heeded. He suggested a different climate, one that might soothe her lungs, somewhere far from the bellowing factories and thick air of our industrial city."

"Well, Colorado certainly is far from Philadelphia."

"Yes, I thought it a bit drastic. But Stephen visited Denver with Father once, and took a liking to the West."

It was the first time he'd spoken his brother's name, and Millie found it difficult not to flinch. She thought she hid her reaction well, until she saw him watching her intently. When she offered no comment, he hesitated then continued.

"At any rate, since he's the one who'll be living here, taking care of our mother, it seemed only fitting to allow him his choice of locations."

"You're not staying?" The question escaped before she could stop it.

"Only until I see my mother settled with a proper nurse and fitted with a household staff." Grim humor entered his eyes. "I'm afraid the wilds of Colorado didn't hold much appeal for the serving class of New England. Our advertisements in the *Philadelphia Inquirer* and other papers received abysmal responses. Even our existing staff members were reluctant to accompany us west. A coachman, a nurse, and a lone kitchen maid were all that could be persuaded to make the journey. At least, of my mother's servants." He opened his mouth as if to say more then shut it.

He's trying not to mention Stephen again. His caution did little good. Stephen couldn't help but occupy her thoughts, not with his brother standing four feet from her. She saw her former love in the nuances of John's every expression, from the lift of his brows to the unsettling impact of his gaze.

Suddenly Millie's forehead furrowed. "If your mother's nurse came with you, why are you looking for a new nurse?"

"Because the old one ran off with the coachman shortly after our arrival." A wry grin played about his mouth. "A fine turn of events, isn't it?"

She almost smiled. "How terrible."

He spread his hands wide, eyes earnest. "Will you help us?"

Please don't ask it of me.

"My mother needs you."

Her dry tongue could barely form the words. "Your brother's wife— would I be expected to—to—" She tried again. "Are you sure she's with child?"

A faint blush tinged his cheeks. "As sure as a man without a wife of his own can be."

"I see."

He trained his focus on his black oxford shoe, which was creating circles in the hooked rug. Abruptly he lifted his head. "I've no choice but to beg your assistance, and believe me when I say that if I had other options, I wouldn't be troubling you with this."

The retort that formed on her lips died when she looked more closely at him. She saw the tension in his face, the strain in the lines on his brow. She hardly knew him, having rarely talked to him when they were children. But now she sensed his desperation, and it was enough to convince her that his mother's need was real. And Stephen's wife would require care during her time of confinement and delivery.

A storm of emotions filled Millie. How could she face a months-long ordeal of caring for the very woman who belonged to the man she'd once loved, the man she'd counted on spending her life with?

She grasped at a feeble hope. "There must be other nurses who'd be willing to take the position."

"Perhaps, but none in Glenwood Springs."

"There are other towns in Colorado."

"True, but who would see to my mother while I conducted such a search? Besides, how many backwoods mining towns do you know that boast nurses who trained under a renowned Baltimore physician?"

She suspected he was flattering her to secure her help. She wanted to study him but was afraid to. There was something in his eyes, so like Stephen's—and yet so different—that she couldn't quite decipher. *I'm sure he still thinks of me as that bedraggled little girl from Nantucket.*

"I'll think about it," she said at last.

Time ticked by.

She knew he was weighing her.

She glanced up...and nearly lost her breath. In the blue-eyed depths of his gaze, she was transported to another time. Helpless against the memories his scrutiny uprooted, she remembered the stark, unconcealed devotion she'd seen in another pair of blue eyes, looking down at her.

In that moment, a brick-like weight settled into her spirit. This man had cost her a lifetime of happiness. *I can't forgive him, I can't.*

"You must pardon me," she said, a tremor in her voice. "But I fear I have other duties to attend to."

She knelt to retrieve her soiled rag, straightened, and swept past him, apron rustling as she went.

Chapter Two

*J*ohn left the doctor's office, his head pounding. A revitalizing breeze wafted over him, the gust as clean as the pristine mountain peaks from which it had blown. He relaxed his clamped jaw and inhaled deeply.

He couldn't deny that seeing Millie after so many years had shaken him. *Did I even manage to utter a single sensible word in there?*

Fearing the answer, he hurried down the path to the hitching post and mounted his horse. He urged the animal forward, hoping to leave thoughts of Millie behind. The effort met with failure.

The girl had become a woman, that much was clear. She possessed that subtle. . .something. . .that came only with the arrival of womanhood. And like other fair members of her sex, she now had the ability to turn him into a flustered schoolboy.

Though if he were being honest, it wasn't the first time she'd rattled him. With a pang, he remembered that particular Nantucket twilight, when he'd had trouble meeting her damp-lashed eyes. One glance at her, and he'd noticed the new fullness of her figure, the constrained rise and fall of her chest that probably concealed a thousand mysterious emotions. But one of them was obvious—pain.

He tightened his jaw once more. He'd done what he had to do.

And today I did it again. Millie hadn't accepted the position, but he'd offered it nonetheless. And he wasn't about to concede defeat without a fight.

A new thought occurred to him. *Even if I persuade her, our troubles will be far from over.* His mother would be outraged, which would prove unpleasant, to say the least. And an ailing woman certainly didn't need to be distressed, a fact that stung his conscience. Had he done the right thing for her? He reminded himself that he'd had little choice. Still, he shuddered to think what she'd say when she heard he'd offered Millie the position.

He reined in his horse, deciding a slower pace would be better. It was childish, he knew, but he wanted to put off the dreaded confrontation as long as possible.

Too soon, he reached the board sidewalks of downtown, where he'd turn west and head toward his mother's house. As he glanced over the row of two-storied brick buildings and false-fronted wooden structures, he noted that there were only one or two of each type of business. Grand Avenue boasted a mercantile, a dry goods store, two banks, a post office, a furniture store, two saloons, a hotel, a restaurant, and a drugstore. *What a contrast to the many skyscrapers and smoke-spewing factories of Philadelphia.*

Glenwood Springs lay in a narrow valley surrounded by rugged hills on all sides. Toward the east, the hills loomed tall and steep, lushly covered in trees. Toward the west, an immense red-rock mountain, aptly named Red Mountain, created a stark but colorful sight. From certain vantage points, the white-capped Sopris Peak could be seen in the distance to the south, while Glenwood Canyon, carved between sheer cliffs, served as the gateway to the northeast. Like many other settlements in mining country, this one had begun as an unruly place, filled with gamblers and prostitutes. It was becoming civilized, as evidenced by the tranquil church steeple that rose above the houses of town. Such things often progressed slowly, if the seedy-looking establishment he'd passed earlier on Bennett Avenue was any indicator. At any rate, he found that the town's slower pace lessened the tension inside him—a tension that reappeared the moment he arrived at his mother's house.

He'd scarcely gotten through the carved oak door when he was met by two servants, one he'd just acquired and the other his mother's faithful kitchen maid, Beatrice. In addition to the servants, the entrance hall reverberated with the stomping boot steps of the men he'd hired to unload the furniture. He'd offered good wages to anyone he could find out and about downtown. His workers included the town scavenger, the coal-delivery man, the fire bell ringer, and what appeared to be a tramp.

John dodged past the servants and tried to edge around the workers, but the coal-delivery man, a beefy fellow with a soot-blackened face, called out to him.

"Hey mister, where do ya want this—this whatnot?"

John paused. The item in question was a rosewood furnishing of sorts, porcelain knobs and miniature drawers suitable for a dining room—or bedroom—or drawing room.

"Just leave it in the entrance hall." He surged forward once more.

The maids scurried along behind him, unable to match his longer strides. He stopped outside his study door, and they caught up.

"This came for you, sir." Beatrice held out a thin, square envelope.

He took it, broke the seal, and read the bold print.

DOUGIN SELLING SHIPYARD SOONER THAN EXPECTED *Stop* ACT
NOW OR NEWBOLD WILL *Stop*

John sighed and rubbed his temples. Realizing that Beatrice was waiting for a response, he retrieved the stylographic pen he kept in his vest pocket and scribbled a message on the back of the telegram.

He returned the paper to her. "Go find my brother and tell him to send his coachman to the telegraph office with this."

She turned at once to do his bidding, telegram in hand. Before he could blink, the other servant, a chambermaid named Sally, stepped toward him.

"Your mother wants to know what you'd like for dinner, Mr. Drexel."

"I'm not hungry."

He darted into his study and shut the door behind him. He crossed the blue Oriental rug and sank onto his desk chair.

There, in the glorious silence, dark cherry walls all around him, his thoughts began to slow. He gazed absently into the cavernous depths of the hearth, cold and ashy this time of year.

The telegram had reminded him that miles away, he had an estate to manage and holdings to oversee. Many of his investments were like ticking bombs, in need of his most timely attention. He imagined his desk back home, piled high with unanswered telegrams from his New York City broker and unsigned contracts and financial statements from his clerk.

Other images plagued his mind as well. He envisioned his mother, wheezing and pale, her helpless eyes fixed on him. He saw his brother's wife, the picture of health but pregnant with a powerless babe, mother and child looking to him. And finally, he saw the wood-frame house he'd just left. He knew it served both as a medical facility and a home for Dr. Murphy and his daughter. Reportedly, the man had left a thriving practice in Baltimore when he'd heard about the desperate need for doctors out west. He'd settled in Denver and remained there until medical care became plentiful; then he moved to Glenwood Springs, once again meeting a dire need.

A simple white house without even a proper front porch—and a man's whole world is inside it. In that moment, John envied the doctor.

Please, God in heaven, help me do right by my family, whatever the cost.

His prayer was interrupted by a sharp rap on the door. He recognized that particular knock and groaned. He glanced up at the ceiling. *Are You testing me?*

"Come in," he called, but his mother was already tottering into the room, leaning heavily on Beatrice's arm.

He contrived a smile. "I see your helpful maid told you where to find me."

17

"Yes, she's quite a loyal girl." His mother had no sooner spoken the words than she was seized by a ferocious series of coughs.

John half rose from his chair, the hair on the back of his neck rising along with him. His mother's coughing spasms had grown more violent lately. He sank back down when Beatrice circled his mother's waist with a sturdy arm and offered her a lace-edged handkerchief. The girl's movements were unsteady, but to her credit, she didn't flinch away from the unnerving task.

His mother's coughs subsided. She took the handkerchief and wiped her mouth with trembling hands then gave Beatrice a feeble nod. "You may return to your other duties now."

Beatrice curtsied and left the room.

His mother gripped the edge of the desk and eased her waiflike body onto the chair opposite John. "I hear you declined dinner this evening."

As if I'm a child to be scolded. "I wasn't hungry."

She raised one reddish-blond brow. "Not even for beef soufflé?"

He shrugged.

Her appraising gaze swept over him. "You weren't able to find a new nurse, were you, son."

His knee jogged up and down. "You may as well know, Mother, the only nurse in town is Millie Cooper."

Her eyes widened, and she clutched at her plum-colored shawl. "Little 'Sconset-girl Millie Cooper? That lowbred fisherman's daughter—a nurse?"

"Yes, and a good one, if the doctor is to be believed."

She moaned, a pitiable sound. "I should never have allowed my darlings to play with that child. Why did our cottage have to be built so unsuitably close to a fishing quarter?"

Their cottage wasn't merely close to a fishing quarter, it was in a fishing quarter. The 'Sconset neighborhood boasted both Nantucket's premier vacation homes and an assortment of crude fishing shacks.

"I share your regret, Mother." He hesitated. *Just say it.* "Because if we'd never met the girl, she might be more inclined to help us now."

His mother's spine grew ramrod stiff. "You didn't offer her a position, I hope?"

He pushed the words past uncooperative lips. "Yes, I did."

"John, how could you?" she cried. "All the pains we took to rout that girl from our lives six years ago, and you invited her back in?"

He shook his head. "Surely Stephen is past his boyish infatuation by now." *Isn't he?* He loosened his cravat, suddenly uncomfortable.

His mother's voice shook. "Your brother's feelings are not to be taken lightly."

"I only meant that Stephen has Florence and the children to think of now. Please don't be upset."

She sniffed and dabbed at her eyes with her handkerchief. "That girl is not of a certain quality, you understand. Her kind never lacks ambition. Their aims are almost always—" She lowered her voice to a whisper. "*Tawdry.*"

He frowned. "I hardly think it's fair to compare her to—"

She cut him off. "Mark my words, if you employ her, she'll disrupt our lives." His mother regarded him a moment, head tilted. "One way or another."

He steepled his fingers together and stared at her for several seconds. *She's terrified that Stephen's happiness will be derailed again.* "Your son is content," he said gently.

"Is he?" She gave him an odd look.

She's so terribly pale. He forced another smile. "You know, Mother, now that I think about it, dinner sounds excellent. Shall we see if that Mrs. Winters knows how to soufflé a beef?" Hilda Winters was the cook he'd hired only that morning.

His mother brightened, troubles seeming forgotten already. "I'll tend to it at once."

John rang the bell, and Beatrice appeared at the door.

He waited until the girl helped his mother to her feet and escorted her from the room before he flopped back against his chair. Visions began hurtling about in his mind, primarily one of his pallid, sickly mother, joined by words like *tawdry* and *lowbred*.

Does Millie think that's why I kept her from marrying Stephen? Because I thought those things about her? He groaned and buried his head in his outstretched arms, no longer able to withstand the tide of memories the day had wrought.

Millie had been bursting with energy as a child, he remembered. He'd seen her on several occasions, jumping about in the surf with Stephen and Rena, eyes crinkled and full cheeks scrunched up in spirited laughter.

What a contrast to the moment she arrived at that clearing in Kramer's Wood. Nantucket's coastal mist had woven through the gold-and-red fall foliage that night. The dim light had shone from the lampposts on either side of him. Footsteps approached. The mist gave way to a whispering wind, and John could see her face clearly. He knew of course that she'd expected Stephen. But he still felt a twinge of envy at knowing his brother elicited a very different response from women than he did. He watched her countenance fall, saw the wariness in her gaze. . .the dawning heartbreak. Youthful ivory skin and a childishly upturned nose couldn't diminish the soulful beauty of her eyes, a soft shade of brown flecked with gold and green. Those eyes reproached him.

In that moment, it had been impossible to think of Millie pragmatically. Before then, he'd thought of her as what she was—an obstacle that needed to be dealt with. *But that was before she looked at me that way.* It had taken every ounce of willpower he'd possessed to hide his misgivings from her.

And truth be told, he'd do it again.

A steely resolve, chased away by the strain of the last few days, crept back into him. Lamentable though the past was, a few girlish tears couldn't change the priorities of his life. True, that wrenching look she'd given him had twisted his stomach with guilt and his heart with. . .he didn't know what.

Nor could he afford to find out. His single-minded focus was what kept this family afloat. They depended on him to provide for them, to see to their health, to manage their estate, handed down from generations. They required his full attention.

And he would give it—starting with finding a way to persuade the only nurse in town to join his mother's household staff.

Chapter Three

*M*illie carefully peeled the gauze back from the wound. She'd soaked it in warm water, but it still clung to the burned skin. Her freckle-faced patient gritted his teeth against what must have been excruciating pain.

"You're doing well, Freddy—so well."

The boy's mother stood in the corner of the room, visibly pale.

"This won't take long," Millie assured her with a smile. She reached toward the medicine counter, where a bowl of soapy water awaited her. She'd prepared it ahead of time, along with a clean cloth and fresh bandage saturated with iodine.

She wrung out the cloth and leaned back toward Freddy. His entire body trembled, and his bare heels drummed incessantly against the side of the examination table. *This could prove difficult.* But to her surprise, he allowed her to lift his injured arm once more.

Millie studied the wound with an experienced eye. In spite of the blisters and dead skin that coiled around the angry red center, the burn was healing nicely. She'd seen the opposite many times. Patients who waited too long to visit the doctor often arrived with high fevers, their sores oozing and emitting odors that nearly made her recoil.

She began dabbing at Freddy's arm. The boy cried out, a sound echoed by his mother. Millie's forehead grew damp at the painstaking effort of keeping her touch light while still thoroughly cleaning the wound.

Finished at last, she grabbed a towel off the counter and patted the wound dry then loosely bandaged it. As usual, Dr. Murphy's voice rang in her mind. *"Never put too much pressure on a burn."*

"And. . .we're done!" she announced as she secured the two gauzy ends together with a pin.

Freddy's legs stopped swinging. His gaze dropped to his bandaged appendage, and a quavering grin spread across his face. His mother rushed over and lifted him into her arms.

Millie realized she was clothed in perspiration. The effort to be as gentle as possible had gotten the better of her.

She gave her patient a well-deserved peppermint stick and escorted him and his mother to the front door. After instructing him to keep his arm clean and return to see her in two days, she waved goodbye and shut the door behind her. With a long exhale, she sagged against the door.

She'd encountered worse injuries, certainly. At least Freddy had been cooperative instead of hysterical. *Then why am I so depleted?* And where was her usual satisfaction at a job well done?

But she knew. Her present state had nothing to do with her trying task, and everything to do with yesterday's visit from John Drexel.

She'd been unable to sleep last night, her mind plagued by his audacious offer. It was ridiculous to imagine accepting such an offer. It was unfair of him to even ask it—which proved he hadn't changed at all. He was still the same unfeeling man who'd derailed her happiness six years ago.

But she couldn't erase that desperate look she'd seen on his face. The memory caused a roiling disquiet within her.

She did her best to ignore it, and she returned to the examination room. She washed the bowl in the nearby basin, dried it, and shoved it into a drawer in the medicine cabinet.

"Do the bowls really go there?"

The quiet question caused her to jerk toward the doorway, where Dr. Murphy stood, his patient eyes creased by lines of age and his frequent, barely there smile.

She glanced back down at the drawer. *No, of course they don't.* She opened the drawer, retrieved the bowl, and put it in its rightful place in the cupboard above the cabinet.

There was a lengthy silence.

"Care to talk about it?" he ventured.

She knew what the "it" was. "No."

He shrugged and ambled off. She went to the door and watched as he entered his office and sat at his hickory desk facing the wall. She stood motionless for a moment then hurried after him.

"The truth is," she said to his broad, solid back.

He swiveled around.

"The truth is," she said again.

"You knew him."

It wasn't a question, so she didn't answer.

There was another lengthy silence.

"How?"

"I almost married his brother."

He replied slowly, "I see."

She leaned against his narrow secretary, a furnishing hardly able to hold the stacks of research papers and medical records he kept inside. "He objected to the match."

The doctor waited, eyes alert.

"Stephen and I had grown—" Millie faltered. "Fond of each other one summer. He returned to Philadelphia in August but promised to come back in the fall, to elope with me. He even gave me a locket, a family heirloom, to assure me of his intentions." She could still remember the weight of that golden treasure in her palm. She'd traced the engravings with her fingertips, her heart full of hope. *How can something that happened so long ago pierce me like this now?*

"And then?" Dr. Murphy prodded.

"I went to meet Stephen, as we'd agreed. Only he wasn't there. John was. He told me that Stephen wouldn't be coming, that he needed to make a more 'advantageous' match.'" The word burned like acid on Millie's tongue. "I couldn't believe Stephen would agree to such a thing. 'He isn't like that,' I said. 'He doesn't care about money and position.' But John just shrugged. I told him I'd wait, that Stephen was bound to be back next summer, and we'd renew our affection then." She could feel her eyes darkening. "John didn't even let me finish before he said, 'That isn't going to happen.' I asked why ever not, and he told me that Stephen understood his familial obligations, and by this time next year, he'd be traveling the Mediterranean on his honeymoon...with another woman."

"And you believed him?"

Millie tasted the acid again and nodded. "He offered to reimburse me for my troubles, and at first I refused. But the more I thought about what it would be like, staying in Nantucket with all my memories of Stephen, the more inclined I was to accept the money." For the first time, she smiled. "It helped me get to Denver—to you. I'd heard that Colorado was a place with plenty of opportunities for a girl willing to work. It turned out to be true. I got the position at the boardinghouse after knocking on only a few doors."

Dr. Murphy grinned. "Who would have thought that a humble serving girl would have such a knack for delivering babies?"

Millie had discovered her gift late one night at the boardinghouse, when an overdue pregnant woman sent her husband for a doctor. Dr. Murphy arrived, and before long recognized the signs of a complicated delivery. Millie, whose room was above the woman's, had been awakened by her cries. She slipped downstairs to see if she could be of use. Desperate for assistance, Dr. Murphy accepted her help.

Now he gazed steadily at her. "I think I must ask—" He paused and began again. "We've been through the thick of it on many occasions, you and I. Folks in the midst of all kinds of crises—and you've done well by them all. So I know you aren't an impulsive, heedless girl. But this. . ." His voice lowered, became intense. "Millie, have you sought the good Lord about this offer?"

She looked away. A whisper inside, one she'd tried to dismiss last night, arose once more. No, she hadn't prayed for guidance. Hadn't listened to that whisper. "If you knew how impossible the very idea of working for him, of seeing Stephen every day—" She couldn't continue. Despite the many hours she and Dr. Murphy had spent laboring together, it still seemed strange to reveal her deepest feelings to a man. She finished with a soft question. "How can I know if God wants me to do something, when the very idea of it fills me with horror?"

"You'll know." He leaned back in his chair, arms behind his head. "After all, you knew when you were meant to work for me, didn't you?"

Oh yes. She'd known.

She could never forget catching that slippery, red-faced infant in her hands. Later, she'd smoothed the mother's brow, and a warm glow enveloped her at the realization that she'd brought a fellow woman deliverance and helped usher a tiny human into the world.

Now she chuckled. "I've never pleaded so hard with anyone in my life, as I did when I asked you to take me on as your assistant."

"And I only agreed because I was too overworked not to. One of the better decisions I've ever made, young woman."

She flushed with pleasure at the compliment.

"Frankly," he added, "I'd be sorry if you left. But I hope you'll follow the path that's right for you." He held up a hand when she started to protest. "I'm not telling you what's right or what isn't. I simply don't want you to decline Mr. Drexel's offer out of fear or bitterness." He glanced around, expression rueful. "One thing's sure—if you took the position, you'd be bettering your lot in life."

"But I love this place."

"In all its glory," he murmured.

A blanketing stillness descended, like the peace of the first snowfall in winter.

"Where will the Drexels live?" Millie asked after a time.

Dr. Murphy seemed puzzled. "Haven't you heard? Mr. Drexel bought Captain Perry's house. Stephen and his wife will live in the guesthouse on the west end of the property."

The captain's house was an immense Victorian mansion, built on a hillside overlooking town. The guesthouse had originally been intended for the captain's sister and her husband, but they'd decided to remain in the east. Shaken by the unexpected death of his wife, Captain Perry had returned to Richmond to be nearer to his family. For months, folks had been speculating about who the new owner would be. Very few families in town could afford such luxury.

"It's so grand," Millie said. *And so intimidating.* Would it soon be her new home?

Before the doctor could respond, the scuffle of footsteps on the porch drew their attention to the front door. The sound reminded Millie that people were depending on her, whether her future was settled or not.

The door opened and Ben Albright, a millworker who lived on the outskirts of town, tromped inside. He greeted Millie and Dr. Murphy with the simple words, "I reckon it's time."

That said, he turned and lumbered off in the direction he'd come from.

Millie moved forward to retrieve her bag from the examination room, but Dr. Murphy stopped her with a hand on her arm.

"You've had enough troubles today without adding an all-night vigil."

"But you might need my help."

His eyes twinkled. "Luella May Albright has given birth to five fat, healthy babies. I'll send for you if I need you."

Millie nodded, too weary to argue.

The doctor left to gather his things, and before long she saw him crossing the entrance hall toward the door, black bag in one hand and gray bowler hat in the other. He paused and gave her an almost bashful look.

"He was a fool, that boy."

"Pardon?"

"Your young man. He was a fool to let you go." The doctor placed his hat on his head and proceeded out the door.

Millie had to face it then—the question she'd suppressed for years.

Yes, John Drexel had interfered in her life. He'd shattered her hopes and dreams, persuaded her to surrender, to accept a mere monetary token in exchange for love.

But what about Stephen?

Dr. Murphy's statement was a potent reminder that there was another element in this story. *Stephen.*

Had he simply been too weak to stand up to his brother, misled by some sort of brother-knows-best mind-set? Or had he, in reality, never loved her at all?

Millie wound a curl around her trembling finger. She knew that she could contemplate the question for days and not arrive at an answer. She also knew that it made no difference, what Stephen felt back then. *No difference at all.*

Yet if it didn't matter, why had Dr. Murphy, one of the wisest men she'd ever met, mentioned it?

❤

The cot was kept folded beneath the examination table for nights like this, when Millie worked late. Dr. Murphy's daughter, Ann, fretted about Millie walking home after dark, and her fellow boarders didn't enjoy being awakened by her arrival. Ann's presence in the house kept the sleeping arrangement from seeming improper. Tonight, Millie had been detained past eleven o'clock by a child with croup, and when Ann insisted she stay the night, she'd gladly complied.

Now she wished she hadn't.

Why does this cot have to be so narrow? And why couldn't she ignore the questions that pelted her mind without reprieve? Every one of them revolved around Stephen's wife. Millie couldn't help wondering—was the woman beautiful? Graceful and refined? A devoted mother?

She remembered back to a time when she'd grown aware of her own lack of social graces and unkempt appearance. Her father, well-meaning though he was, couldn't arrange her hair or sew her clothes in any way that resembled elegance. Nor could he teach her to behave like a lady. She'd gone to primary school as a child, and knew how to read and write, but didn't learn ladylike manners or educated speech until she met Ann, who became her dedicated tutor.

No doubt Stephen's wife attended the best finishing schools in New England. The woman was probably brought up by nursemaids and governesses, like Rena. Taught to speak in a modulated tone, to hold her teacup just so, and ensure that her skin was white as the driven snow.

Yes, Millie had noticed the difference between herself and the daughters of the wealthy families that summered in Nantucket. *But I didn't think any of that made a difference to Stephen.*

A tightness seized her chest and wouldn't recede. No, she refused to think of him.

She also wouldn't think of the man who'd kept them apart. John Drexel had never considered anyone's feelings but his own. Perhaps he didn't actually have feelings.

Deep down, she knew she was being unfair. Maybe even absurd. Especially when she recalled the pained look in his eyes yesterday, when he'd said he had no choice but to ask her for help. *How would I feel, if I were desperate to rescue a loved one, and couldn't?* But Millie knew. She knew too well.

She also knew that therein was the cause of her sleepless state.

I cannot do it, dear Father. It was expecting too much to ask her to give up her safe, familiar existence and reenter the Drexel family's lofty world.

♥

That night, Millie had the dream again.

The hard-packed dirt beneath her feet was warm, tepid with the muggy heat of summer. A limp breeze blew through the window, a ghostly whisper. The sound mingled with the moans coming from the bed, where a woman lay tangled in her damp sheets.

The small dwelling seemed to close in around Millie, to trap her inside with the sickening odor of willow bark and soiled linens, the latter of which were heaped on the ground in the darkest corner of the room.

The woman moaned. The guttural emission came from the depths of her suffering.

Do something, do something, Millie's mind cried. She tried to move her legs, but they wouldn't budge. She tried again. *I have to help her.* But her feet were stuck to the claylike surface on which she stood.

Do something, do something. The words kept repeating themselves, over and over. They pulsed along with the pounding of Millie's heart.

And kept on pounding, more and more urgently.

Millie jolted awake. Her whole body shook, and her gaze darted wildly about.

The sights around her, the neat rows of medicine in glass bottles on the counter, the stethoscopes hanging where they belonged on the wall, filled her vision. Slowly her heart ceased its mad race. She relaxed against her pillow.

Then she heard it, the pounding on the front door. A mimic of all that had haunted her sleep.

Millie slipped off her cot and slid her feet into her shoes. She threw her shawl over her nightgown, grabbed her bag, and walked quickly out into the entrance hall. She lifted the latch to unlock the door, and opened it just far enough to peer out.

There, fist raised to commence pounding again, stood John Drexel. He barely met Millie's eyes before he spoke, voice tense and words rushed.

"My mother is having an attack. I need help."

Chapter Four

The first thing Millie did after hearing John's jarring announcement was to tighten her shawl over her shoulders. Despite the heat of summer, she secured the woolen fabric in a clutched fist, a shield against all that awaited her.

"The doctor is away," she said. *I'll have to do this on my own.*

John gave her a "well then" look and, without hesitation, turned toward the pathway. He clearly expected her to follow.

She did.

Millie was faintly aware of the crunching of pebbles under her feet, of the sidestepping horse at the end of the path. *No carriage?* But then, there wouldn't have been time to harness a team.

John stopped without warning, and she almost ran into him.

"Do you ride?"

"I'll manage."

He continued forward and untied the horse from the hitching post then flung the reins over the animal's glossy neck. In one fluid motion, he gathered a fistful of mane and mounted. He reached for Millie's hand and pulled her up behind him.

She straddled the horse awkwardly, her nightgown hiked around her legs. Before she could think, John tugged her forward and wound her arm around his middle. She nearly jerked away when she bumped into the warmth of his back, clothed only in a nightshirt. A flush invaded her cheeks.

But this wasn't the time for prudishness.

Without wasting another second, John urged the horse into action.

Millie held tightly to him, medical bag clasped in her free hand. As they raced along the lane through town, her wobbly knees clung to the horse's sides.

Henry Hyde Salter. He wrote the book on asthma, didn't he? Something about pathology. Yes, that was it, *On Asthma: Its Pathology and Treatment.*

She remembered the book, but could she remember what she'd learned from it? Now, when it counted, could she recall the answers she'd so ably given when Dr. Murphy quizzed her on the subject?

If only I had more experience with the illness. A rapid thumping intensified in her chest.

The horse sped past the rows of two-storied buildings to the clusters of little wood-frame residences. Every window was dark this late at night, despite Glenwood Springs being one of the first hydroelectrically lit towns in the country. Fortunately, the moon shone brightly and illuminated the way. John turned the horse westward, where they paralleled the flowing emerald waters of the Grand River then climbed the steep dirt lane that led to the daunting Victorian mansion.

At last they came to a halt. John dismounted and turned to reach for Millie. She felt his hands on her waist briefly before her feet touched the ground.

Bag in her grasp, she hastened up the brick pathway to the house.

No sooner had she entered through the oak door, its stained glass window a colorful maze of shapes, when she heard the sound of racing footsteps on the stairs. The servants were frantic.

Help me, God.

The entrance hall was like a whirling carousel in Millie's mind. She surged ahead to join a young maid on the staircase. She ascended in swift strides, not stopping when the girl glanced back at her, a question in her eyes.

"I'm a nurse," Millie told her.

Then the room ceased its whirling.

Her thoughts grew more collected. Emergencies were familiar territory to a nurse, something she could manage.

Millie reached the top of the stairs and followed the maid along a narrow hallway.

The scent of cinnamon greeted her as she entered a dark room. The lamp beside the bed cast a dim glow on the wall. For an instant, Millie's vision traced the wine-colored pattern of the wallpaper, tiny countryside scenes bordered by flowers.

Her attention was pulled downward to the immense headboard of the four-poster bed, then to her rigid patient.

Millie propelled herself forward. Another maid, older than the first, relinquished her place at the bedside. Millie knelt and slipped her hand onto Katherine Drexel's clammy forehead and glanced down at her taut body.

Even worse than I thought.

Her sweaty red hair lay in a tangled mat, her head pressed back against the pillow as though trying to burrow through the mattress. Her back was arched, chest distended, eyes bugged out in distress.

Then Millie heard the most futile sound imaginable—an attempt at inhalation, a hissing rasp.

Dear God, she's going to suffocate.

Millie became dizzy, almost unable to breathe herself.

She heard John's voice from the doorway. "Do something." The words were low, desperate.

Do something. Do something.

And by some miracle, Millie remembered the odor she'd smelled when she first entered the room. What was it? *Cinnamon.* Words she'd once recited in monotone to Dr. Murphy flooded back to her.

"Ascertain the state of the air he is breathing, if there is in it any known or unknown irritant. . .let the removal from these influences be the first step taken."

Perhaps Katherine's lungs couldn't tolerate cinnamon. *It isn't so common as hay or dust, but. . .*

Millie rose and hurried to the window. She fought her way past the clinging lace curtains and unlatched the lock. With a vigorous thrust, she opened the two enormous panes, and fresh air flowed inside.

She turned and addressed the maids, who stood huddled against the far wall. "Where is the smell of cinnamon coming from?"

One of them pointed to the adjoining room. "There's a s–sachet," the girl stammered. "In the water closet. For freshening the air."

"Take it downstairs," Millie ordered.

The maids scurried off, and Millie returned to her patient's side. She sensed John approaching behind her.

A gust of wind from the window swept over them, and Katherine gasped. Tried to breathe again. This time, a slow, suctioning noise ensued.

Better.

But the panic in the wide blue eyes remained.

"Place your patient in a favorable position; get him out of bed and bolster him up in an armchair."

"Can you lift her up?" she asked John.

In reply, he scooped his mother into his arms as if she weighed no more than a baby chick, and Millie pointed to a velour armchair in the corner of the room.

"Put her over there."

Mercifully, he did as asked without question, setting his mother carefully onto the chair. She slumped against it, limp and helpless as any being Millie had ever seen.

"Place before him a table of convenient height, with a pillow on it, on which he may rest his elbows and throw himself forward."

Millie's gaze shot about and landed on the only possibility in sight, a large dressing table that included a cheval mirror.

"Help me move that dresser."

"Now?"

"Yes, I want to prop her up on it."

He muttered to himself but moved to assist her. Together they hefted the burdensome piece of furniture and edged their way across the floor with it. They set it in front of his mother, and Millie did just as her training instructed. She snatched a pillow from the bed and plopped it on the dressing table, she then grasped her patient's elbows and pulled her into an upright position.

Propped on the cushioned surface, Katherine attempted to breathe once more.

Millie squeezed her eyes shut. *Please, God.* She hardly dared to peek from her eyelids.

Katherine's chest rose and fell in a single, frail breath. A little color, just a hint, tinted her cheeks. But her panicked gaze sought John's.

"Your son is right here," Millie soothed. "There's no hurry, he's staying right here."

Katherine inhaled another quick, ragged breath.

"No hurry," Millie repeated. "Everything will be all right."

This brought on a slower breath. Then another—then a third, one that seemed to accomplish a lifesaving calm.

Relief, like water bursting from a collapsed dam, poured over Millie. She held fast to the dressing table for support and simply stared at her patient. Watched her breathe.

She's not so intimidating now, is she?

Millie hadn't seen much of Katherine Drexel growing up. But occasionally, she'd been the recipient of that sharp, birdlike gaze.

Age had begun to show on the woman's pale face. She possessed a few wrinkles about her mouth and a sag in her cheeks. Her limbs appeared twiggy, like they'd snap in two under the smallest weight.

A sudden sound drew Millie's focus to the doorway. The maids had returned, and they entered the room together, faces nearly as pale as Katherine's.

Millie smiled. "Perhaps your mistress would like a cup of coffee— good, strong coffee."

♥

About twenty minutes later, John joined Millie out in the hallway.

"She's much better." He closed the bedroom door behind him.

"Yes, the coffee should help her recover."

He gave her a quizzical look. "Isn't that an odd drink for the middle of the night?"

"It's been reported that asthma sufferers are aided by it."

His head fell back against the wall behind him. "That was quite an ordeal." His eyes slid shut.

Yes, it was. But unlike him, Millie had an energy singing through her veins, an inexplicable strength she always received during times of crisis. It sustained her still, though the scare was past.

She took the opportunity to study him. Straight nose, sensitive-looking mouth—an anomaly, to be sure—and fringe of dark lashes. Medium height, slim build. Through his flimsy nightshirt, she could see he was well proportioned, lean muscles defined.

You're staring at the man. Her cheeks grew hot.

"I should look in on your mother." Millie started toward the bedroom. "I just needed to collect my breath, is all."

John stepped in front of the door, blocking her path. "Beatrice and Sally are seeing to her now. I wonder if I might talk to you."

She backed the couple of feet it took to create distance between them and waited.

He turned sleep-deprived eyes on her. "I'm asking you, Miss Cooper—won't you reconsider being my mother's nurse?"

I have reconsidered it, a dozen times. Every time, she'd felt as though she was about to drift out to sea in stormy waters, and the waves would swell until they drowned her. It reminded her of the disciples in the boat on the Sea of Galilee, terrified of the lightning, the crashing breakers, the pelting torrent. Each time, she heard the question the Master asked His followers on that day. *"Where is your faith?"*

The potent query was accompanied by memories of the dream. She'd see again the black, brittle curls fanned out on the damp pillow, the eyes glassy with delirium. She'd sense it again, the cloistering atmosphere of the room, the aura, almost an odor, of sickness. Her mind would scream at her to do something.

Well, now I can.

Oh, but she didn't want to. *Please, no.* If she took that route, the tempest lay ahead, dark and foreboding. Yet the stormy sea wasn't vacant, nor limitless in its power. Jesus Christ of Nazareth stood in the boat in the midst of those tumultuous waves, arms outstretched. Lord of the storm.

In truth, His was the voice Millie had heard, prompting her to accept the position. It wasn't a trumpet blast from heaven's gates, just a whisper in her soul.

Not only did her Master ask it of her, her past asked it of her. And her present all but demanded it. She couldn't bear knowing that a fellow being would suffer. *Not when I could be of help.*

She realized that John was waiting for an answer. She fidgeted with the woolen ends of her shawl. "Your mother has changed." She was stalling, and she knew it.

He didn't comment.

Silence prevailed. Finally Millie spoke in an even voice. "Yes, Mr. Drexel, I will accept your offer."

His every feature eased, as if his troubles had been released and drained away. "I expect you'll need time to gather your belongings come morning, before we send the carriage for you."

She nodded, stricken by the chilling jolt of reality. The energy that had so sustained her, surged through her veins and kept her upright, vanished. *Am I truly doing this?* She thought she might faint.

"Do you think you might be ready by ten o'clock?"

She nodded again.

"Where may we find you?"

"The doctor's office will do," she heard herself say.

He hesitated. "And Florence?"

Millie searched her wits. *Florence must be Stephen's wife.* She drew upon every fiber of her resolve. "Yes, I'll see to her too."

His expression was impassive. "I'll go fetch my brother's coachman to take you home." He turned to leave but paused after taking only a few steps. "Thank you," he said softly, his back to her.

Then he was gone.

♥

"I hear I missed some excitement last night."

The words intruded into the serenity of John's hideaway. This study, with its unadorned cherry wainscoting and orderly shelves of gold-stamped books, had become a refuge to him.

He glanced up from his musty pamphlet and reluctantly marked his place with a woven bookmarker. "Smelting the Ores." That's where he'd left off. He'd recently invested in several Colorado mines and a smelting company and wanted to educate himself on their processes before visiting.

Which he planned to do soon.

But first, he had an unhappy caller to address.

He pushed back from his desk with a creak of brass wheels. "Hello, Stephen."

His brother flung the door open wider and entered the room. Seemingly as an afterthought, he jerked off his hat and gave his dark hair a perfunctory pat. Unlike their mother and Rena, he didn't possess the customary Drexel locks. *Well, it's really Mother's people, not the Drexels, who have red hair.*

"Care to tell me what happened last night?"

John summoned a pacifying smile. "Mother had an attack, but she's much better now. You needn't worry."

Stephen smiled too, but it didn't reach his eyes. "Needn't I?"

John would have dearly loved to be halfway to Leadville before word of their mother's new nurse entered his brother's ears. Alas, it was not to be. *He already knows.*

Stephen locked his arms behind him, hands clamped together. Since childhood, he'd stood that way whenever he was angry or upset. "Seems you've been making some pretty significant decisions without me."

Isn't that the way it's always been?

His brother must have guessed his thoughts. "This time is different, and you know it."

"The decision had to be made. Urgently."

"You didn't think it prudent to include me in this one, brother?" The too-soft tone foretold of trouble.

Distract him. John considered his options. *Can't send him to the races, there aren't any.* The wilderness of Colorado didn't likely boast a gentlemen's club either. But it would have been an excellent idea, shipping Stephen off to play billiards with a group of jolly, cigar-smoking clubmen. *What about Denver?*

John tried to appear regretful. "This move hasn't been easy for you, I realize that now. Perhaps you'd like a diversion, something to take your mind off your difficulties here? Say, a trip to Denver?"

Stephen's laugh was devoid of humor. "Sorry, the lollipop and pony won't work this time."

John stared at his brother for several seconds. Then he surrendered with a sharp exhale and gestured toward the chair across from him. "Why don't you sit down."

Stephen complied.

John picked up a pen and turned it, end over end. He stopped abruptly and folded his hands on the desk. "I hired Millie Cooper last night to fill the position of Mother's nurse and Florence's midwife."

Stephen's expression revealed nothing. "Yes, I know. Fletcher told me."

Jay Fletcher, Stephen's loyal coachman, would be the most likely of the servants to turn informant. "Look, Mother needed a new nurse—direly. Miss Cooper is qualified in every way for the task, and no one else in this backwoods town, save the doctor who trained her, would even be adequate. What did you expect me to do?"

Stephen shrugged. "Oh, I don't know. . .ask me first?"

John knew his brother had a fair point, but he wouldn't let on. "There wasn't time."

Stephen emitted a sharp, jagged sound. "I was going to marry the girl, John. *Marry* her."

John didn't reply.

He should thank me, that's what he should do. Stephen had a beautiful wife and two healthy children to occupy himself with. One of them was a fine son to continue the Drexel name and follow in his father's footsteps. *Whatever those might be.* Even before the death of their own father, Charles Hammond Drexel II, Stephen had been an irresponsible playboy who charmed all in his path but accomplished little.

John wondered if he'd ever had a forthright conversation with his brother. Ever really pounded things out until they knew where the other stood. *Just tell him you're sorry for hiring Millie without consulting him.* And he was. But the words wouldn't come.

He became gradually aware that Stephen was studying him, mouth held at an odd tilt.

The silence grew conspicuous. Stephen slowly shook his head and rose from his chair. He walked to the door, and then turned.

"Just so you know, if you'd asked me about hiring Millie, I would have said yes." Then he strode from the room without giving John a chance to respond.

♥

Millie's trunk lay open at her feet, her belongings piled on top of the narrow bed. She had no particular attachment to this boardinghouse room, with its spindly iron bedstead and faded painting of hunting dogs chasing a fox. *But at least it's familiar.*

On the brink of entering her new life, Millie longed to cling to everything she'd known before. When her gaze fell on a particular age-worn envelope protruding from a particular leather-bound book, she snatched it up and held it tightly against her breast. She could only guess the worth of the locket inside that envelope. It didn't matter; she'd never sell it. It contained something far too precious to her. She held the envelope a moment longer then returned it to its place inside the book.

A soft tap on the door hailed the arrival of yet another comfort. This was a real, flesh and blood comfort, one Millie had learned to rely on over the years.

Ann Murphy poked her blond head through the door and smiled. Her smile, like her doctor father's, was faint and fleeting. "May I come in?"

"Please do."

Millie had decided long ago that though Ann might not be called beautiful, the contrast of her brown eyes and fair hair lent a certain appeal. Her usually serious demeanor made it all the more delightful when those dark eyes lit with humor.

Ann entered the room, and in one glance seemed to take in the disorder, the heaps of untidy clothes, books, and keepsakes. She pushed up her sleeves and set to work, folding, stacking, arranging. "I'm going to miss you, Millie."

Millie didn't trust herself to speak. She and Ann had seen each other nearly every day for the past five years. "I'll visit often," she managed at last.

"See that you do."

"We'll talk at church too." But Millie felt like crying. Once a week and an occasional formal visit weren't enough.

"Ann."

Her friend stopped folding and refolding a calico Sunday dress.

"I'll miss you too."

Ann's lips trembled, and she clasped Millie's hand in hers. She squeezed gently then brushed her fingers across her eyes with a little laugh. "Oh, this is absurd. You'll be across town, not in the next county."

Millie wiped at her own eyes. "Yes, and the time apart might make our visits all the more special."

Ann resumed her work, and Millie followed suit. She rolled up a pair of silk stockings and set them in the trunk beside undergarments of equal softness. She lifted the worn book from the bed and placed it in the trunk amid the cushioned folds.

"Do you still have the locket?" Ann asked.

In response, Millie reached down once more and retrieved the envelope from the thin pages of the book—her mother's Bible—a beautiful old volume with hand-sewn endbands. She lifted the envelope's top fold and slipped out the exquisite piece of jewelry.

"Oh, it's lovely," Ann breathed.

The gift from Stephen, passed down from generations of Drexels, was made of pure gold, its rounded edges embellished with carved rosebuds. At its center was a perfect pearl, surrounded on four sides by emeralds. On the back was the letter *D*, written in a scrolling script.

"Do you think you'll return it to him now?"

Millie's eyes widened. Such a thought hadn't occurred to her. The locket was so tied to what she'd stored inside it, she didn't know how she could ever relinquish it. "I tried to send it to him years ago, but couldn't come by his Philadelphia address. But of course I should give it back to him now."

Ann smoothed the delicate chain between her thumb and forefinger. "Does the sight of it bother you?"

Millie weighed her answer. "No, not really. At least, it hasn't for a long time. I was busy, you see, learning from your father, focused on my nursing. But now. . ."

"It must be hard, all of this resurfacing." Ann hesitated. "Will it be difficult, being near Stephen every day?"

Millie knew she could tell Ann anything, that her friend would never betray a confidence. *Just as I would never reveal a secret of hers.* Like the fact that Ann was sweet on the young minister, Louis Warren. She'd confessed as much to Millie one night after an evening service. It made sense—Ann would be the ideal minister's wife. She was cultured, educated, selfless. She taught Sunday school and made jams and quilts for charity fundraisers. She and Reverend Warren worked well together. He seemed to enjoy her company, and everyone seemed to view them as an obvious match. Yet he still hadn't declared himself.

Millie had decided months ago that her friend should consider other options. The emotional ties to the reverend might be keeping her from other opportunities. But when Millie broached the subject, she'd met with staunch silence.

None of this explained Millie's difficulty in confessing her innermost feelings regarding Stephen now. *Maybe it's because I don't understand them myself.*

"I don't suppose being in his company will be terribly comfortable," she said finally. "I was engaged to the man. Now he's married, happily settled, no doubt." It stung, but it was the truth.

Later, after Ann departed, Millie closed the trunk and turned the key with a final-sounding click. She walked downstairs to the rough-hewn main room and said goodbye to the boardinghouse matron, a sharp-tongued miner's wife who took in boarders for "extry cash."

Next, Millie went to the doctor's office and packed whatever supplies were hers, along with a few items Dr. Murphy insisted she take with her.

That goodbye was harder.

All the while, as she bade farewell to her old life, Millie tried to ignore the shadow that snaked upward from her heart to her mind. Surely it couldn't be so bad, nursing one old woman and delivering a single small baby. . .could it?

Chapter Five

"This will be your room." The maid opened the door, which banged against the bed in the tiny upstairs compartment.

Millie leaned through the doorway and glanced about. The ceiling sloped down to meet the wall, attic-like. The wallpaper was feminine but garish, strewn with large posies and mint-green leaves. *Was this once a ladies' dressing room?*

Millie turned to the maid, who'd introduced herself as Sally. The girl was all elbows and angles, and had stiff yellow hair. "Mightn't I stay in the servants' quarters with the rest of you?"

"Well. . ." Sally looked one way, then the other. She edged closer to Millie. "The missus said you aren't to be treated as one of us, being her particular nurse and all."

Millie gazed again at her new residence, so silent and bare, and felt her shoulders droop. The bed was covered by a red paisley quilt, an appalling combination with the posy wallpaper. There was no mirror on the wall, no water pitcher on the dresser. Millie tried not to notice the way the looming wardrobe blocked the light from the window. "It's just so secluded."

"At least you got yer own space."

"But what if I'd rather be below stairs with everyone else?"

A shuttered look entered Sally's eyes. "Doesn't seem quite possible,

miss. You're not to be treated as an equal. 'Specially by a chambermaid."
With that, she turned and walked off, but added over her shoulder, "The
missus will see you in her sitting room when you're finished getting
settled."

Millie watched her leave then stepped through the doorway. The
floorboards squeaked as she crossed the room to her trunk. Stephen's
coachman had brought it upstairs and, evidently, plunked it in the widest
space available, in front of the wardrobe.

She didn't mind that her new quarters were so small. The bareness
was nothing new either. Her boardinghouse room hadn't been the least
bit elegant, not to mention her father's dingy fishing shack in Nantucket.
At least Papa was there with me.

Millie fought the sudden sting in her eyes. How lonely her new life
seemed. She glanced out the window and saw that the town lay below
to the east. The sight of it was a reminder of what she'd left behind.
She'd spent countless hours among its citizens, binding wounds, cool-
ing fevered brows, ushering indignantly squalling babies into the world.
After a long day of making house calls, she'd always loved hearing the
peal of bells as H. B. Waltz clanged down the street in his ice-delivery
wagon, chased by a mob of hot, thirsty children. She loved the wild,
savory aroma of venison that drifted up from Katie Bender's restaurant,
the sterile, medicinal scent of Will Parkison's pharmacy. She even loved
the cheap, brassy perfume of the red-light district. Though hardened and
cynical in manner, residents of the brothels knew her by name. With
ailments not proper to speak of, they always greeted Millie with a desperate sort of gratitude.

Of course they did. They needed me.

But then, didn't Katherine and Florence Drexel need her too?
Though from very different backgrounds, and with all the advantages
wealth and status could provide, these two women might just be as desperate as the girls on Bennett Avenue.

At the thought, Millie sniffed away her childish tears.

It took a great deal of heaving, but she finally shoved her trunk away from the wardrobe doors. She unlocked it and began hanging her dresses in the wardrobe. When the task was finished, she laid her undergarments in the dresser drawers and propped her little mirror on the wooden surface. She unpacked her few books, cherished works by Dickens, Shakespeare, and Emily Bronte, and stood them in a neat row beside the mirror. Lastly, she lifted out her Bible, careful not to let the envelope slip from the worn pages.

A squint in the mirror and quick pinch of her cheeks, and she was ready to face her new patient.

As Millie made her way down the hall toward the staircase, every step felt like a risk. The chance of seeing Stephen, his expectant wife, or domineering older brother, was very real. In spite of recent glimpses into a softer side of John Drexel, Millie still felt wary. If he proved to be the callous man she'd suspected he was all along, she'd do well to avoid him. And anyway, whatever kind of man he was, the fact remained that he'd hurt her once. *Or was it Stephen?* Millie had difficulty believing her former love capable of hurting anyone. *No, it was John.* So she must be vigilant to safeguard herself from him.

Fortunately, she reached the bottom of the stairs without seeing anyone. She glanced around the entrance hall, a spacious, high-ceilinged room that contained a crystal chandelier and immense Oriental rug. In the middle of the rug stood a lace-covered table that displayed a bountiful floral arrangement. *Which room is the sitting room?* Her gaze went to and fro between four different doorways.

The door at the back opened, and a maid appeared. Millie recognized her as one of the maids who'd been attending Katherine during the night. Sally was the other.

"I'm looking for the sitting room," Millie said. "Would you be so kind as to direct me?"

"You're wanting Mrs. Drexel?" Unlike Sally, this girl seemed self-possessed, with tidy brown hair and even features.

Millie nodded.

"She'll be in the sitting room in her bedroom." The maid gestured to the door on the right. "Not here, in the formal drawing room."

If the girl intended to make Millie feel ignorant, she'd succeeded.

The maid peered in either direction, like Sally had, then drew nearer to Millie. "See, miss, the missus doesn't venture downstairs often. Daren't go against the orders of her doctor in Philadelphia. He was mighty particular about keeping her from too much excitement."

Millie's hackles lowered. "But why keep her shut in her room like that?"

The maid shrugged. "A patient in her delicate condition shouldn't be climbing up and down stairs, I suppose. And the doctor practically forbade her to go outside." She lowered her voice. "I'm Beatrice, by the way."

Millie smiled at her. "I'm Millie."

"Yes, miss, I know who you are. But you're to be Miss Cooper to us."

Millie sighed inwardly. She must mend this uncomfortable situation with the servants as soon as possible. *And poor Mrs. Drexel—it can't be good for her to be cooped up in that dark room all the time.*

Beatrice departed, and Millie returned upstairs. She went down the hallway and rapped softly on Katherine's door.

"Come in," said the reedy voice from inside.

Millie entered.

In an alcove off to one side, there was indeed a sitting room, partially blocked from view by a large dressing screen. Half-lying, half-seated on a floral chaise, was the woman of the house herself.

In the light of day, she didn't seem quite so fragile. Her red-blond hair was swept into a knot at the base of her neck, her mouth tinted with a rosy flush. And though her breathing sounded congested and the skin over her cheekbones appeared paper-thin, there was nothing weak about her gaze. She stared with piercing eyes at Millie.

"Don't just stand there, girl. Go get—" A series of coughs interrupted her. "Go get my sachet."

"The cinnamon one?" The words came out on their own, apart from Millie's dazed wits.

"Yes. It's in the water closet."

"B—but I told the maids to—"

"And they did as you commanded." Katherine primly lifted her tea-cup from the porcelain tray-table in her lap. She brought the cup to her lips and took a sip. "The sachet is mine. I want it."

She's spoiled, Millie realized, emerging abruptly from her daze. *Like a child.* Another awareness seeped in. Her new patient might well prove complex, difficult, and shrewder than she appeared. Only one thing was certain. *She's not going to be sniffing any cinnamon sachet today.*

The nurse within took over. Millie met the icy-blue stare without blinking. "I think you might be adversely affected by cinnamon, Mrs. Drexel. Perhaps by several things. I cannot risk provoking another attack by exposing you to so strong an odor."

"Mighty high-sounding, aren't we?"

Katherine said no more, and Millie knew she'd won the first battle. She softened her tone. "Would you like some more tea? I'd be glad to refill the pot for you."

Two clawlike hands swooped down and grasped the delftware tea-pot, preventing Millie from taking it.

Millie almost laughed. She hesitated only a second then knelt and reached to touch Katherine's forehead, like she had the night before. She paused. It was one thing to act so boldly during an attack, when the woman was hardly aware of anything but her own struggle for life. *But now she's awake. Will she pull away?*

The motherless child within Millie wasn't quite ready to find out. She withdrew her hand and sat back on her heels. "How are you feeling this morning, Mrs. Drexel? Feverish at all?"

Katherine sniffed. "I would feel better if I had a proper nurse."

Millie bit her tongue. *If I'm not a proper nurse, why are you making the servants tiptoe around me?* She stood and smoothed the wrinkles from her dress. "It's a lovely day. Maybe you'd like to venture outdoors? I would assist you of course." *Please say yes, it might do you some good.*

Somehow, although Millie was the one standing, Katherine looked down her sharp nose as she replied under her breath, "And risk being seen in the company of the fisherman's daughter?"

Millie scarcely heard the woman's words, but hear them she did, and she felt as if a spray of cold seawater had washed over her. "Pardon?"

This time there was no subtlety. "Don't think for one moment that I've forgotten your common origins, my dear."

Millie's spirit sank. Katherine Drexel considered her beneath the family. *I should have expected it.* After all, John had implied as much that night in Nantucket. But this was different. The matter was confirmed, instead of merely suspected. Even more humiliating, the truth of that night was finally revealed. If John was anything like his mother, he'd kept her from marrying Stephen because he thought she'd be an embarrassment to his family.

Millie wanted to seethe at the woman, to rage. *Can't you see it doesn't matter? Can't you see that your son is married to someone else now?*

Instead she bowed her head, stomach roiling. The thought of spending day after day with this woman made her nauseous. She was trapped, with no escape in sight. The velvety walls around her, the thick valances at the windows, seemed to cage her in. If only she could flee, race down the stairs and burst through the front door into the sunshine. Breathe and breathe of the pure mountain air.

"My other nurse used to read books to me." Katherine's voice was as matter of fact as a young girl's, as though nothing unpleasant had happened. "I don't suppose you know how to read."

"Yes." Millie spoke the word with undue force. "I do." Katherine waved her hand toward a bookcase on her left. "The books are over there. Sensible volumes, every one of them. I can't abide those frivolous fairy tales girls read nowadays."

Millie nodded numbly and went to the bookcase. She skimmed the various titles with a grimace. There wasn't a single book that looked interesting. Beautiful though the covers were, all seemed to contain droning works. Men of old, masters of science and philosophy, abounded here. *An ailing woman doesn't need to hear lectures and essays.* Katherine should be immersed in inspiring stories, tales that raised her out of her troubles.

Millie's gaze quit roving across the titles abruptly. *I don't know why I should care.*

She selected a wide volume that promised to recount the particulars of the rise and fall of Athens, and then returned to her haughty patient.

❤

Soft snores told her that Katherine had fallen asleep. Millie laid aside the book, carefully lifted the tray-table from Katherine's lap, and set it on the nearby table.

A single labored breath caused Millie to stop short. *Please, please don't have another attack.* Not right now. Not when it took all her might to bear up under the words that continued to mock her.

"Don't think for one moment that I've forgotten your common origins."

Oh, she wouldn't. This wisp of a woman with the narrow chin and all the strength of a newborn calf had made certain of that.

The snores began again, more steadily this time, and Millie reached for the tray and moved toward the door. She knew this was an excellent opportunity to examine her patient, but she couldn't summon the energy just now.

She went in search of the kitchen, ever alert to the possibility of meeting one of the Drexel men—or the other Drexel woman. Of course, even if she managed to delay the encounter, she would eventually be obliged to call on the younger Mrs. Drexel. To meet the beautiful children she'd borne to Stephen. *Unless the child she's carrying is their first.* It was a feeble hope, and at any rate, what did it matter? They'd all gone on with their lives, and so should she.

She did her best to focus on her mission and soon arrived in the entrance hall. She opened the first door she came to, a dining room. The next was a library, and after that a study. The door at the back of the hall opened to a staircase with only three stairs, and she descended them into a dimly lit corridor. A crashing sound, a banging of pots and pans, led her to the kitchen. When she entered, the noises came to a halt.

Two feminine occupants stared at her for a moment then returned to their work. One of them, Beatrice, stood toward the back of the room in the scullery, washing dishes in a copper basin and setting them to dry on a wooden drainboard. The other, an older woman wearing a white cap atop her gray-flecked black hair, pounded dough on a sturdy worktable in the main room.

"I'm here to bring back the tea tray." The flat bricks of the floor and dense stone of the walls seemed to absorb Millie's words.

The woman kneading the dough jerked her chin toward a set of shelves across from her. "You can put it over there."

Millie walked to the shelves and set her burden down. She started back toward the door then stopped. "I don't wish to cause you any trouble. But it's just the three of us, and I've been wondering—it's awfully quiet in the house. Are there only you two and Sally?"

The woman nodded curtly.

Beatrice joined them from the scullery and began making a list on her splayed fingers. "Mrs. Winters here is the cook, Sally is the chambermaid, I'm the kitchen maid. We still need a coachman, and perhaps a butler or footman."

"Perhaps?"

The maid shrugged. "It's a small house."

It is? Then Millie remembered that Beatrice had accompanied the Drexels from Philadelphia, a city with many houses larger and finer than this one.

Mrs. Winters put her hands on her plump hips and shot Beatrice a look. "Miss Cooper's place isn't below stairs, my girl. Best we let her be on her way."

Millie knew she'd just been asked to leave, and she moved to comply. But again she hesitated. She wanted to ask them about John, she realized. Surely it wasn't strange to wonder if the master of the house was lurking around some corner, ready to judge one's every deed.

"Is Mr. Drexel at home?"

"Which one?" came a voice from behind her.

She turned and saw Sally, straw-like hair, bony limbs and all, in the doorway.

"I couldn't help overhearing," the girl told Mrs. Winters. "The butler's pantry is awfully close by, you know."

Mrs. Winters threw up her stout hands. Flour puffed everywhere. "You girls will be the death of me, with all your eavesdropping ways. Fraternizing amongst ourselves"—she inclined her head meaningfully toward Millie—"will be permitted only below stairs."

Sally emitted a gleeful squeal and scooted over to the table. She wedged herself between Beatrice and Mrs. Winters and selected a carrot from a silver platter. She looked at Millie as she took a big chomp. "Which Mr. Drexel are we trying to dodge?"

Both. But Millie wasn't willing to admit such a thing. "I was surprised, is all, not to see the elder Mr. Drexel today. He lives here, doesn't he?"

Sally nodded. "But he's gone," she said around another bite of carrot. "He's at Mr. Stephen's, helping find more servants."

Or avoiding me? The question was hard to ignore, even with three sets of eyes on her. It seemed that John wasn't a bit keener on seeing her than she was him. *Or perhaps he's merely eager to escape a house filled with women.* Or maybe Stephen truly did need his help. Whatever the case, his absence suited Millie just fine. It was easier to conceal her bitterness toward him if he wasn't there.

"Is it really so important that I don't associate with any of you?" she asked.

Beatrice and Sally exchanged glances.

"The missus was most insistent on it," Beatrice admitted.

"But why?"

Sally gulped down her bite of carrot and took another. "There's servants, and then there's *servants*. You know, lady's maids, governesses, and the like. 'Least, that's what I learned since coming to work in this uppity house."

Millie remembered the governesses she'd seen strolling babies along the sidewalk in Nantucket, their only companions their small charges and each other. Like them, she was to be virtually friendless.

A creeping suspicion wound its way into her mind. *Katherine Drexel doesn't consider me above anyone.* Millie wasn't being treated with respect because of her station, she was being deliberately ostracized, made to feel unwanted and alone. Her depressing new room verified the fact as well. These were calculated attempts to cause her to resign her post.

Millie gave Sally and the others a determined smile. It was time to return to her duties upstairs. Whatever Katherine Drexel thought of her, the truth remained that she was responsible for the ailing woman. And she'd care for her, if it killed her.

Chapter Six

*T*he often fruitless quest for servants and lack of sleep had taken its toll on John. Millie's arrival had helped, but he still lay awake at night, sure his mother would have another attack. *I hope Millie and Mother are getting along all right.* He'd steered clear of those particular deep waters, intent on avoiding distractions. Millie, he feared, would prove to be exactly that.

He glanced around Stephen's study. No mounds of paperwork, or any other kind of work, cluttered the desk, only an expensive-looking collection of tin soldiers in a wooden box with a glass lid. A nearby bookshelf held more treasures, souvenirs from exotic lands. A rifle hung over the door, and above the hearth was a majestic elk, three-fourths of the wall dominated by its antlers.

Stephen, who'd escorted the latest candidate to the front door, returned and plopped onto his chair. "How many contenders have we seen now? Twelve?"

John didn't reply. He gestured toward the elk. "How much did that little hunting expedition cost me?"

Stephen grinned. "A beauty, isn't he?"

John sighed. *Yes, brother, your achievements are remarkable.* He rubbed his face with weary hands. "Thirteen. Thirteen applicants for the position of Mother's coachman. None this drunk though."

Stephen chuckled. "He managed to win the prize, didn't he?"

"What are we going to do?"

His brother shrugged. "Nothing."

"Oh, now there's a fine idea."

Stephen reached for the box of soldiers and began standing them in a row on his desk. "Mother scarcely leaves the house. There's no hospital to rush her to, and even if she gets well, she can't be expected to traipse off and shop at Wanamaker's. There *is* no Wanamaker's." He knocked down the first soldier, which knocked down the next, and the next. "Why the devil does she need a coachman?"

John opened his mouth to answer then paused. Why indeed? A woman in their mother's condition wouldn't require a carriage often, and when she did, she could simply send for Stephen's coachman. "Would Fletcher mind, do you think?"

His brother shrugged again. "I don't know why he should. He'd probably just as soon drive Mother as drive me or Florence—or worse, our savage children."

John laughed in spite of himself. "They're not savage."

"Let's just say that we miss the good Miss Wenton."

Miss Wenton was the children's former nursemaid, a kindhearted but stern Pennsylvanian reared by Quaker parents. Not wishing to be parted from her family, she hadn't accompanied the Drexels to Colorado.

"Without her," Stephen said, "the children have become unruly. I don't blame Florence, not when she's so tired."

John pretended to examine one of the soldiers. "Yes, I've noticed she hasn't been quite herself."

It was a broad hint. He wanted Stephen to tell him, officially, the cause of Florence's recent fatigue. It was a delicate topic, he knew, even when broached in private. *But does he imagine I won't notice when his third child suddenly appears?*

"My wife hasn't been feeling well lately." Stephen shot John a sidelong glance. "A blockhead could deduce the reason why."

A grin twitched John's lips. *Fair enough.* "Talk to Fletcher, Stephen.

Dividing his duties between the two households would increase his workload, and he should be forewarned."

"Of course."

"We can't afford to lose another servant, especially one we've little hope of replacing."

Stephen's eyes darkened. "You think I don't know that?"

I think you'd rather be hunting or playing billiards than overseeing your staff. "Forgive me. I'm sure you do understand." Not a bit sincere, but he had no desire to make things worse between him and his brother.

Stephen's mulish manner faded, soon replaced by a firm squaring of the jaw. "Jay Fletcher is a good man. He won't let us down."

John studied his brother a moment. An inkling wormed its way into his mind. Was it possible that Stephen cared more about managing his own affairs than he'd let on? Had he actually overseen his household with some degree of competence? Earned and kept his servants' loyalties?

No. Stephen was simply a charmer. It required little effort on his part.

John rose from his chair and clapped his hat on his head. "I should be going. I have a train to catch first thing in the morning."

Stephen rose as well and walked with him to the doorway. "How long will you be away?"

"It depends. This is the first time I've had the opportunity to visit our mines here. I sent my agent, and if he's to be believed, we're in just far enough with the coal. But something tells me a controlling stake in the smelting industry will become vital soon. I'm considering pulling out of some of our silver interests to invest more heavily in smelting." He didn't know why he was telling this to Stephen. *He's not even listening.* His brother kept fidgeting with the door lock, flipping the brass latch back and forth.

"Sounds fun," he said.

"Fun is not a requirement for conducting business."

The dark flash returned to Stephen's eyes.

"Just. . .take care of things here, will you?" John attempted a smile. "Please."

Stephen hesitated then nodded.

John couldn't help pressing the matter. "If anything happens with Mother, you'll—"

"I'll send for you. Or see to the problem myself. Now go."

And so he did.

But as he followed the trail through the grove of pines to his mother's house, a seed of doubt began to make itself known. Wasn't it risky, after all, to leave an ailing woman in Stephen's care? Was John's earlier hope realistic, that there might be more to his brother than he'd realized? *How many times did Father pay bail to that two-bit Philadelphia jail because of Stephen?* For silly crimes too, such as throwing rotten eggs at a neighbor lady's window, or starting a brawl at a local tavern. *He's sure to muddle things up, like he has so many times before.* Like he would have six years ago, if John hadn't intervened.

No. He couldn't leave his family in Stephen's care.

He entered his mother's front door and proceeded into the entrance hall. With a sideways step, he circumvented the table and its gigantic bouquet of flowers. Each movement felt weighted. He was growing aware of an increasing urge to talk to someone, to share his burdensome load. For so long, he'd carried it alone. It had become second nature to grit his teeth and keep pressing on. He'd thought it unfair to expect another human soul to shoulder what should be his to bear.

Yet now he lifted his eyes to the heavens, to the One whose voice he'd been taught by his mother to heed, from his earliest memories. *Where do I turn?*

It was subconscious, he was certain. It couldn't have had anything to do with his prayer—surely the Lord knew how to direct earthly affairs better than that. But somehow he found his steps leading him toward the kitchen, where the servants often gathered. *Maybe she'll be there, fetching coffee or something.* Then he could speak to her without his mother overhearing.

He'd almost reached the door at the back of the entrance hall, when it swung open and Millie appeared. She glanced up and skidded to a halt when she saw him.

"Careful," he said, and instinctively reached to steady her.

She backed away. He withdrew his hand. *Not a very promising beginning.* He toyed with the brim of his hat. "I see we're continuing with the coffee treatment." He nodded toward the silver coffee service she held.

She tightened her grasp on the tray and backed farther away. She hit the door behind her, and it closed with a bang. The sound seemed thunderous in the silent room. It echoed off the ceiling and walls and vibrated off John's frayed nerves. *Am I an ogre, Miss Cooper, that you cringe away from me?*

She loosened her hold on the handles and released a suppressed breath. "You startled me. The house is usually so quiet, with only us women about."

He stood frozen for an indiscernible amount of time. How was it that he'd forgotten the effect of those down-swept lashes? Forgotten how her pixie-like features made him want to strap on a sword and march out to defend her against some unseen foe?

This was a mistake.

He called upon his flagging willpower, to no avail. Fascinated, he stared at her strong, determined chin, complete with its winsome dimple. *Of course, it's not terribly strong now when it's trembling.* Her full lips, indented on top, must have been dry, because she licked them. *Dry mouth, trembling chin. . .* What could he have done to make her shrink from him like this? He'd never spoken harshly to her, at least not that he could remember.

She gave him a skittish glance, half a smile, and suddenly, he knew. Intuition hadn't revealed it to him, nor had experience. He had neither where women were concerned. But somehow, he'd solved the mystery.

She's flustered. Not scared, flustered. He was unable to stop himself then from finding her gaze. . .and holding it until she blushed. He'd disarmed her, and it filled him with a before-unknown mix of power and tenderness. *A ladies' man might take advantage of this situation.* But smooth, polished ways with women had always eluded him, so he did the only thing he knew to do—get straight to the point.

"I'm leaving for Leadville in the morning. I thought you should know."

❤

Why is he telling me this? He certainly hadn't bothered giving her an account of his comings and goings so far. Not once since she'd arrived at his mother's house had she even seen him. The words she'd stammered were true. In these few short days, she'd grown accustomed to her all-female surroundings. Which made him seem all the more. . .mannish. To make matters worse, there was an appealing, woodsy scent about him, like the depths of the forest after a rain.

"Is there something you need from me before you go?" she blurted out.

He shook his head. "No, I simply wanted someone else to know of my whereabouts, in case anything unexpected should happen."

"But why me?" She hadn't meant to speak the thought aloud and wished she could take it back.

At that moment, the drawing room door opened and Sally emerged into the entrance hall, feather duster in hand. She hummed as she dusted the sconces a few feet beyond them.

John watched her briefly before inclining his head toward the study. "Will you come with me, Miss Cooper?"

Millie followed him. Once they were alone in the study, she stood numbly holding the coffee tray. She was hardly aware of her aching arms. What she did notice was how his woodsy scent grew stronger in the confines of the room.

John set his hat on the desk and took the tray from her, his sleeve just brushing hers. It was an accident, she was sure, as was the light sweep of his hair against her cheek. Still, she jerked away from him.

He lifted his brows but didn't comment. He placed the tray alongside his hat and circled the desk to seat himself.

She sat as well, and with the comforting bulk of the desk between them, said, "I hope I didn't sound rude earlier. I was just surprised to be informed of your plans." Somehow the statement seemed too personal.

"Why?" His voice was soft.

Because you don't see me as an equal and never have. The whispered thought came from a part of herself that she'd temporarily forgotten, the part that resented a particular past moment with him. Of course she couldn't talk about it now. He would know he'd gotten under her skin if she did. She sought the blank pages of her mind for something to say. What emerged was worse than what she'd kept inside.

"I was surprised that you included me in your plans, because you've been avoiding me."

His brows lifted again, higher. "Oh?"

She bit her lip and looked away. *He's going to deny it, and I'll be so mortified.*

But curiously, he said the last thing she expected him to say. It followed a long, unsteady exhale.

"Has it ever occurred to you, Miss Cooper, that it might be difficult for me to converse with beautiful women?"

The confession brought her gaze flying upward, mouth agape. Thankfully he was staring down at his hands, folded tightly together on the desk.

In the past, she hadn't considered him at all, other than to think it was a shame how he worked so many hours and never made time for friendships or leisurely activities. But now she wondered. Could it be that he'd immersed himself in business for reasons other than ambition? Perhaps being in a man's world simply put him at his ease. *If he's intimidated by me, I needn't be by him.*

The conciliatory thought did little to soothe her. He'd as much as admitted that he found her beautiful, and it had an unnerving effect. It took her a moment to realize he was speaking again.

"So you see, if I weren't desperate, I wouldn't have sought this interview with you."

How very charming. "Thank you."

He shot her a tense look. "Please don't misunderstand me." He drummed his fingers on the desktop, over and over. Then he grasped the edge of the desk and pushed away from it. "Frankly, it doesn't matter."

This was the tone she remembered. The brisk dismissal of all that wasn't business. *Ever sensible.* The recollection of who he was, who he really was, stiffened her spine and pricked her mind with flashes of unpleasant memory.

"I just want to ensure that I can be reached while I'm away." He rummaged about in a drawer, pulled out a paper, and gave it to her. "This is my itinerary, so you'll be able to contact me by wire if necessary. Leadville is my first stop, Pueblo my last."

She looked down at the page, at the tidy notations of dates and places. *The same man who once sent me on my way without remorse is now entrusting his family to me.* "Why?" she whispered.

"Because if I don't leave this with you, I won't be able to leave at all." His chair creaked as he leaned back in it. "My brother has many worthy qualities, but I'm afraid careful heed to details isn't one of them."

What makes you think it's one of mine?

"Women are often better at these things," he said, as if he'd heard her.

"You have several women in your employ."

"Yours is the highest ranking position among them."

So that explained it. Everything made perfect sense now. The lord of the manor didn't wish to leave his household in the care of maids. *It's because I'm a nurse.* His speech about being nervous around beautiful women had merely been an attempt to soften her. *To make me pliable, so he can do as he pleases.* His methods seemed sincere, but they were not. And she'd almost fallen for them.

Her expression must have reflected her hostile musings, for his gaze darted away from hers. The silence between them lengthened, thickened.

"How is Rena?" The question practically leaped from her.

He blinked. "Rena?" His befuddlement was obvious, but he answered her. "She's well enough, I suppose."

"I haven't seen her in so long. That last summer, when your brother and I—when we were—" She stopped, cheeks warm. "When we were—"

"Please just say it."

But she couldn't. *When we were in love.* Even if she could voice such a private sentiment, she was determined that no piece of her heart should be exposed to this man. "Rena was at finishing school that summer," she said instead. "So I didn't get to see her, or say a proper goodbye. Will she be joining you here in Glenwood Springs?"

"Unfortunately, no. She did well in finishing school, I can tell you. Then she had a good season, the year she debuted. She's married now."

"I wish I could have seen her at her coming-out party."

He smiled. "She was awfully self-possessed, nothing like the little sister in braids and skinned knees I grew up with. Like a stranger, graceful and poised."

Which I was not. Millie's chest constricted.

"At any rate," he said, "her husband is quite immersed in his work in New York City."

The words wrenched from Millie without permission. "Did you manage to arrange an 'advantageous' match for her too?"

A faint glimmer, just a spark, flared in his eyes. He seemed about to retort but was interrupted by a noise that came from the entrance hall. It was followed by two swift knocks, then the study door swung open.

Millie twisted in her chair to see the cause of the disturbance. . .and felt the blood drain from her face.

Stephen stood in the doorway.

Chapter Seven

*H*er childhood sweetheart, who'd once held her heart in his hands, looked at her only an instant before his gaze fairly flew elsewhere.

Stephen is standing right in front of you.

This bit of knowledge had a profound effect on Millie. Her traitorous heart, which had leaped at the sight of him, now pounded like a drum. Her extremities grew colder with every unforgiving beat.

He blocked the light from the entrance hall, his thicker chest and stronger arms denoting a change from the slim youth she'd once known so well.

At such a moment, it was odd that she should notice John's gaze flick toward her, a replica of his brother's hasty glance. She wondered what he was thinking.

"I regret barging in like this," Stephen said, "but I'm in need of assistance."

John rose and reached for his hat, but Stephen shook his head. "Assistance from your nurse."

"Our mother's nurse." John looked his brother up and down with a scowl. "And you look hale as a horse."

Stephen rolled his eyes toward the ceiling. "Not for me. For Florence." A flush appeared beneath his tanned skin. "My wife is in her time of. . .well, that is, she expects—" He broke off and drew himself up with obvious effort. "My wife is pregnant."

The indecorous word hung in the air like a toxic vapor. Millie was aware of John brushing nonexistent dust off the desk, his eyes trained on the movement of his hand.

Stephen forged ahead. "She hasn't tended to panic in the past. At least, not when she was expecting the others. So you'll understand that I cannot dismiss it when she says she's concerned. She's had some symptoms today of, well, pangs and. . .perhaps other—" His flush deepened. He gave Millie an apologetic look. "This is an awkward topic indeed."

Sure that her ashen face betrayed her, Millie rose from her chair. "I'll fetch my bag."

She turned to John but didn't quite meet his gaze—things hadn't ended well between them. Or more precisely, things had never been well between them. "Mr. Drexel, could you see that Beatrice knows I'll be away for a time? She's proved adept at caring for your mother."

He nodded, expression unreadable.

Stephen waited until she brushed past him then followed her through the door and across the entrance hall.

"I'll be right back," she told him when they'd reached the stairs. She hurried up to her room, retrieved her black bag from the foot of the bed, and returned to him.

"After you," he murmured once they were outside.

The setting sun warmed Millie's face as she led the way through the pines to Stephen's house. It quieted her thoughts, that warmth, soothed her skin where the breeze caused gooseflesh to arise. There was a snap in the air, she noticed, an orange tint to the leaves that fluttered on the oak shrubs. *Autumn is approaching.*

She could feel the way Stephen's larger form blocked the wind at her back. If she stopped, he would run into her, his chest level with her head. If she glanced backward, she would see the way the breeze blew the dark thatches of his hair across his forehead, almost into his eyes. *Like it always did during a windstorm on the seashore.*

The air around Millie seemed to grow still as memories swarmed over her. The crunch of their footsteps was the only sound in the fading light. Part of her wanted to turn, say something real to him. Ask him how he'd been. The other part was determined to remain detached, just as he was.

Though little time had passed, the trek seemed endless. Stephen didn't say a word. She kept waiting for him to, but he never did.

"Is your wife resting now?" she asked when the silence became unbearable.

"She is, yes."

"And these pangs she's been suffering, are they sharp and intense, or more like an overworked muscle?"

"Duller, I think."

There were other things Millie needed to know, but she wouldn't ask him if her next breath depended on it. *Still, I hope his wife is all right.*

That last thought reminded Millie that there was a frightened patient at the end of this pathway, a woman possibly facing complications with her unborn babe. Nothing else mattered in light of such a concern.

She quickened her pace.

Soon they arrived at Stephen's house. Though by no means small, it looked like a little dollhouse against its looming backdrop, Red Mountain. Millie paused, and Stephen came around her to unlatch the gate.

"There's a trick to it," he explained. He flipped the latch up, down, and back up again, and the gate swung open.

They proceeded into the house. Once they were in the entrance hall, he gestured toward a winding staircase.

"My wife is upstairs."

Millie didn't delay but swiftly ascended the steps, Stephen's heavier tread thudding behind her. At the top, she passed a harried-looking maid, ruffled mobcap askew over pinned curls. She gripped the hands of two small children, a brown-haired girl and a stout little boy.

A door to the right was cracked open, and Stephen strode past Millie to rap on it. He opened it just enough to lean his head inside. He must have found waiting eyes upon him, for he said, "The nurse is here."

The door opened wider, and a petite blond peered out at Millie with a tired smile.

"Do come in."

Millie entered the room, noting that it was less showy than Katherine's bedroom. The walls were papered in pink tea roses, the bed covered in a simple eyelet lace spread.

The woman—Florence—closed the door on Stephen and stood awaiting instructions, her bottom lip tucked between her teeth.

"Why don't you sit there on the bed," Millie suggested.

Florence complied, and Millie went to a nearby dresser. She set down her medical bag and drew out her stethoscope and thermometer.

"I'm not ill," Florence said quickly.

Millie paused. Generally she preferred to discover such information herself, but in this case, her patient clearly had something on her mind. Millie put her tools back in the bag.

"Your. . .husband mentioned you've been having some pangs?"

Florence nodded. "Just achy, and down low."

Millie sat on the bed beside the woman and assured her that such a symptom was common.

"Well. . ." Florence fixed her gaze on her lap.

"Yes?"

Given a few gentle prompts, Florence soon revealed what was truly troubling her. It wasn't a worry Millie hadn't heard before, with five years' experience tending to expectant mothers. "Tell me, Mrs. Drexel, this bit of blood you saw, did it follow a time of strenuous activity?"

A defensive look stole into Florence's eyes, but she nodded. "There's much to be done, having recently arrived at a new home. And of course, there's the children."

"I understand." *Please, let it be just a simple case of overexertion.* "When, by your estimation, will your children's new brother or sister arrive?"

"January, I think."

Five months' gestation then. Millie looked down at Florence's abdomen and assessed it with a practiced eye. While gazing at the maternal swell, she remembered that this woman was Stephen's wife. The woman he'd married, the woman he—or was it his brother?—had chosen over her.

In spite of the toying fingers, droop of the lips, and perspiring brow, it was plain that Florence wasn't only beautiful, she was patrician. *Unfailingly upright posture, skin white as porcelain, ladylike voice. . .a perfect debutante.* Her softly rounded belly, the beatific form of a Madonna, only enhanced the lovely picture she presented. With an ache inside she couldn't quite vanquish, Millie again silently cried to God for help.

"Have you felt any quickening yet?" she asked.

Florence brightened. "Yes, there have been some movements."

"When did they start?"

"A few weeks ago."

"Are you still feeling them?"

Florence nodded.

Millie rose from the bed and spoke in a clinical tone. "Well, Mrs. Drexel, I can tell you that you're the proper size for this stage in your time of expectancy. As to your foremost concern, the bit of blood you saw, it might well be attributed to overexertion. If you're careful not to overdo, and to acquire plenty of rest in the coming weeks, it's my belief that you can look forward to a healthy infant come winter."

A smile eased over Florence's face. She reached up to clasp Millie's hand in hers and squeezed it. "Thank you."

"Certainly." Millie freed her hand and stepped away. She collected her bag, reminded her patient to get plenty of sleep, and departed.

She'd nearly escaped the upper floor of the house, with only the stairs and entrance hall left, when she spotted Stephen. He sat with his children on a wooden bench beside the window. He leaped to his feet like a jack from its box and came forward as best he could with his daughter clinging to his leg. In his arms he held his little son.

"How is she?" He bore the same harried look the maid had earlier. His children pulled him in opposite directions, and he stumbled sideways to avoid stepping on his daughter. He repositioned his son, whom he'd almost dumped on the floor.

"As you can see, we're a bit, ah—" He stopped as his daughter careened, so sharply her enormous bow came undone and her long hair flew every which way.

Stephen staggered, righted himself once more. "Nettie!" he hollered.

The maid appeared from a door at the end of the hall and approached carrying a tray filled with colorful little jars. She addressed the girl. "Would you like to come with me, Lucy, and do some painting?"

The child nodded and scrambled to her feet. She bounded over to the maid and they went off down the hall.

"A spirited one, that." Stephen's smile was feeble.

It occurred to Millie that they were alone again, except for the boy. *But he's scarcely more than a baby.* She glanced at Stephen's tall form, at his jade-hued eyes, so diligently avoiding hers. She felt his presence acutely and wanted nothing more than to flee.

Beyond them, in the little recess beside the window, scattered toys were illuminated by two lit sconces. Millie's gaze took in the wooden blocks, cloth doll, and tipped-over rocking horse.

"Painting seems to be my eldest child's favorite activity, at present," Stephen said. "Next week it will be something else entirely." He tightened his arms around his son's generous belly to prevent the boy, who was straining toward the floor, from falling. "She paints with quite a flourish too." Abruptly he looked at Millie. "What have you discovered about my wife? Is something wrong with the babe?"

Though his gaze reached clear to her very center, she'd expected the question and had an answer ready. "There are things I must keep watch for, just to be certain. But at this point, I see no cause for alarm."

His eyes closed, his lips moving as if in wordless thanks.

His son, meanwhile, peeked out at Millie from under his woolen beret, a faint grin on his plump face. He seemed agleam with a look of...kinship. Millie's throat suddenly closed over. *Stephen used to have that exact expression when he was a child.*

"Did you—" Stephen paused. "Would you tell me what we need to keep watch for, concerning Florence?"

Not in a hundred years. It simply wasn't something one discussed with a man, especially this man. "I'm sure Mrs. Drexel will inform you of whatever she feels is necessary."

"Yes, but I prefer to hear it firsthand, from a proficient on the subject." He wiped his palms on his trouser legs as though they were sweaty. "Discomfiting as it is."

He's changed. It was subtle, but she could see it. New lines around his mouth told of more frequent grave expressions. The half-impish, half-tender light in his eyes had matured into a steady, almost hard look. *He's a father now, with all the cares that accompany that role.* And she was being forced to speak of intimate matters with him, this father of another woman's children.

He spread his hands wide. "Won't you tell me how I can ensure the safety of my unborn child?"

A simmer began inside her. It joined the deluge of other emotions she'd experienced on this whole dreadful evening and grew to a boil. *Does he think this is easy for me?*

She faced him with trembling chin. "Ask *her*," she spat. "She's your wife."

And then, hot-cheeked and battling tears, she rushed from his presence. She fled down the stairs, across the entrance hall, and out the door.

Chapter Eight

*J*ohn barely heard the rapid *thump, thump* as the conductor punched a hole in his ticket. The clanging sound of the wheels beneath his feet muffled lesser noises.

The train had been spewing its black smoke for several minutes now, but there were still miles of mountain passes to conquer before reaching Leadville. Come morning, John planned to visit Iron Hill, where his family owned stock in a silver mine.

He reached for his carpetbag under the high-backed seat in front of him. A trunk was preferable for proper travel, but he'd had little time to prepare for his journey. He'd stayed up late last night studying. . .and stewing. The studying had readied him for the task ahead, the visits to mines and refineries. The stewing had accomplished nothing. It circled around his responsibilities as head of the family and sole provider, keeping him awake until almost dawn and causing him to oversleep—hence the haphazard packing.

John rummaged through his bag until he found the book he'd brought, *Geology and Mining Industry of Leadville Co.* He started reading the chapter titled "Descriptive Geology of Leadville and Vicinity."

"Powerful, ain't she?"

John dragged his gaze from the book to the passenger beside him, a man wearing a broad-brimmed Stetson. "Pardon?"

"The train," the man explained. "She's quite a force, ain't she?"

"She is."

The Stetson-man acquired a dreamy look. "Puts me in mind of a horse I once had, down south, in El Paso. A regular charger he was, ran like a crack of raw thunder. You ride?"

"Some. I've dabbled in breeding, actually." He didn't add that the horses he owned were blooded Thoroughbreds, one a descendent of the great Derby winner Diomed—sire of the Godolphin of America, Sir Archy.

"I've made my peace with these newfangled engines," the man said. "I'll admit it's a novelty, wheels churning beneath a man's feet like mad. But nothing beats an old-fashioned horseback ride, where a body can feel the wind and smell the sunshine and leather."

John agreed but didn't have time to say so, because a lad came by selling newspapers. The Stetson-man occupied himself with fishing for coins in his pocket then began to read.

His words stayed with John. He closed his eyes and imagined his hands gripping the reins as he sped across the rolling green pastures at Gentry Valley Stables, where he boarded his horses. How soon, he wondered, could he return?

The servants were in place now, except for a nursemaid for Lucy and Charlie. And for the time being, Florence seemed content to look after the children herself. *Although, with possible complications with the babe. . .* The situation warranted close observation, that was certain. He'd also need to observe the new staff members, ensure that they proved satisfactory. But his mother's health was the chief factor. It would be unwise for him to leave for Philadelphia if her attacks became more frequent.

Deep inside, in a place he didn't wish to dwell, he knew he could lose her. Asthma sufferers, he'd learned from doctors in the East, could pass into eternity during milder attacks than some she'd endured. *I must speak to Millie and find out how Mother is truly doing.*

He stared out the window, watching the trees speed by like shuffling decks of cards. Occasional open spaces revealed layers of mountains in the distance. *I'll wager it's much colder up here.* Glenwood Springs was tucked between the tall peaks around it, sheltered from the wind.

He knew he'd bungled things between him and Millie last night. She was necessary to his family's well-being; he couldn't hope to find a more qualified nurse, and he'd upset her. He still remembered the words she'd cast at him before Stephen arrived on the scene.

"Did you manage to arrange an 'advantageous' match for her too?"

They'd been speaking of Rena when Millie voiced that particular resentful remark. Now, free from her disarming feminine presence, he realized he'd been mistaken when he thought she was flustered by him. Ill at ease, perhaps even intimidated. But not flustered. "Flustered" was what she was when Stephen appeared in the doorway.

The thought made John feel like clouting something. *Plainly, she still cares for him.* Stephen, on the other hand, had been harder to read. Only one conclusion could be drawn about him, and that was that he'd interrupted their conversation. *It cost me too.* John's standing with Millie, the very person he needed to communicate with, was now uncertain at best.

He forced his attention back to his book. Yes, seeing Millie again was a daunting prospect, but he couldn't allow it to keep him from his work.

♥

Katherine sniffed, a derisive sound. She looked sharply at Millie, who sat beside her on the royal-blue settee in the entrance hall. "This is a wildly ill-advised excursion, you know."

We're attending a two-hour church service, not conquering the heights of Mount Everest. "It's just for the morning, Mrs. Drexel. We'll be home well before your afternoon nap."

Katherine scowled and drew a little mirror from the recesses of her beaded black reticule. "I find it incomprehensible," she said as she fussed with her hair, "that the advice of a skilled, reputed doctor from the East is being so carelessly discarded. My good Dr. Philips told me many times, if he told me once, that I should avoid the outdoors, and too much stimulation." She returned the mirror to the reticule. "This outing"—she cinched the drawstrings closed with a snap—"is both."

Millie didn't reply. She thought she detected a hint of eagerness beneath Katherine's protests. *And anyway, if she didn't want to go, nothing could persuade her otherwise.* Still, Millie hesitated. Was there cause for concern?

This past week, she'd somehow persuaded Katherine to leave her room and come downstairs more often. It hadn't done any harm, but venturing outdoors was another matter.

Millie surveyed the rise and fall of Katherine's chest and studied her face for answers. The flesh around her eyes, Millie noticed, was puffy and red. Her nose was drippy and clogged, plagued by some mysterious irritant. Either that or she had a relentless cold. But the wheezing sound in her breaths had lessened lately, as if her lungs weren't quite so congested.

The improvements seemed to begin when Millie permanently banned the cinnamon sachet, after finding it in Katherine's water closet for the third time. *She's proved more tenacious than I'd expected.* Further progress came when Millie vanquished all colognes, lotions, and other heavy scents. And she'd asked Sally to be thorough in her dusting. There was nothing worse for delicate lungs than dust.

But what if this outing causes another attack?

Millie knew she needed to make up her mind quickly. Stephen would be here soon to collect them in his carriage. She chafed inside, remembering how she'd lost her composure with him the other night after seeing to Florence. How she'd failed to mimic his impersonal, formal manner. The one day she'd seen him since, he'd acted as if the incident hadn't occurred. *Well, I certainly recall it.* She had no desire to repeat it, which might mean avoiding him altogether. Yet with John away, she had no choice but to discuss important matters, such as her patient's health, with Stephen.

Who happened to be knocking on the front door at this very moment.

"I'll go," Millie said, as though there was a danger of Katherine doing so.

Impersonal. Formal. Millie seared the words into her mind as she reached for the doorknob.

She opened the door, and though she'd expected him, a thud still thumped against her rib cage at the sight of him. He wore a simple black lounge coat, silk vest, and gray trousers—all of which were made of the finest materials.

She stepped aside and let him in.

Once past the threshold, he paused and nodded at his mother. He studied her briefly then turned and spoke to Millie in a lowered tone. "Is my mother equal to this?"

Must maintain distance. Millie took a step back. "That's what I hoped to talk to you about. She's only had one attack this week. It was a few days ago, after dinner, and quite mild."

He clasped his hands behind him, his posture straight as could be.

A new thought occurred to Millie. Could his formal behavior be an attempt to avoid the fact that there had once been something between them, and now could never be? *No, he probably simply doesn't care anymore.*

"Do you foresee a problem?" A slight flush rose in his face. "Not to say that you haven't considered the question already."

"It's all right, I would ask the same questions if I were you." She watched Katherine pin on her hat, a velvet creation trimmed with an array of purple feathers and satin ribbons. The woman didn't seem interested in their conversation, but one never knew.

Millie lowered her voice to a whisper. "There's no way to be sure. Her doctor in Philadelphia advised her to avoid the outdoors. But I wonder if she might have been plagued by the air there—by factory smoke or some other impurity."

He gazed at his mother, head tilted. "Let this be a trial then. We'll observe her closely, and return her home at the first sign of trouble."

The tension in Millie's shoulders loosened with the knowledge that he agreed with her.

Together they escorted Katherine to the carriage, Millie on one side, Stephen on the other. It came as no surprise to Millie that the woman ignored her and clung to Stephen.

When they arrived at the carriage, Lucy clambered down from the front seat, where she'd been sitting next to the coachman. Neither Florence nor Charlie were present.

"Is your wife unwell, son?" Katherine asked.

"No, just a little tired. And she thought it best to stay home with Charlie. He's too young to behave himself in church just yet."

With Stephen busy talking, Millie hurried to climb into the coach. She didn't want to give him the chance to offer her assistance.

Katherine ascended next. Her ample yards of skirts claimed an entire seat, so Stephen was forced to sit beside Millie, Lucy in his lap.

Once everyone was seated, the carriage jolted to a start.

As the horses trotted down the lane, Lucy wriggled and squirmed in her father's lap. She chattered on and on, oblivious to the way he and Millie leaned as far from each other as possible.

How I wish I could have gone with the others. The chambermaid, Sally, had enlisted the services of her brother, who lived just down the hill. He'd come in his wagon to collect his sister and the other servants and take them to church. Millie had longed to join them but of course knew she must remain near Katherine.

"Such terrible dust," the woman said, lace-edged handkerchief pressed to her nose. She lowered the cloth to her lap. It appeared to be damp and limp after the contact with her nose, but no more so than usual.

At least her sniffles aren't worsening in this outside air. "Let's have a look at that pulse," Millie murmured.

Katherine sighed like a martyr and surrendered her wrist. Millie held it for a few seconds and took note of the steady beats.

"Perfect." She let go and sat back against the cushioned seat. The instant she was settled, Lucy, who was still squirming, inadvertently kicked her in the side. The breath whooshed from Millie's lips, and the child's eyes widened.

"I'm sorry!"

"No harm done." Millie patted Lucy's hand and returned her gaze to the other side of the carriage. She must keep watch over Katherine, her primary responsibility. She cataloged each symptom she saw. *Eyes still puffy, nose still runny, skin still pale...but breathing about the same.* She was thankful for that.

"Perhaps, Miss Cooper," Katherine said, "you might turn your attention to my poor restive granddaughter, instead of making a show of concern for my health."

Stephen, who'd admittedly had his hands full containing his daughter, went still. He didn't say a word, but by the change in Katherine's demeanor, Millie knew he'd conveyed something by his look.

Katherine clamped her mouth shut, and the rest of the journey continued in tense silence.

The churchyard came into view at the end of the leaf-scattered lane. Several conveyances dotted the lawn out front, ranging from lumbering farm wagons to sporty black traps. The bell tower reached upward toward a cloudless sky, the bell ringing in perfect harmony with the chorus of chirping birds.

Millie felt like a rain cloud in the midst of a sea of sunshine. *I'm tired,* she realized. *Tired of tiptoeing around this family.* Where was the zest that had possessed her as a young woman? What had become of the bold girl who'd traveled unescorted to the wilderness of Colorado and learned a new trade?

She'd find her, she determined. Beginning with holding her head high around the man beside her. *He did this, after all, not me.* Whether his brother had persuaded, coerced, or flat demanded that he quit seeing her, in the end, Stephen had surrendered. And Millie refused to give him the impression that she still carried a torch for him. A girl had her pride.

The carriage wheels rolled to a stop, and Millie raised a prayer to the One who ruled every storm.

This time, Stephen offered his hand to assist her, and she accepted it. She stepped to the ground, doing her best to ignore the feel of his palm, warm against hers. She turned to Katherine with a bright smile and looped her arm through the woman's rigid, clenched elbow. "Shall we go inside?"

♥

Millie eagerly searched the array of churchgoers for Ann as she and Katherine followed Stephen and Lucy down the center aisle. She'd forgotten how pleasant it was to be greeted by hearty handshakes and broad smiles. Each face shone with welcome—from courageous Eleanora Malaby, the first bride to arrive in Glenwood Springs, to prim and proper Mrs. B. T. Napier, whose husband owned the dry goods store, to roguish but good-hearted livery stable proprietor, George Banning.

As usual, the little building was filled to bursting. This was the one day a week in which the more isolated homesteaders saw another human soul, and they took full advantage of the occasion. It was a colorful sight, Sunday-best boots and women's swishing skirts—poplin or checked wool, with an occasional taffeta or silk thrown in. *A far cry from Mrs. Drexel's finery.*

The woman clung to Millie out of necessity. She tired easily when walking without assistance, and needed a barrier between herself and the jostling crowd. *People would never guess that veiled disdain on her face isn't for them—it's for her nurse.* A pain welled up inside Millie, difficult to ignore.

Just then, she heard a deep, familiar voice behind her.

"Well," it said, "I see that my departed associate has come to say hello at last."

Millie spun around to behold Dr. Murphy standing a few feet away, a twinkle in his eyes. His tweed suit and faint scent of pipe tobacco were so fatherly, so comforting, it was all she could do not to rush over and fling her arms around him. Instead she gave him a curtsy. "Good morning, Dr. Murphy."

Stephen walked over, Lucy in tow, and Millie knew he'd come to meet the doctor, compelled by the demands of good form. So she made the introductions.

"Dr. Murphy, this is Mr. Stephen Drexel, his mother, Mrs. Katherine Drexel, and his daughter, Lucy." She shifted her gaze toward the doctor. "And this is Dr. Calvin Murphy."

Katherine inclined her head in a queenly but civil nod, and Stephen shook the doctor's hand.

"I hear you once had a practice in Baltimore?" Stephen inquired, even as he leaned sideways to keep Lucy from escaping his grasp. She strained away from him, clearly eager to be off to the next adventure. "You must miss the convenience of the city, the ready access to hospitals and supplies."

"Yes." Dr. Murphy appeared about to say more, and perhaps he did, but Millie didn't hear him.

She'd spied, through the press of milling bodies, her fair-haired friend. "Ann!" she cried, arms opening wide.

As the two women embraced, tears pricked Millie's eyes. *This is what it feels like to be unreservedly loved.*

Ann stepped back, her brown eyes shining. "I've been so anxious to see you, Millie. I thought Sunday school would never end."

Millie's brows rose. "You wanted Sunday school to end? I don't believe that for a second."

"The children were dears as always of course. But a certain deacon's closing prayer was so very length—" Ann seemed suddenly aware of the presence of the three strangers. "That is to say, his prayer was so very—" Her expression grew helpless, and she smiled a sheepish smile that included them all. "How do you do."

Millie introduced her to the others, and the appropriate greetings were exchanged.

Ann knelt before Lucy. "Good morning, Miss Drexel."

Lucy just looked at her, round-eyed and for once, silent.

"Say good morning to the lady," Stephen prompted.

"Good morning," Lucy echoed.

Ann tapped her finger against her chin. "You know, you seem almost big enough to begin learning Bible stories."

Lucy nodded. "That's because I'm already four."

"My, that does seem old." Ann rose and met Stephen's gaze. "If it wouldn't be too much trouble, sir, we'd love to have her join us for Sunday school."

Stephen flashed his absurdly handsome grin. "That might be arranged."

Ann ducked her head shyly, and Millie groaned inside. *Even a girl so sensible as Ann, instantly charmed.*

"Lucy's mother would be pleased," Stephen said. "She likes to see the children learning the ways of the Lord. We have a boy at home, but I'm sorry to say he's too young for Sunday school at present."

Ann glanced toward Katherine. "How lovely it must be, Mrs. Drexel, to have your grandchildren living so close by."

Katherine gave a reply that Millie didn't heed. She was distracted by Dr. Murphy, who'd caught her attention and leaned closer to her.

"Your patient is looking fit as a fiddle," he whispered with a wink.

His approval soaked into her spirit like rain into desert sands.

Unfortunately, she wasn't able to bask in the refreshment for long. Reverend Warren was making his way to the front of the church, an indication that the service was about to start. When he passed by her, she couldn't help looking over at Ann. Millie hurt inside at the rapt way her friend gazed up at the young minister. *Why does she still care for him so?*

Stephen murmured, "Nice to meet you" to the Murphys and gathered Lucy's hand in his. He led the way to a pew occupied only by Mr. Bennett, owner of the sawmill west of town.

Millie and the Drexels seated themselves, Lucy between Stephen and Millie, Katherine on the end.

When Reverend Warren raised his arms and said, "All rise," Millie stood with the others, but her mind wasn't on the service. She was remembering the very moment she'd stood across from John Drexel, in the hall outside his mother's room, and accepted this position. She'd made the decision to listen to God's compelling voice and become Katherine's nurse—to embark upon these stormy waters.

"Let us turn in our hymnals to hymn number sixty-seven," Reverend Warren said. "How Firm a Foundation."

Millie turned the pages and found the hymn. Then for a time, she stared down at the open hymnal. The congregation sang around her unheeded. Never had the meaning of a song seemed so alive to her. Verse two, in particular, seemed written just for her.

When through the deep waters I call thee to go,
the rivers of sorrow shall not overflow;
 for I will be with thee, thy troubles to bless,
and sanctify to thee thy deepest distress.

Millie grasped the words and clung to them. She wasn't alone on this tumultuous voyage. She never would be.

As the sermon began, Millie continued thinking about the hymn. *Sanctify thy deepest distress.* What did it mean? Could God really sanctify her distresses? Bless her troubles? It was as if He'd promised to bring good out of her trials. But Millie had long suspected that blessings were reserved for heaven.

Though assured of God's presence, she found herself unable to accept such a promise.

Chapter Nine

*M*illie paused outside the drawing room door. She'd gone upstairs to fetch a book, and dawdled as long as she dared in hopes that Katherine would be asleep when she returned. *Like she should have been last night.*

Three times, Millie had been roused from her slumber at the whim of her restless patient. She'd left the comfort of her bed to reheat the stone at Katherine's feet, fetch her a glass of warm milk, and shut her drapes, among other trifling errands.

Now Millie stole into the drawing room as quietly as possible.

Alas, Katherine sat wide awake in her Venetian chair, potted ferns on one side and stained glass lampshade on the other. "How relieved I am to see you, my dear. I was certain some dire calamity must have befallen you, that you were so detained."

Millie longed to reply in kind, sweet as could be. *As you can see, Mrs. Drexel, I'm quite unharmed. But I sincerely thank you for your concern.* Instead she crossed the room, set the book on the table beside the coffee tray, and seated herself on the sofa. "This is the Christmas story I told you about, the one by Mr. Dickens."

Katherine harrumphed and said nothing.

"Is your throat feeling any better?" Millie asked.

There was a stony silence.

"I suppose so," Katherine said finally.

Well, will wonders never cease? For three days, the woman had complained of a sore throat. Millie had checked and rechecked her temperature, stared into her open mouth multiple times, and stewed over whether or not she had streptococcus—or even more terrifying, scarlet fever. Millie almost sent for Dr. Murphy but decided against it. Katherine's fever only climbed high once and didn't last long.

Still, this news of improvement was welcome.

"You needn't look so triumphant, Miss Cooper. As if you'd somehow managed to seat yourself in the place of the Almighty, and might claim a hand in my recovery."

Millie's facade, the mask of the impervious nurse, began to slip. Without warning, it dropped off altogether. "Believe me, Mrs. Drexel, if I had the power of the Almighty at my disposal, your rather too choosy throat would not be my first concern."

This time the silence was deafening.

Katherine lifted her spoon from the coffee tray. "My, that's an impertinent tone for a servant to take, don't you think?"

Was that a. . .smile. . .in Katherine Drexel's voice?

Millie watched the woman scoop sugar into her porcelain cup, each flick of her wrist more assertive than the last. She showed little sign of amusement. She set the spoon on the tray. "I wonder, Miss Cooper, if my son knew of your tendency to lose your temper when he engaged your services."

No, she's definitely not amused. "I'm afraid he didn't say."

Iron glinted in Katherine's eyes.

But I dearly wish he'd have warned me about you, madam.

They stared at each other, patient and nurse, a wordless colliding of wills.

Millie was the first to look away. How, she cried inwardly, had it come to this? Instead of getting better, her relationship with Katherine continued in the same injurious vein. She wondered, as she had before, if God had chosen the best person for this position. *Surely there's someone more suited to it. Mrs. Drexel clearly doesn't want me here.* The last thought made her ache inside.

Seconds later, a knock sounded on the front door, and Millie practically fled to answer it.

Their visitor proved to be Nettie, one of Stephen's maids. "Mrs. Drexel sent me to see if you'd come, miss. Charlie is feeling poorly, and she says it would ease her mind if you'd come look in on him."

The cold grip that seized Millie whenever a cry for help concerned a small child took hold again. She snatched up her medical bag, stowed beside the door for times like these. "First I must ask someone to stay with Mrs. Drexel. *My* Mrs. Drexel, I mean."

Nettie grinned. "Yes, miss, I knew which missus you meant. I'll wait here."

Millie hurried back to the drawing room. In spite of her urgency, her years of experience warned her not to fling open the door and announce that Charlie was sick. *It would only frighten her.* She nudged the door open. "It seems I'm needed at your son's house, Mrs. Drexel. I shouldn't be long, just a quick examination."

Katherine was instantly on the alert. "An examination of whom?"

I should have known I couldn't fool her. "Charlie."

Alarm sharpened the woman's features. "Whatever is the matter with the boy?"

Millie almost drew nearer to her, almost clasped those thin hands in her own and vowed that Charlie would be well cared for. *But she wouldn't accept such comfort, not from me.* "I don't know for sure. His mother sent for me though, so I should go to him."

"Yes. Go."

Millie found Beatrice in the kitchen and asked her to look after Katherine, then she rejoined Nettie on the porch. Together they descended the steps and followed the trail to Stephen's house.

A flushed and breathless Florence answered the door when they arrived. "I'm so grateful you've come." She moved aside and bid them enter. "Charlie is upstairs in the nursery."

Millie wasn't ready to leave the feverish-looking woman just yet. "Are you feeling quite well, Mrs. Drexel?"

The blue eyes pooled with tears. "Oh, please don't worry about me. Tend to Charlie first. He's so hot and miserable, poor boy, and his father won't let me go to him. He fears exposing me to danger. Our dear Tansy is with him now, but he wants his mother." She appeared ready to cry.

"Your husband is quite right. And I'll see to Charlie right away." It wouldn't be prudent, after all, to allow an expectant woman to become hysterical—especially not one so delicate. *No wonder Stephen frets over her so.* Florence possessed a fragile quality, sure to secure a man's sworn protection. She made Millie feel as dainty as an ox. Though the mirror in Millie's bedroom assured her there was nothing unsightly about her, her figure was rather curvier than Florence's. But such things didn't matter right now. Not when a wee patient awaited her.

❤

Charles Hammond Drexel III tossed about in his bed, white sheets twisted around his chubby knees. A buxom woman whom Millie assumed was Tansy sat beside him, a kerchief tied around her tight black curls.

"Glory be," she said when she saw Millie. "You's here." She heaved herself out of the chair. "I was shore you'd be Charlie's daddy, who don't know much about soothing a poor sick baby. He at the store getting molasses taffy. It's Charlie's favorite."

Millie chose her steps with care. She avoided several strewn toys, among them a red ball and a myriad of wooden alphabet blocks. She placed her bag on the nightstand and claimed the chair beside the bed.

"You need anything afore I save my supper from being burned black?" Tansy asked.

Millie shook her head, and the woman departed.

The bed seemed huge compared to its occupant, whose legs fought against his tangled sheets, each bare toe splayed with effort. Millie almost smiled. *Well, he certainly isn't feeble.*

"How are you doing, young Master Drexel?"

He stopped squirming and looked at her. She was struck again by his resemblance to his father—with one charming addition, a leftward dimple, which now flashed into view.

"Papa is bringing me canny."

Millie had no desire to correct his pronunciation. The real impulse, which his mother likely succumbed to often, was to gather him in her arms and cover his face in kisses. Instead she simply gestured toward the sheets.

"I see you're a bit tangled there."

A scowl drew his brows together. His attention returned, with a vengeance, to his former predicament. One knee jerked, then the other, then both in rapid succession. Millie kept her amusement to herself and reached down to unwind the sheets. She observed him carefully as she smoothed and tugged. *His nasal breathing is a bit clogged. He's coughed more than once. His eyes are alert, not dull with fever.*

Further examination revealed that the child had a fever after all. But it was nothing alarming, and Millie concluded that Charlie's ailment was a common head cold.

She relayed her findings to Tansy, who'd returned, her supper having been salvaged.

The cook beamed upon hearing that her little charge wasn't seriously ill. "I'll be shore to tell his mama. She took Miss Lucy for a walk in the woods." She shook her head, horror and wonder in her eyes. "Never did see the like of that girl. She hustling and restless as a summer rain."

Millie chuckled and snapped her bag shut. "Please see that camphor oil is applied to Charlie's chest if his breathing grows more labored, and that he's offered plenty of warm broth. Tell Mrs. Drexel to send for me if he doesn't improve in the next few days."

Tansy nodded.

Millie said goodbye to Charlie, collected her bag from the night-stand, and left the room.

The upstairs hallway that led from the nursery to the play area was littered with marbles. She'd only proceeded a few cautious steps when she heard footsteps approaching.

They did not belong to a woman.

Millie's chest seemed to cave inward. She didn't have the strength to face Stephen now, not after being wrung out and left to dry by his mother.

But when she raised her gaze to behold her intruder, it wasn't Stephen. . .it was John.

She became aware of a strange, unexpected sense of reprieve. She told herself that the one brother wasn't better than the other. The last time they'd spoken, she'd been angry with John for a reason. And he'd rejected her in Nantucket, had considered her unworthy. *Like his mother does every waking hour.*

So far his eyes had been on the marbles. When he looked up and saw her, he came to an abrupt halt and raked his fingers through his hair. "Miss Cooper."

She'd forgotten how red that hair appeared at times, particularly now, illuminated by the setting sun that streamed in from the window behind him.

"You're home," she said lamely.

"Yes, just got in, actually." He glanced past her, down the hall. It was silent, the doors all closed. "I came looking for Stephen, but it would seem he's away at present."

She nodded. "He's gone to the mercantile, or so I heard."

"And you're here to. . . ?" He moved sideways and lifted one foot to see beneath it, as if finding the cause of some discomfort. A marble rolled out from under his shoe.

For some reason, she remembered what he'd said before, that it was difficult for him to talk to beautiful women. *Well, that certainly can't be plaguing him now.* She knew how disheveled she must look, windblown from the rushed walk over, eyes puffy from her sleepless night. "Little Charlie isn't feeling well. I came to examine him. He just has a cold in the head though, and should recover soon."

He leaned against the wall beside him. "I've been wondering—daily, as a matter of fact—how things have been going here. I wasn't able to speak with my brother before I left, and he seemed concerned about his wife that last night."

"Mrs. Drexel is doing very well. Her husband's worries have come to naught." *And I'll say no more on the subject.*

"He must've been relieved to hear it."

She detected the same emotion in him as he'd attributed to Stephen. *Yes, everybody dotes on Florence, I know, I know.* She could feel the strain of the past few days getting the better of her.

He peered at her in the dusky light, and his voice came in a low but clear murmur. "Things seemed a little. . .off-kilter, between the two of us that night as well."

She had to force herself not to gape. He could have asked about his mother, or more about Florence's or Charlie's health, or talked about his visits to the mines. Instead he'd brought up their parting conversation.

He stood less than two feet from her in their shared narrow hallway. His suntanned forearms bore witness to the fact that he'd spent time out of doors while he was away. His simple blue work shirt looked soft and inviting.

He's waiting for a reply. "I—I wasn't myself at the time. Surely you'll understand, I was still settling into my new position. The newness of it had me a bit on edge. Things are better now."

He gave her an even look. "You asked about my sister. I don't see how her marriage or my role in arranging it so 'advantageously,' as you put it, can have much to do with nursing my mother."

She tried to brush the incident aside. "I was overwrought. Please don't concern yourself, it won't happen again."

"I should hope not. My sister isn't likely to require more than one husband."

"No," she said without thinking. "Not with her big brother there to make sure her match was so very profitable."

His lips flattened. "I won't apologize for caring for my family."

"Your mother will thank you most fervently for it, I'm sure."

His forehead suddenly creased. "What does she have to do with it?"

Again, Millie spoke before she thought. "She was once saved from a repugnant, irrevocable association with the fisherman's daughter."

He blinked, as though uncomprehending, then frowned. "She said that?"

Why did I have to bring her into this? Katherine Drexel, no matter how condescending, didn't need to be dragged through the mire before her son. A pang filled Millie. She'd failed her patient once again. "Please, Mr. Drexel," she whispered, "just let me return to my work."

He reached out as if to clasp her arm, but stayed his hand. "Has my mother been hard on you?"

The breeze drifted in from the windows, rustling his hair and bringing his woods-after-the-rain scent to her. His hand hovered near her sleeve.

Inexplicably, she couldn't remember what he'd just asked. *Why are you confusing me, John?*

She had no idea what possessed her to call him by his given name, even in her thoughts. She'd scarcely considered him as anything more than "Stephen's brother" when they were children. He always seemed so much older, so distant and serious. *But he's not distant now.*

"It doesn't matter," she said at last.

"Yes. It does." But he withdrew his hand.

"I should get back to your mother. She was quite worried about Charlie, and I must tell her that his illness isn't serious." Millie glanced out the window overlooking the pine grove, where Florence had taken Lucy for a walk. "I should also ask a servant to find his mother with the good news, and Stephen—" She stopped short at the change that overcame his expression without warning.

He straightened and folded his arms over his chest. "So he's *Stephen* to you, is he?"

Hasn't he always been? "I'm sorry, I'm afraid I don't understand."

He laughed, but there was no joy in the sound. "Don't apologize,

Miss Cooper. The reminder was timely, I assure you."

Millie had no response to that.

Which was just as well, because the dancing patter of little feet on the stairs marked Lucy's return.

❤

The following morning, before the curtains had even been unfurled from the windows, Millie escaped the house. She slipped into Katherine's room first and made sure her patient was sleeping comfortably then fled her cloistering Victorian prison.

Her breath made a puff of air outside as she descended the front porch steps. She donned her shawl and headed east, toward the Roaring Fork. Once she was safely out of sight of the house, she inhaled the damp, pine-needle-strewn air. She relaxed her neck, one taut muscle at a time.

She arrived at the river to find that an early morning fog had wended its way through the stately cottonwoods along the bank. A breeze fluttered the yellow and red leaves of delicate shrubs at the water's edge, a fairyland of mist and wonder. A family of pheasants fluttered up from the vibrant bushes. Somehow, their noisy flight didn't disturb the tranquility of the morning.

Ah, Father, Your creation is so beautiful. I'd nearly forgotten.

Millie walked south along the river until she came to a little clearing in the underbrush and beheld a fallen log, just right for sitting on. She sank down onto it, feeling the coolness that arose from the water, reminiscent of an ocean spray. She let her eyes slide shut and simply listened. The rhythmic current splashed against the rocks, the aptly named Roaring Fork creating a rushing sound in her ears, very like the roar of the sea.

For a moment, Millie sensed it, the *knowing* she'd experienced when she'd given her heart to the Lord Jesus one glorious spring day as an eleven-year-old girl. Her decision had followed a long but earnest lesson taught by the very old Sunday school teacher at the First

Baptist Church of Nantucket on the corner of Summer Street and Traders Lane.

It was a special kind of knowing, both then and now. God was real, His love a surety.

But Millie recalled her recent burdens, felt again the weight of wanting to be a good nurse, while nearly buckling under the demands of her frail taskmaster. The servants, though sociable when below stairs, didn't often enter Millie's sphere. Stephen seemed determined to treat her with formal courtesy. *He isn't even a friend.* A tightness filled Millie's throat. As for Florence, she was simply too perfect. In her presence, Millie was very aware of her girl-from-the-fishing-quarter roots.

And John. . .

She wasn't sure what she'd done to anger him. It had to do with Stephen, that much was obvious. It was somehow connected to her mention of his brother's name. *I wouldn't have thought him so changeable.* But perhaps he was. For that very reason, among others that sprang from the painful past, Millie couldn't allow herself to trust him.

Time passed as she sat there in her riverside haven and communed with her Maker.

I long to be the nurse You created me to be, dear Father. To pardon Mrs. Drexel for her condescension. To forgive her sons for their part in destroying my dreams and treat them lovingly, as You would have me do.

But her prayers seemed to rise no higher than the treetops. Maybe it was because she didn't really believe she could accomplish what she was asking, even with God's help.

She realized she was humming the same tune she'd sung in church, the one about the firm foundation. *"The rivers of sorrow shall not overflow. . . I will be with thee, thy troubles to bless."*

Would God truly bless her, deliver her from her troubles?

He didn't before.

The thought wove its poisonous way into her heart. It seemed a betrayal of the One she loved. But she was haunted by memories. She recalled the dirt under her knees as she knelt beside a tousled bed in a dingy shack and begged God to spare a life. She remembered herself as a young woman in love, on the verge of what should have been her happiest moment.

Millie knew then, with a heaviness she couldn't overcome, that her inability to trust another went far deeper than her doubts about John Drexel.

Chapter Ten

 John stopped by the bank and asked the cashier, Mr. Fesler, to add Stephen's name to their account. He told Mr. Clark at the post office that the mail would be collected by his brother for the foreseeable future. Now he rang a bell, summoning his mother's staff to the entrance hall.

His hands grew damp at the thought of seeing Millie. At least the presence of the other servants would ensure a formal atmosphere, unlike the last time they spoke. Why had he been so testy? *As if I cared about her feelings for Stephen.*

Better to dwell on things he understood, such as business contracts, holdings, lines of credit, or anything else wonderfully straightforward. He needed to stay focused, to keep his mind sharp for his upcoming meetings with his clerk, broker, and the several titans of industry whose enterprises he'd invested in.

Not to mention the meeting he'd just called with his mother's servants. *I wonder what's keeping them?*

He was about to ring the bell again when the door at the back opened. They filed into the entrance hall and faced him in their stiff white aprons—the chambermaid, kitchen maid, and cook. *But no nurse.* He noticed that their appearances were neat as pins, except the good Mrs. Winters, whose arms were dusted with flour.

"Where's Miss Cooper?" he asked.

"She's mixing an elixir for your mother in the dry goods pantry," Beatrice answered.

A prickle ran up his spine. "My mother hasn't been having more of her attacks, has she?"

"No sir," Mrs. Winters assured him. "She's just not breathing as easy as usual today."

He didn't care for the sound of that, and he determined to talk to Millie before he left. *However much I dread the encounter.* He returned his attention to the servants. "I assume you know that I'm leaving for Philadelphia this afternoon."

They nodded.

"Any needs or concerns should be taken to my brother in my absence." At their uneasy exchange of glances, he gave them an encouraging smile. "He'll see to things, you needn't worry."

"Pardon me for asking," Beatrice said, "but what if Mr. Stephen finds himself too busy with his own affairs to bother with us?"

"He won't." But John had asked himself that very question for days. Abandoning this kindhearted little group of workers who'd come to rely on him was more difficult than he'd anticipated. Particularly since he was turning them over to Stephen. *At least they have Millie. She'll send for me if need be.*

The servants made no further objections, simply bobbed their curtsies and said their goodbyes.

He found Millie right where Beatrice said she would be, in the pantry. The room was adjacent to the kitchen, two steps downward. Shelves lined the walls, stocked with dry goods—sacks of flour, crates of potatoes, jars of spices. Braided dried garlic and onions dangled from the ceiling.

John ducked through the doorway and Millie glanced up from the paper bag she was filling with dusty lumps. She froze at first but then continued in her task, expression as cool as the air that rose up from the stone floor.

"Your mother isn't well," she said, "or I would have come to the meeting with the others."

She thinks I'm here to reprimand her? "I hope you'll always consider your duty to my mother to be above your duty to me, or to anyone else."

She thawed a little but maintained the distance between them.

He gestured toward her bag. "What's this?"

"Gingerroot. Earlier today, I remembered an elderly woman in Nantucket telling me that ginger tea soothed her husband greatly, before he passed on." Millie dropped another lump of ginger into the bag and folded the top. "I would have thought of it sooner, except she never said his illness was asthma. But now, looking back, I think it was. Anyway, boiled slices of ginger make a good tea, mixed with lemon and honey. I'm going to steep a pot for your mother."

A tightness squeezed his chest. "Is the matter truly so urgent?"

"Maybe not. But I like to act without delay, when something might help her."

There was a brief silence.

"How is my mother, really? And please, don't keep anything from me. I'm leaving in a few hours and cannot depart without knowing."

Millie met his gaze, a fact that threatened to unnerve him. "Some days she has trouble with her breathing. Not a severe attack, just labored. Today is one of those days. I can't explain it. We've been careful to keep dust and other irritants, colognes and such, from her. Other than a few strolls outdoors, she's been very sheltered. She's had several minor attacks, but nothing like the first one you and I witnessed, that night you came to me for help."

John knew he should have kept abreast of his mother's condition, regardless of how uneasy he was in Millie's presence. "I've been remiss. You've done much to ensure my mother's well-being, and I haven't even been aware of it. I'm grateful."

She shook her head. "It's my privilege to see to her."

"And it's mine to see to you."

Her gaze faltered. He encountered a mad impulse to draw nearer to her—much nearer. *How soft she is. How lovely.*

"You needn't worry about me, sir," she whispered.

Am I to be "sir" to her forever? It appeared so, and it rankled him. "On the contrary, I must 'worry' about all the persons in my employ."

Her demeanor altered, and she drew herself up. "Never fear that I've forgotten my place."

He battled the unseen foe of his guilt. If it weren't for him, her place in this house would be a very different one. *But that was years ago.*

John didn't enjoy his inner turmoil. He also didn't have time to sort through it. The train wouldn't wait, and his estate in Philadelphia had waited long enough. *Perhaps it's for the best that overseeing Millie will be another man's task now.*

Which was something he should mention before he departed, he realized. "Your role here is important. Never think otherwise. But I must go now, and my brother will manage this household in my absence." The indifference he longed to convey failed him. "Will this present a problem for you, Miss Cooper?"

Her eyes flashed. "No sir. It will not."

By her tone, he knew she understood the implication of his question. She clearly resented the suggestion that her former attachment to Stephen might be lingering, might interfere with her work. Piqued as they were, her mossy-brown eyes still drew him, a pull stronger than any quicksand.

Her voice shook. "May I go now?"

"You may." He forced himself to say no more.

She brushed past him. His shoulder moved once with the impact when she bumped against him, but he didn't take a step.

Didn't go after her.

❤

Millie sat in a rosewood chair she'd borrowed from the nearby dressing table. She held her stethoscope in position over Florence Drexel's heart, and took note of the steady beats with as much care as she took in avoiding the woman's eyes. The bedsprings creaked, the eyelet lace quilt stretched taut under Florence's cumbersome weight.

In the weeks since John's departure, Millie's days had been blessedly uneventful. She hadn't needed to seek out Stephen, because there hadn't been any upsets with the servants or Katherine's health. The few times she'd seen Florence, she merely asked about her diet, sleeping habits, and the baby's movements. She made sure there was no more bleeding or any sharp pains, and instructed her patient to send word if anything changed. But those interactions were brief.

Today was different.

She pulled the stethoscope from her ears and removed the thermometer from Florence's mouth. *A wonder of an invention, this little glass cylinder.* It was able to ascertain a patient's temperature in only five minutes.

Millie looked at the colored bar inside the glass. "Well Mrs. Drexel, it would seem that you're a healthy young woman."

Florence smiled shyly. "Do call me Florence. It's so confusing with two Mrs. Drexels."

"Very well." Millie slipped the thermometer into her medical bag. "Why don't we proceed with examining the baby, Florence?"

A rosy hue tinged the woman's cheeks. "Will you be, that is, will I be expected to—"

"Nothing invasive, I promise. I'll just be feeling your abdomen." Millie reached out and placed both hands on Florence's swollen belly.

The baby, Millie soon discovered, was lying sideways—and responded to her examination with a swift kick. She grinned. "For such a tiny foot, this little one has quite a kick."

There was wonder in Florence's eyes. "That's where its feet are?"

"Yes, and this"—Millie grasped Florence's hand and guided it to the opposite side of her belly—"is its head."

Florence's fingers moved in gently stroking circles. "No one ever explained such things to me before." After a moment, she frowned. "This is where it should be? The head, I mean?"

"Yes, the baby doesn't transition to the head-down position until closer to time to deliver." Millie withdrew her hands. "Be assured, everything seems to be progressing beautifully." *If only Florence weren't so beautiful herself.* Millie tried to dismiss the sour thought, but it lingered.

"I haven't been quite as worried about this baby as I was when I carried Lucy or Charlie. But one does wonder. As I mentioned, my doctor in Philadelphia didn't school me in such matters." Florence brushed her halo of blond curls away from her alabaster brow. "But then, I never asked him, since he was a man." She suddenly grasped both of Millie's hands in hers. "It's lovely to have you here instead, Millie. May I call you Millie?"

"Of course." Millie fought the urge to disengage her hands.

Florence released her hold and ducked her head. "You see, I feel that I already know you. My husband told me you used to be playmates, that—"

She was interrupted by a thump on the door, followed by a scuffling noise. Lucy burst into the room, her long brown hair streaming out behind her. Her father strode after her, but she dodged him and dived into her mother's lap.

Had Millie not been convinced that babes in wombs were sheltered in an encasement fashioned by the Almighty Himself, she would have been alarmed at the sight.

Florence winked at Stephen. "Do come in."

"I tried to stop her, but. . ." He blew his hair from his eyes and started again. "Darling, where is Nettie? I can't seem to find her anywhere, and it's past time for—"

Florence laid a hand on his arm. "We're nearly finished here."

"Mama," Lucy said, "Papa says I must play quietly in my room. But I want to go outside. I don't care if it's raining."

Florence unwound Lucy's arms from her waist and transferred them into Stephen's strong grasp. "Just take her downstairs, will you?

I truly won't be long." Mischief glinted in her eyes. "Or perhaps you'd rather stay here and discover all there is to know about the miracle of childbirth?"

A deep blush invaded his cheeks. He tightened his hold on his daughter while still gazing at his wife. Slowly he shook his head, eyes reproaching her even as his struggle not to laugh was all too apparent.

In that moment, Millie glimpsed his heart. *He cares for her.* More painfully, he and Florence had become friends. Somewhere along the way, they'd come to share what she'd once shared with Stephen herself.

In the confines of the room, she could detect his cologne. *It's like taking a deep breath on the sandbar during a storm.* She remembered that scent well. It had always seemed so reckless, uniquely Stephen. And somehow, it brought the past to life, shredded every last remnant of her inner calm.

"Come, Lucy." Stephen smoothed his daughter's hair. "Let's go see if your brother has awakened from his nap." He turned and walked toward the door, his hand stretched out behind him. To Millie's surprise, Lucy ran after him and caught his larger hand in hers.

In the quiet that followed their departure, Millie remembered Florence had been about to say something. *Something Stephen told her about our past.* But any interest Millie had in that, or any subject, had been vanquished by the look in Stephen's eyes when he'd gazed at his wife.

"My poor husband has been trying for weeks to find a nursemaid for the children. He's having difficulty keeping his patience with them, and doesn't understand why I feel differently."

Millie feigned interest. "Oh?"

Florence rested her palm on her abdomen, a motherly action that caused Millie a wistful ache.

"I'm not certain of the reason myself," Florence said. "But looking after Lucy and Charlie, trying as it is at times, brings me joy. It would be shocking in Philadelphia of course, children being attended by their own mother, but here. . ."

Millie nodded.

"Perhaps it's my upbringing. My mother was a member of the old guard, you see. She took pains to raise me with old-fashioned values. A well-bred young woman didn't expect to be waited on hand and foot, she must learn to do for herself. We *had* servants, it was just considered in poor taste to depend upon them too fully."

Millie lifted a brow. "That's a good policy in this case too, isn't it? Your servants certainly won't wish to birth this child for you."

Florence laughed, a delightful sound. "No, certainly not."

She reminds me of Ann, Millie realized. Oh, not in appearance. Though both women had fair hair, Florence was the more beautiful, and came from greater wealth. She was a cherished wife and mother. Ann still pined for a man who scarcely noticed her. *Perhaps the similarity isn't easy to define.*

Florence hesitated. "It's what drew me to him, you know. Stephen was so kind, not haughty toward his servants, or people who were considered beneath him, like other men in my set were."

Millie wished she didn't feel compelled to be polite. "Where did you and he first meet?"

"At a party in Boston given by my aunt, who was acquainted with one of his father's business associates. During the evening, Stephen asked a girl whose family had recently lost their fortune—due to a scandal, mind you—to dance with him. She'd been slighted at every turn. I thought it brave of him."

"Yes," Millie managed. "I'm sure it was." She gestured to Florence's belly. "It would seem that your child is to be fitted with a good father."

Florence nodded and began speaking of other things—namely, her baby.

Outwardly composed, Millie answered the woman's many questions on the topic. But inside, she was grasping for a reason to dislike this woman. *Things would seem easier if I could.*

♥

"He gave the cap a parting squeeze, in which his hand relaxed; and had barely time to reel to bed, before he sank into a heavy sleep."

Millie let her voice fade into silence. She once again sat at the bedside of a patient, this time with Dickens's *A Christmas Carol* in her lap. Though Katherine pretended to turn up her nose at such "fictitious drivel," she nonetheless leaned forward eagerly whenever Millie opened the red-and-gold cover. But tonight, drowsiness prevailed, and she'd fallen asleep.

She looks like a wax doll, lying there so still and white. She'd been docile and quiet all evening. There was a strange hum in her breathing—a tiny catch and a hint of a wheeze. It went away before nightfall, so Millie put it out of her mind.

The lamplight cast an orange glow over Katherine's face. A cold draft, its source a mystery, caused the filmy canopy that enveloped the bed to move in a ghostly flutter.

Over the past weeks, Millie had come to the conclusion that Katherine Drexel would have died if she hadn't moved to Colorado. She'd improved since Millie first came to be her nurse. Millie was sure it was due to escaping the smoke-chugging factories of Philadelphia. Whatever else she felt about John Drexel, she had to admire him for loading his family onto a train and prodding them to the depths of the Rocky Mountains, whether or not they wished to go.

She'd thought about him tonight, in the kitchen when she brewed Katherine a pot of ginger tea. The tangy, spicy aroma had reminded her of that encounter with him in the dry goods pantry. She'd longed to finish their conversation, to be the last one to speak, to hurt him as he'd hurt her. How plain he'd made it, that his concern for her was only as her employer. And how cutting he'd been, when he asked whether it would be a problem for her to work for Stephen.

She glanced down at Katherine's nightstand, at the little teapot, hot and fragrant on its silver tray, shadowed by the massive headboard.

Her heart all but stopped at the sound of a sudden whoosh of air emerging from Katherine's open, gasping mouth. Millie stared at the distended blue eyes, fixed on nothing. At the thin, hunched shoulders, head thrown back against the pillow in seizure-like rigidity. Every vein on the woman's neck was corded as she tried to draw in breath. Her dry lips worked as though to cry for help. But no words emerged.

"Shhhh." Millie reached for Katherine's upper arms and held her steady. "Don't try to talk, Mrs. Drexel. I'm right here."

She knew from her studies that in the throes of such an attack, the woman would scarcely be able to move, speak, even make the smallest gesture. Nothing but the agonized sputter of thwarted air escaped her throat.

In that instant, an aura of death, a fragility of body and spirit, seemed present at Katherine's bedside. *No, it must not win.*

"All will be well," Millie soothed. "I'm right here with you." She tugged Katherine forward into an upright, sitting position and loosened the ribbons at her throat. "There, that ought to ease things up a bit." She pleaded silently with the Almighty. *Please, please help her.*

A hissing sound, one that might pass for a breath, emerged from Katherine's mouth. Color ebbed into her ashen cheeks. The first breath was followed by a second. *Weaker, but better than no breath at all.*

Millie shakily poured a cup of tea. She lifted it toward Katherine's nose. "Here, Mrs. Drexel, it's the ginger tea you like so well. Doesn't it smell good?"

Miraculously, the woman seized the cup in both hands and took a small sniff.

She took another sniff.

Then an actual breath.

The tea seemed to be helping. It was as if the scent somehow calmed her and allowed the air to seep into her lungs.

Or perhaps it's the very breath of God.

Katherine's breath caught again. She gripped the cup in one hand and clung to Millie's sleeve with the other.

"You're going to be just fine, Mrs. Drexel. Just fine."

Katherine's hold loosened, but she didn't let go. Only when her breathing grew less sporadic did her hand slip down into her lap. Her look of childlike dependency slowly faded as the attack receded and her breaths returned to normal.

"Do you know," she croaked, "when Stephen was a child, he once came dashing into—" A series of fierce coughs interrupted her speech. She took a drink of tea. "He came dashing into our summer cottage, shouting that Rena had fallen and injured herself. I hurried, along with my lady's maid, to the beach, and there, sitting in the sand beside a jagged piece of driftwood, was my crumpled daughter." Katherine stopped, panting as though she'd just run a race. "You were sitting next to her, Millie. And while the maid was bandaging that skinned little knee, you stayed there, stroking Rena's hand." She drew in a long, wobbly breath. "You refused to leave her side."

"So did you," Millie said softly.

"Yes." Katherine gave the teacup to Millie and lay back against her pillow. "Of course I did. I'm her mother."

Millie imagined what it must have been like, growing up as this woman's child. Katherine Drexel would have insisted on nothing but the best for her offspring. She would hasten to their defense, that subtle strength able to defend them from most any foe. *The Drexel children were privileged in more ways than one.*

"I'm very tired," Katherine said suddenly.

"Would you like me to read to you some more?"

"No, I don't think so."

"I wouldn't mind, truly."

Katherine sniffed. "I should hope you wouldn't. It's your duty to see to my needs." She paused. "You ought to go to bed, child."

Millie rose then hesitated. "I'm glad you're feeling. . .more yourself, Mrs. Drexel."

"I haven't felt like myself in ages." An edge hardened Katherine's voice. "People who are the picture of health, most often rustics, cannot know what it is to carry an ailment about one's neck like a millstone. Always aware of it but never speaking of it."

"Oh, but I—"

"A simple island vagabond like yourself cannot understand."

Over the years, Millie had learned to suppress the curse of her hasty temper, passed down from generation upon generation of her mother's Irish predecessors. But she couldn't quite manage it tonight. "Perhaps, if you'd broaden your mind, Mrs. Drexel, you might find that a simple island vagabond understands more than you think." *And cares too much about what a frail old woman thinks of her.*

Millie lifted the tray from the nightstand and fled the room. She didn't look back, unwilling for Katherine to see the tears that had gathered in her eyes.

❤

In her sleep, she heard them again, the pitiful moans, the delirious murmurings. Saw the black curls fanned out on the perspiration-drenched pillow. Felt the heat that rose from the rash-covered skin.

"Baby, get a cloth for her head. It's hurting her somethin' fierce."

She could smell it, the scent of the most dreadful disease she'd ever encountered. The soiled confines of the shack caused her mind to reel and her temples to pound as though she'd contracted the illness herself.

"Here's the cloth I brought for you, Mama. Wake up, Mama, wake up!"

But her mother didn't.

Millie jerked upright in her bed. She looked about her room, gazed at the sloped ceiling, the posy-strewn wallpaper until she knew, really knew, that she was back in the present.

A sliver of light shone from the window and fell across the worn Bible on the dresser. The envelope protruded reassuringly from the pages, its contents creating a bulge in the leather-bound book.

I still haven't returned that locket to Stephen. She'd do it, sometime. But it was all that tied her to her early history, to the memories she both feared and hoped would fade.

Millie swung her legs out of bed and walked over to the dresser. She slipped the envelope from the Bible and slid the locket into her palm. She pushed the tiny, spring-loaded button, and the gold encasement popped open. A choking lump filled her throat as she beheld the coil of black hair, nestled against the velvet lining.

She stared down at that silken lock, shiny as a crow's wing, and felt just as she had when she'd hurried from Katherine's bedroom. . .like a lost child.

Chapter Eleven

$\mathcal{D}$espite the bitter cold of the Pennsylvania morning, John reveled in the sounds that came from the rows of stalls. He liked the rhythmic cadence of pitchfork into hay, the stomping of restless hooves.

His newest foal, a six-month-old Thoroughbred beauty, looked at him with wary eyes from her place in the corner of the stall. He knelt down, trying to be soothing. "Aren't you a little darling," he crooned. He continued to speak in low tones until she returned to munching hay.

Sid, the stable manager, approached on bowed legs, the mark of a man who spent much time in the saddle. He entered the stall and gestured toward the foal. "I see you've found the newest member of your family, Drexel."

John stood and held out his hand. "Sid Delaney. It's good to see you."

Sid shook his hand. "Been wondering when you'd get tired of Colorado."

John smiled. "As close to heaven as this place is, I'd get tired of just about anywhere else."

It might seem a strange remark to make in a stall that hadn't been mucked yet this morning. But John didn't find the distinct, earthy smell of horse manure unpleasant.

Sid nodded. "Your pa felt the same way."

It had been their special outing, his and his father's, coming here to the Gentry Valley Stables. Charles Drexel was a horseman, and John inherited the love from him. "I can't stay away, even in two feet of snow—any more than he could." The words were laden with memories.

He'd left the city before dawn, hoping to see if the foal, whom Sid had written him about, was ready to sell. But then, any excuse would do, when faced with mounds of paperwork and an overzealous clerk back at his estate.

He returned his gaze to the foal. "She'll be worth a tidy sum one day, I'd wager."

"Her bloodlines say so. . .and so does she." Sid shook his head, eyes full of admiration. "What a beauty."

The silky mane and long legs were the least of the foal's good looks. *It's something in her eyes.* They shone with a keen intelligence. "You think I should sell her yet?" John asked. *Please say no.*

"Well, she follows nice and gentle on a lead rope, and she's been eating oats for a while now."

John's heart sank.

Sid gave him a knowing sideways glance. "But she could use some more training yet. Still a little skittish."

"That's what I like to hear." John knew that Sid suspected what he himself was just realizing—he'd never sell this foal.

Sid chuckled. "You make a first-rate businessman, Drexel. Turn quite a profit when it comes to horses."

John laughed, and Sid slapped his back. "Come on out to the paddock, I have something to show you."

The "something" turned out to be a blooded bay stallion that nearly robbed John of breath. There was raw power in the animal's every movement. The sheen of his dark coat, slightly dappled beneath the surface, stood out in sharp relief against the white-railed fences and snowy hills of the Pennsylvania countryside.

The stallion pawed the snow with effortless agility. He was pure grace as he lifted his head at the trainer's prodding and cantered in a circle on the hard-packed trail.

His trainer stood in the center of the paddock, beaver hat over his ears. He communicated with quiet commands and the smallest twitches of his mitted hands. *I'd gladly trade places with him.* John's palms fairly itched to hold the lunge line and be nearer to that magnificent animal.

"Like him?" Sid asked.

John let out a low whistle.

Sid grinned and rested his elbows on the rail. "His sire's a sheer bolt of lightning called Night Stalker, shipped from England a few years back. His grandsire, Night Tempest—he's the first of the Nights—made quite a name for himself across the Atlantic."

John jutted his chin toward the stallion. "What's his name?"

"Night Hawk."

"It suits him."

As John watched the commanding steed gallop around the paddock, he knew he'd be back next week, and the week after that, to pay a visit to Night Hawk.

❤

The warm blaze in the library hearth at the estate should have been comforting. The familiar gilt-framed portrait of the Drexel patriarch above the hearth was illuminated in the flickering light. The painting captured the intensity of the man's eyes, vivid green beneath his thick brows. With his dark sideburns and curvy mouth, Charles Drexel more closely resembled Stephen than John. *In many ways, unfortunately.*

John looked down at the letter in his hand and nearly groaned. "He bought a hotel," he said to the empty room.

The letter indeed contained the news that Stephen had bought a hotel. And not just any hotel, but the former Fancy Leona's, an institution whose origins were easy to guess. When Glenwood Springs had grown from its crude beginnings and started to resemble a proper town, the hotel was bought by a businessman from Ohio. He'd done his best to make it a respectable establishment. But it was cheaply constructed, already falling apart. Even the grounds were in sore need of attention.

Stephen explained in his letter that the owner had wanted to sell because he'd been lonely ever since his son went away to college. The boy had remained back east, and his father decided to join him there. *More likely, the man sold out for lack of paying guests.*

John turned to the second page of the letter. *"I think with some renovations,"* Stephen had written, *"the place would really come into its own."*

John read no further. Why had he left his brother in charge of the family. . .and its resources? He should have hired a clerk in Glenwood Springs to oversee their financial affairs. But how could he have known this would happen? Stephen had never shown an interest in business before, seeming content to leave those matters to John. *Which clearly was the prudent course of action.* Now they'd be saddled with a money-draining facility, and he would be responsible for keeping the venture from becoming a disaster. *My brother has no idea the thin ice we walk on sometimes.* Buying and selling, guessing and wagering, was a dangerous game, even when a man knew the rules.

John rose and poured himself a glass of port. He held it by the sturdy stem and stared into the hearth, his mind drifting miles away. He thought about Glenwood Springs, about the majestic mountains that sheltered the town from the outside world, the merging rivers that were the lifeblood of the valley, the little white church that burst at the seams with sincere believers. He thought about his mother, about Stephen and his family. He thought about Millie. *I've missed her,* he realized. He reminded himself that the woman wasn't exactly keen on him just now, given their parting conversation.

And yet. . .

He took a sip of his drink and listened to the clock on the wall strike its slow, monotonous hour. He pictured Millie, saw the injured look in her eyes when he'd asked whether working for Stephen would prove too difficult for her.

And suddenly he knew he'd never felt more alone.

It was enough to make a man want to throw his glass of port against the wall.

Chapter Twelve

On a clear midwinter day, the jagged mountain peaks white against the blue sky, the town below covered in glittering frost, the unthinkable happened.

While Millie's frail, wheezing patient chugged steadily along, her glowing, robust mother-to-be fell ill.

Millie had encountered this particular illness before, both in wakefulness and sleep. . .in reality and dreams.

She sent for Dr. Murphy to confirm what she already knew, secretly hoping he'd stay at her side throughout the ordeal. But he couldn't be away long, he said. There were two other cases of the illness in town. He had to try and stop an outbreak, confine the patients to their rooms, forbid anyone but himself from visiting them. He must warn the townspeople to boil their drinking water and cease eating raw foods, at least until he learned the source of the contamination.

So it was, in a dark mingling of her past and present, Millie found herself nearly alone in a fight against the disease that had claimed her mother's life. She allowed only Tansy in the sickroom. The cook was familiar with the disease, and knew to wash her hands and cleanse anything that came into contact with their infectious patient.

Stephen vacillated between tending to his children and hovering in the hallway outside his wife's room, where he paced the floor with drawn face and anxious eyes.

As night fell, a silvery moon arose. It shone through the window and cast its dim light over Florence. The woman's fever-flushed cheeks and damp, twisted nightgown seemed to cause a dusk, more real than the darkness outside, to descend upon Millie. She did her best to dismiss the memories the sights evoked, and leaned over to change the cloth on Florence's brow, her own soaked in perspiration. She removed the warm towel and took the cool one Tansy handed her.

The cook wiped her palms on her apron and dug about in her pocket. "I just remembered—the doc sent a message." She drew out a wrinkled piece of paper and gave it to Millie.

Millie read the lines with a hurried gaze then sagged against the bedpost. *Thank You, God.*

"What he say?" Tansy asked.

Instead of answering, Millie looked at the cook sharply, a sudden tension in her stomach. "Has everyone in the house stopped drinking milk, even the children?"

"Yes, we done just like you told us. Boiled all the water and washed the vegetables like they's covered in filth, and ate no cheese or butter or milk."

Millie's tension eased. She let the note flutter to the floor unheeded and turned her attention back to her patient. She laid the cloth on Florence's forehead and smoothed out the edges. Realizing she hadn't answered Tansy's question, she said, "Dr. Murphy writes that he thinks the illness began at Hank Rainer's farm." The farmer kept cows and sold milk to a handful of families, including Stephen's. "Apparently, he hired a milkmaid recently, a German woman new to town. Dr. Murphy went to the farm and warned Hank to keep the maid away from the cows and their milk. Only Florence and a couple others were infected."

"The German gal sick or something?"

Millie unbuttoned Florence's nightgown at the neck and examined her chest. The unimproved, rose-colored bumps caused a sinking feeling in Millie's middle. "No, the maid isn't ill. But after immigrating to America, she lived in Chicago for ten years. The city has suffered several outbreaks of typhoid fever." She dabbed witch hazel extract on a cloth and rubbed it over Florence's chest. The poor woman flinched away from Millie's ministering strokes. "It's all right," she soothed, "this will help." She glanced at Tansy. "Typhoid fever can be spread by someone who's been exposed to the disease, but isn't actually afflicted with it. With no other newcomers to town, Dr. Murphy thinks the milkmaid must be the cause."

Tansy nodded and went to stand by the wall at the head of the bed, a faithful sentinel at her lady's service.

For Millie, every muffled groan from the sickbed, every whiff of willow bark, brought the past to life in a way that made her stomach churn. She felt like that scared little girl again, watching her mother's life ebb away.

But she was jarred to the present when Florence's eyes flew open. The woman reached up and grabbed Millie's arms, her gaze filled with desperation. "My baby," she murmured.

Millie longed to invent a reassuring tale, to give this woman a conciliatory pat on the head. But as she looked into the gaunt, pleading face, she found she couldn't see Florence as just another patient in need of comfort, or even as a rival. Millie saw only a sweet mother, fearful for her child. *She could have been a friend, if I'd let her.* Perhaps, in time, Millie would have.

But time was not a luxury she possessed at this moment. *It's too soon—too soon for the baby.*

"Florence," she said gently, "it's difficult to be sure of how babes in wombs might be affected by an illness. The best thing for both of you is for you to rest. Take as much nourishment as you can, and just try to sleep." She managed a smile. "Can you do that for me?"

Florence nodded, her assent followed by a soft moan. "My head aches."

Millie went to the dresser, where there was a glass of boiled water and a jar of medicine. The medicine, white willow bark, was known to lessen headaches and lower fevers. So far it had succeeded in doing both for Florence.

Millie mixed the powder with the water then hastened back to the bed and helped Florence sit up. Sip by sip, her patient drank the mixture. Once finished, she sank back onto her pillow, lips pursed against the pain but body less rigid.

Millie straightened and stood motionless. She tried to still the spinning of her thoughts, a careening carousel that threatened to overwhelm her. *No, there's no time to stop, no time to think.* "Tansy, go fetch more cool cloths and boiled water, please." *And please, dear God, give me the strength to help this poor, sick woman.*

❤

Three weeks later, Millie sat at Florence's bedside in Katherine's opulent spare room, still keeping her wakeful vigil, the faithful cook still at her side. After that first night, Stephen had brought Florence over to his mother's house, so Millie could be close to both her patients. Katherine was forbidden to go anywhere near the sickroom, and for once, she'd followed orders.

Millie stared at the velvet, gold-colored curtains across from her. She noted the way the two sides didn't quite meet in the middle, leaving a narrow gap between them. Her weary gaze went through that gap, out to the sky, to the stars that twinkled in the inky blackness.

Her limp body molded itself to the chair. These past weeks, the nights and days had blurred together. Hour upon hour she'd labored. She'd administered tonics of willow bark and witch hazel, cooled Florence's fevered forehead, gathered up soiled linens to be taken to the servants' hall and laundered. She'd hardly paused to sleep or eat. Her throat was dry, parched with thirst, her eyes seemingly unable to form tears.

While she sat staring out the window, the sound of her own pulse grew louder and louder in her ears.

Her patient's swollen belly partially obstructed her view. The babe that caused the protrusion, ever in the background of Millie's thoughts, now consumed them. *We could do it—we just might be successful.* It had been too early before, when Florence first contracted the fever. *But now the child might survive.*

Oh, but it was risky. Such a procedure was a terrible danger to the mother. The operation was to be avoided at all possible costs. *Could Florence endure it?*

Millie gazed down at the flushed face and unmoving body before her. Despite every effort, Florence's fever had continued to rise, and was now at perilous heights. Her delirium had increased. The distant look in her eyes grew more pronounced, until her mind seemed to be somewhere else entirely. But even more telling was the unmistakable aura that surrounded her, an aura Millie was all too familiar with. She'd felt it at many bedsides. This precious wife and mother, so worth saving, was dying.

Once Millie admitted the truth to herself, she knew what she must do.

At first, her body refused to obey her command to turn and speak to Tansy. But then, gifted by an energy that sprang up as if from nowhere, she whirled around.

"Tansy, please send word to the doctor, and tell him I need him to come and perform a cesarean section."

The large woman's eyes grew round as could be. In time, she recovered with a shake of her head and bustled from the room.

Silence shrouded Millie, a numbness of mind and spirit that didn't last long.

I'll have to tell Stephen.

She cringed at the very idea. She'd already informed him that his wife's condition was worsening, but she doubted he'd even heard her. Sometime during the past weeks, his anxious pacing had turned into a befuddled daze. He'd wandered the halls of his mother's house, responding to all queries in absent tones. *He won't be so oblivious when he hears this news.* It didn't seem fair, that she had to be the one to tell him.

Millie forced herself to leave the room and walk out into the hall. She looked both ways. Stephen wasn't readily visible, but she could hear a faint noise from around the corner. She moved toward it and saw him sitting on the window seat, head against the pane. He rose when she approached.

"How is she?" He stood waiting for an answer in that way of his, hands clasped tightly behind his back.

Oh, how Millie wanted to reassure him. How she wished he were still in his daze, unable to comprehend what she had to say. "I regret that I have some. . .difficult news."

He waited, sea-hued gaze fixed on hers.

Just say it. "I'm sending for the doctor to perform a cesarean section to deliver your child." *Please help him understand that Florence is beyond saving.*

"Why?"

Her heart plunged. "To save your baby's life."

Still he didn't seem to understand. "Won't it be too dangerous? For Florence, I mean?"

Millie's dry eyes finally, after three parched weeks, flooded with tears. "I'm afraid that it's too late for Florence."

The realization dawned on his face, profound and painful to behold. He pressed his fingers against the bridge of his nose as though bracing himself against an unbearable agony. He remained that way, head bowed. In the careworn, defeated lines of his mouth and brow, Millie could barely see a remaining hint of the boy she'd once loved.

How can this be happening?

Millie reached toward him. "I'm so sorry," she whispered.

He jerked away, eyes flashing. "Don't."

Her lips trembled. "Stephen. . ."

"Just don't."

He spun around and walked away, his aim the stairs, his gait never wavering.

She wanted to collapse into a heap and sob, but knew she couldn't. This wasn't the time to let herself feel, to wonder if he'd ever recover from this moment.

She had a surgery to prepare for.

♥

Everything moved quickly after Dr. Murphy arrived.

A wintry draft entered the sickroom with the physician. Flakes of snow flew up from his overcoat as he took it off. He set his bag on the dresser and strode to the bed. He stooped over Florence, gray brows knitted together.

As if through a long tunnel, Millie heard him ask how close the baby was to its expected date of arrival.

"About six weeks, I think," she replied.

His frown deepened. He studied Florence a few seconds longer, then he straightened and spoke tersely over his shoulder. "We must deliver this child. Now."

The next minutes passed in swift preparation. Only doctor and nurse were permitted in the room.

Millie hastened to the dresser, where she'd put the surgical instruments to soak in a basin of carbolic acid. By the light of the kerosene lamp, she lifted them out one by one—scalpel, syringe, clamp, scissors, and needles—and set them to dry on a clean cloth.

Dr. Murphy wiped iodine low on Florence's abdomen and glanced up from the brownish stain. "Carbolic acid."

Millie gave him the bottle, and he sprayed his hands with the sterilizing solution.

"Chloroform her," he said next.

She grabbed the cloth-covered cone off the nightstand. She knew she must be careful when she dropped the potent droplets on it, but she was having trouble concentrating on anything but the fact that this woman, Stephen's beloved wife, was fading.

For Florence was looking right at her.

The light had nearly gone from her eyes. Her breaths were shallow, cheeks scarlet, fever ablaze. But for one moment, she was aware of her surroundings.

"The bab—" she said in a just-audible voice.

The word was distorted, unfinished, but Millie understood it. She stepped to the bed and stroked her patient's shoulder. "Your baby is still with us, Florence. I promise we'll do our best for him or her."

Little change came over the woman's face. She seemed incapable of making even the slightest expression.

Lord, she was so healthy, so full of life. Now she was an almost empty shell—a shell whose baby might die if they didn't hurry.

By habit, Millie dropped the right amount of chloroform onto the cone. She held it over Florence's mouth and nose and waited until the woman's eyes drifted shut and her jaw went slack.

Millie removed the cone. "She's ready."

Dr. Murphy leaned down until his face was mere inches from Florence's belly. With a steady hand, he made his incision.

Millie worked alongside him in the flickering light. She stymied the flow of blood, handed him instruments, and wiped his perspiring brow by turns. She glanced often at Florence's closed eyes to be sure the woman was still unconscious.

All the while, Millie had difficulty quieting her racing thoughts. Perhaps she'd acted prematurely. Perhaps the baby would never draw its first breath. Dr. Murphy had agreed, thankfully, with her conclusion that there was no time to lose. But that didn't guarantee success. Even if the babe managed to take an initial breath, would its lungs be developed enough to draw all the breaths that needed to follow? *Oh God, please let them be.*

Into Millie's mind came a glimpse, just a flash, of a vision. She could see Him, Jesus in the boat. He was here, the One who'd stood up in a raging storm, spread out His arms, and commanded the wind and waves to be still. He was Lord of the storm. How, she didn't know, but she clung to the vision with everything in her.

Then it happened. The heart-stopping moment when the doctor lifted that scrawny being up from its bloody encasement.

As Millie stared at that tiny baby girl, the world ceased revolving. Even the lamplight seemed to stand at attention, its lurching shadows like statues. Nothing disturbed the hushed, breathless silence.

She's perfect. Beautiful.

But she wasn't crying.

Wee fingers and toes splayed outward. Twig-sized legs scrunched against slimy chest, arms stretched out as though railing in protest. But no sound emitted from the lips. The baby's tummy, dwarfed by the umbilical cord, didn't rise and fall as it should.

Do something.

The two-word echo from Millie's past helped her unfreeze. She snatched the syringe off the nightstand and used it to suction mucus from the baby's mouth.

Dr. Murphy didn't hesitate an instant when she'd finished, but in one rapid motion, turned the infant in his hand, face toward the floor. Millie feared he might drop her.

Smack, went the doctor's palm, flat against the round bottom. And smack, it went again.

A feeble cry, more like a lamb's bleat, broke the silence, followed by breaths.

Thank You, dear God in heaven.

Dr. Murphy returned the baby to her upright position, clamped and snipped the umbilical cord, and gave her to Millie. "Get her cleaned off and into blankets," he ordered. "Take her to a hearth fire and keep her there." He stooped back over Florence without waiting to see if Millie obeyed.

He was right not to hover—Millie cleaned and wrapped the scarcely breathing baby with the utmost care.

Just before she left the room, the infant feeling weightless in her arms, she looked at the bed. Dr. Murphy was suturing Florence's incision with a neat row of stiches, when suddenly he paused and glanced up at his patient's face. Soberly, he drew the needle up, pulled the thread taut, and knotted it off. Then slowly, tenderly, he reached over and closed her eyes.

Chapter Thirteen

Millie paced before the glowing hearth in the library, her gaze on the tiny newborn she held in her arms. She paused and looked at the clock on the wall—again.

An hour had passed since she'd sent for the woman she hoped would serve as a wet nurse. The baby needed to eat soon, while she was still alert. *But is she even capable of it?* The thought that she might not be developed enough to latch, to suck, to swallow, was too terrible to contemplate. Moment by tense moment, Millie feared the infant wouldn't live to draw her next breath. The rise and fall of her bony little chest was so shallow. *So. . .rickety.*

And would the jailer's wife, whose baby Dr. Murphy had delivered three months ago, be willing to come in the dead of night?

A log fell in the hearth, and sparks shot upward. To Millie's tired eyes, it was all a fiery orange blur.

Footsteps sounded in the entrance hall. They grew louder, and then the library door cracked open. The jailer's wife, hair straggled around her chapped cheeks, leaned into the room.

Never had Millie seen a sight quite so beautiful. "Come in, Mrs. Mosley. Thank you for coming so late at night."

"Oh, I hurried right on over when I heard the news. But the snow's coming down like the judgment, and the drifts are that deep." Mrs.

Mosley entered the room. She looked at the baby, and her plain face softened. "Poor little mite. I don't know as I have enough milk to spare for her, though I dearly hope so of course."

So do I. Millie transferred the baby into the woman's stout arms. The infant all but disappeared against the large bosom.

"She must be kept warm at all times," Millie warned.

"Oh, I know. I had an early one myself—my first." Mrs. Mosley held the baby expertly in the crook of her arm. She glanced at Millie. "If I may say so, you look clean worn out. Why don't you go sit a spell, and leave this to me?"

With a compliance born of exhaustion, Millie took the woman's advice. But she paused at the door, hand on the knob, and looked back. How could a babe so small, whose head fit entirely into one's palm, be *living*? Was it because of the prayers, surely lifted to heaven from father, grandmother, and servants? *Yes, and because the babe's mother clung to life long enough to impart strength to her child.*

At the remembrance of Florence, a weight as heavy as rocks descended over Millie. The child had consumed her mind, but now there was nothing to keep her from thinking about the mother. The sweet woman she'd been unable to save.

The thought brought a painful sob. But Millie knew if she allowed herself to cry, she'd fall to pieces.

She left the library and started toward the stairs. In the entrance hall, she met Beatrice, who was on her way to the kitchen to fetch Katherine a glass of warm milk. Shortly after Florence had fallen ill, Beatrice offered to care for Katherine, who'd had difficulty sleeping since learning of her daughter-in-law's dire condition. *But she's my patient. I should see to her.* Millie moved to take the glass from Beatrice, but the slender kitchen maid clung to it with surprising strength.

"You need to get some sleep, Miss Cooper."

Before Millie could respond, she heard footsteps on the stairs above them. She glanced up and froze.

Stephen descended the steps. His hair was disheveled, his eyes bloodshot. His wrinkled shirt hung loose over his trousers, his necktie undone.

And he was looking at her with eyes aflame.

That look enveloped her, caused her soul to sink and her knees to quake. She was hardly aware of her surroundings, of Beatrice's presence. She spoke quickly, soothingly. "Your newborn daughter is in the library. She's eating now, but you should be able to see her soon."

He ignored the words and came to loom before her. "You," he said through clenched jaw. "You insisted on prying into something you knew nothing of. Sent for a butcher to come take a knife to my wife. To *cut* into her. To—" He broke off, a sheen in his eyes. His mouth opened, but he seemed voiceless.

Her reply was tremulous. "I am so sorry for your loss, Stephen. We had to act swiftly, in order to save your baby's life. She's beautiful."

He pointed a rigid finger at her. The voice he'd lost returned with a vengeance.

Even Beatrice shrank from him.

"What gives you the right to risk my wife's life? To take her away from me like that? How dare you come into my family's home and decide whose life should be traded for whose!"

Millie felt so very muddled. She could hardly understand what he was saying. But there was no mistaking his tone. It pelted against her like a hail of bullets. *How he hates me.* In that terrible moment, she didn't blame him. Mightn't Florence have pulled through after all, without the trauma of a surgery?

"I should have known," he continued. "The second I saw you standing in my brother's study, looking for all the world like an innocent girl in need of a big, strong protector. I should have known then that it was all an act. You resented her, didn't you? From the very first. You couldn't wait to—"

"No!" The objection fairly wrenched from Millie's lips. "I did everything I could for her." She felt the heaving sobs, dry and horrible, begin to steal her breath away. She forced them down as best she could and rushed past him. Past Beatrice, whose eyes were wellsprings of sympathy.

Millie fled up the stairs, somehow sure he wouldn't pursue her.

She raced into her room and flung herself across the bed.

Head buried in the billowy softness of her pillow, she poured out her tears. For some time she remained that way, prone and sobbing.

Depleted but unable to sleep, Millie sat up, her back against the wall. The moonlight streamed in from the lone window and lent the room a pale glow. The sight of her mother's Bible on the dresser both comforted and distressed her. It reminded her of the vision she'd so recently seen—Jesus in the boat, standing in a raging storm, commanding the wind and waves to be still. She'd been confident, as she helped the doctor surgically deliver that baby, that her Lord was in control of the storm. But she'd just come from the deathbed of a patient, a patient who'd left this world too soon.

Was Florence's death my fault?

Stephen certainly thought so. Millie forced back another sob. As far as memory served, he'd never been one to raise his voice. That he'd done so to her caused a wound difficult to bear. She tried to wipe her tears, but fresh ones surged up in their place. They arose from a well deep inside her, a marred reservoir. In her heart of hearts, she bore another wound far worse than the one Stephen had inflicted.

It found its root in her faltering faith. *No one* was in control of this storm.

♥

The next morning, Millie opened her eyes and realized she'd fallen asleep sitting up. Her head had lolled onto her shoulder, her tears dried onto her cheeks. The sun streamed in through the window, having just crested the craggy heights of Glenwood Canyon. She'd been asleep for several hours.

Suddenly she tensed. *The baby. What if she wasn't able to eat? What if they haven't kept her warm enough?*

Millie compelled her stiff legs to swing out of bed and hurry across the floorboards, out the door.

When she passed Katherine's room, she glimpsed her patient standing stock still, staring down at a note that lay on the tea table in her little sitting area.

Millie paused.

Katherine glanced up. "Come in," she said tonelessly.

Millie entered the room, the baby still paramount in her thoughts. "The baby, is she—"

"She's being seen to." Katherine stooped and lifted the note from the table. She held it a moment, gazing at it as though it were a living thing, then handed it to Millie. "Stephen is gone."

Millie felt the blood ebb from her cheeks. *Surely he hasn't done a dreadful. . .harm to himself.* "You mean. . . ?"

"It's all in the note."

Millie looked down and read the words scrawled across the page.

"Mother," Stephen had written. *"I find I cannot remain in this place that has become a prison to me. Every room, every once-precious sight, even my children, are an unbearable reminder of all that I have lost. Do not look for my return. I can no longer endure a life in which the woman dearest to my heart has been so cruelly snatched from me."* It was signed simply, *"Stephen."*

Millie let the note dangle from her fingers. She sought her numb mind for something to say. He'd left his family. His home. Abandoned his children. *Surely he wouldn't do such a thing.* "Do you think he really means it?"

Katherine nodded, seeming taxed by the effort. "Even as a child, Stephen was too rash for his own good—but this is different. I'm convinced it's not an impulse of the moment. My son is torn asunder, Millie. Ill-equipped to meet this, his greatest tragedy." Her chin trembled. "I coddled him too greatly when he was young."

Millie tried to speak, to offer some consolation. Instead she just stood there for several seconds, helpless in the face of such anguish. *She looks so stooped, so old and tired.*

But after a time, Katherine straightened, as if bolstered by a dormant strength. "That is as it may be. We must determine what to do now."

Very true. A motherless newborn needed feeding. Two small children needed tending. At present, the children were being minded by a rotation of maids in a house bereft of both mother and father. *But since when has the highborn Mrs. Drexel consulted her lowly nurse on such matters?*

It didn't escape Millie that she was being extended an olive branch. Katherine Drexel had set aside her prejudices, at least for now. *She's astute enough to realize that we must work together.* "It's difficult to know where to begin."

"Yes." Katherine sighed. "There's the baby, and the children. And the servants will require direction of course."

"About the baby—the wet nurse I sent for may not prove sufficient."

Katherine blinked. "Why ever not?"

Millie hesitated. It was an uncomfortable topic to discuss, even for a nurse. "Sometimes a woman's supply of milk doesn't answer the demands of one hungry babe, much less two."

Katherine's ears turned crimson.

In the silence that followed, Millie remembered something. She hated to overwhelm her patient with this now, but it needed to be addressed. "There's the matter of Florence's funeral as well."

Katherine's brave posture began to crumble, like a sandcastle being engulfed in a giant wave. "My son has left behind quite a mess, hasn't he?"

Her endurance is waning. "Why don't you lie down for a while, Mrs. Drexel? I'll help you over to the chaise." Millie clasped Katherine's arm to do just that, and thankfully, the woman didn't resist. She sank heavily onto her seat, head against the floral cushion behind her.

Millie went to the bed to retrieve a pillow, and as she crossed the room, the questions that had haunted her the night before resurfaced. Only this time, they didn't defeat her. Whether she could have saved Florence if she'd acted differently, or whether she should have let the babe live or die as nature dictated, were no longer foremost in her mind. Nor was Stephen's outraged litany of grief, with pale Beatrice looking on.

At this moment, all she saw were Katherine's eyes, drained of their former spark. *How terrible to have lived so many years and still be unable to rely on one's son.* Millie longed to be someone this woman could trust. To show herself different than Katherine had thought her. To overcome obstacles and be of use. *Please help me find a way.*

Millie returned to the chaise and slid the pillow beneath Katherine's head.

Katherine struggled into a more upright position. Once erect, she gave Millie a resolved look. "Our priorities are clear, young woman."

"Yes?"

"First, we must locate a suitable wet nurse for the babe."

Millie nodded.

"Second, we must make arrangements for Florence's funeral."

"I'll see to both as quickly as I can," Millie promised.

Katherine eased back against the pillow and closed her eyes. Her voice came softly. "Stephen would want violets on the casket. They were Florence's favorite flower. Never did he fail to bring her a bouquet of violets every spring. That, at least, my son could be depended on to do."

It was then that Millie knew how she could be of most use. Before she even found a wet nurse or saw to the funeral, she would send a telegram to Philadelphia.

Because you, madam, have more than one son to depend on.

Chapter Fourteen

*J*ohn sat in the cavernous Philadelphia dining room eating a late breakfast. He was alone save the maid, Jennie, who always stood by to refill his coffee cup. He'd just opened the newspaper to the finance page when Dickson entered the room.

"A telegram came for you, sir." The butler held out a small silver tray with his white-gloved hand.

John's knife and fork clattered to his plate as he reached for the telegram. He tried to ignore the knot that formed in his stomach but thought of his mother, and it squeezed even tighter. *It's probably nothing.* He often received telegrams when his clerk was away on business errands.

John slit the seal, flipped up the top fold, and read the few printed words.

"Who is it from?" Jennie burst out, apparently compelled by a curiosity that made her forget her manners.

"My mother's nurse." For an instant, he just stared down at the telegram. Then he dropped it to the table and rose so quickly his chair almost tipped over. He tossed his napkin onto his plate and turned to face Dickson. "Tell Mack to harness the roan. I'm catching the eleven o'clock train."

"But sir," the butler protested, "it's ten forty now."

"I can do it."

And John dashed from the room, fully intending to make good his promise.

❤

Two days later, carpetbag in hand, he entered his mother's house in Glenwood Springs. The walk from the train depot had been long and frigid, and he was chilled through. He didn't stop to hang his hat in the entrance hall but headed straight for the staircase, toward the ruckus that came from the second floor.

He followed the noise to the spare room, a somber affair with dark green curtains and a gold-colored map of the world hanging on the wall above the dresser. He stood in the doorway unnoticed.

Lucy sat "reading" a book to her brother and her dolls. Charlie, rather than heed the story, busied himself wrapping a curtain cord around one of the doll's heads. The children looked so small and helpless in that corner, dwarfed by that enormous curtain.

John glanced at the opposite side of the room and watched as Millie heaved one end of Lucy's four-poster bed, Sally the other. *They must have moved the children's things over here from Stephen's house.* Both women breathed heavily, hair stuck to perspiring foreheads. Millie, in particular, appeared so dead on her feet that John wanted to rush over and lift the bed from her. Indeed, he stepped forward to do just that, but before he could, a feminine shriek arose from the corner.

He whirled to see Lucy pointing at Charlie, who was now swinging from the curtain, a human pendulum.

Both women dashed toward him. Millie snatched him up midair, and he squirmed and tried to launch himself from her grasp. His flailing boot struck her in the chest, and the white strain around her lips indicated she was struggling not to cry out.

Before John could blink, Lucy burst into tears. "Charlie almost falled," she bawled.

Not a second later, from the room across the hall, there came a piercing wail. The baby had evidently awakened from its slumber.

With the children in disarray and the furniture askew around her, Millie looked up and saw him standing there. He knew she'd seen him by the way her eyes grew round with dismay. Charlie's gaze followed hers, and his eyes widened too, but with glee. The boy gave a great, rocking lurch, and Millie nearly dropped him. She recovered and set him safely onto the floor. He sped, Lucy close behind, to John, who fought a lump in his throat at the sight.

He dropped his bag and knelt to welcome them. He felt the impact of their clinging arms like a blow to the stomach. His mind couldn't settle on one thought. *Florence is really gone. My brother left his children here to flounder.* Seeing them so. . .lost. . .made it real. And what about the baby? Millie's telegram had said something about it being fragile.

John gave his niece and nephew a squeeze and stood to his feet. He strode into the room, both children scurrying after him. "Sally, please take Miss Lucy and her brother and see that they are presented with more restful activities."

Sally curtsied and moved to obey.

Millie reached for the maid's sleeve. "Would you also find Josie and tell her the baby is awake?"

Sally nodded. She lifted Charlie onto her hip, took Lucy by the hand, and proceeded out the door.

With maid and children gone, the room was silent, other than the still-crying baby across the hall.

John looked at Millie. He noticed the wrinkles in her dress, the pins that had come loose in her hair. There were dark shadows beneath her eyes, which were red-rimmed and somehow. . .wounded. *Thank you, brother, for that.* Or so he assumed. He longed to march this woman straight to bed. When, he wondered, was the last time she'd really slept?

But he knew he couldn't part with her, not yet. He needed her. *Soon, Millie, I'll see you properly cared for.*

♥

Millie stifled the urge to lift a fluttery hand to her hair. *I must look a sight.* John hadn't mentioned it nor commented on the disarray that greeted him when he walked through the door, but he must have seen both.

He removed his hat and coat and set them on the dresser. With the movement, a cold scent of snow wafted up from him. In spite of his wintery aura, she had the sudden, overwhelming desire to be in his arms.

Absurd.

She had no strength to further examine the yearning, to wonder at the change in her. She'd all but flown from him the last time they'd spoken. He'd driven her away with his provoking remarks about Stephen. *I assure you, sir, working for your brother was easy compared to managing his household without him.* But the thought of Stephen still stung.

Since becoming Katherine's nurse, Millie had been condescended to and sniffed at. Katherine had implied that her "rustic" presence was unwelcome, and John had hinted that she still possessed feelings for his married brother. But only Stephen had been cruel enough to suggest that she'd done less than her best when Florence lay dying.

And he certainly left me in a lurch when he took off in the night.

She'd borne the burdens of the past few days alone as best she could, having no other choice. But now John was here. Steady, strong, capable of rescuing her. Still, the nurse in her, trained to confront a crisis and see it through to the end, refused to be coddled.

And anyway, he'd no doubt be appalled to find himself holding his mother's weeping nurse in his arms. Especially now, added to everything else. *He must be reeling, just like the rest of us.* Though Katherine had written him when Florence first fell ill, nobody kept him abreast of her worsening condition, at least, not that Millie was aware of. Her telegram must have been a shock to him.

He took off his gloves, and she saw that his hands were reddened with cold. "How is my mother holding up?" He blew hot air into his cupped palms.

The question puzzled her, though in her present state, anything might. "She's in her room," she said finally.

"And how is she doing?"

"Fairly well, I think."

He knelt to put his gloves into his bag. "It's good that the children are not still at Stephen's house." He inclined his head toward Lucy's bed. "I see you've brought their things over here."

"We considered letting them stay in their own home, in familiar surroundings, but thought it best for them to be with their grandmother and baby sister."

He glanced up at her. "It's a girl then?"

"It is."

The light that brightened his eyes was chased away by a frown. "You wrote that the babe is fragile."

"We're hoping she'll prove tenacious." It was the best Millie could offer.

His frown deepened. He stood.

"We decided to delay Florence's funeral until you came home, sir. Provided you arrived promptly."

He lifted a brow. "You doubted that I would?"

She shook her head. "No, but I'm amazed by how quickly you responded to my telegram. I'm glad you're here." She blushed. "That is to say, we're all relieved, I'm sure."

He held her gaze for an instant longer then tilted his head back as if tired of bearing its weight. "What must be done for the babe?"

"We're keeping her warm constantly, and I've engaged the services of a wet nurse."

He gave her a questioning look. "And when might I meet this woman you've hired to nourish my niece?"

Millie gestured to the hall. "Miss Josie should be with the baby now, in the trunk room. We've converted it into a makeshift nursery."

His brows rose again. "Miss?"

Beggars cannot be choosers. Millie kept the thought to herself, though it was true. When she'd realized that the jailer's wife wouldn't be able to produce enough milk for two, she'd scoured the town looking for another woman with a nursing baby. The only one she could find was Josie Swanson, an unwed, uncouth miner's daughter.

"With you and your brother absent, I haven't discussed specific wages with her." Millie moved toward the door. "But I did promise her generous compensation. It was the only way she'd come."

He didn't comment, simply followed her across the hall.

She tapped on the door. It opened a sliver, and Josie's bucktoothed face appeared.

"That baby won't eat, *no* how," the girl stated.

Millie's heart sank. She felt John stiffen beside her. He drew close and spoke low in her ear. "Is this a common occurrence?"

I'm afraid so. She didn't answer but smiled brightly at Josie. "We're doing our best though, aren't we?"

"It ain't my fault," the girl huffed. "My own Sadie seems pleased as pie with what I got."

Millie groaned inwardly. *Can't she at least pretend to be genteel?*

"Perhaps," John whispered to Millie, "a proper interview might be in order."

She hoped Josie hadn't heard him. Offending the girl would be a mistake.

Josie's pronounced chin came up. "I ain't stupid, sir. I done everything Miss Millie told me to do. Twice I tried to—"

Millie shook her head sharply, lips pressed together. She shuddered to think what the girl had been about to say. A glance to her right told her that John's cheeks were aflame, gaze fixed on the ceiling as though it merited his full attention.

But Josie wasn't finished. "Twice I tried to—"

Again Millie shook her head, and again, John reacted as might be expected. He wheeled around and started across the hall.

"Excuse me a moment, Josie." Millie went after him. "Mr. Drexel, I'm sorry, but this—"

"It's delicate, I know."

"It's also needful."

Even in the dimly lit hallway, she could see his concern for his niece. He nodded toward the nursery. "Do what you must. I'll speak with Miss Josie later."

Millie turned from him, but he spoke softly to her back.

"Thank you."

Alongside a struggling infant, a bereaved family, and a household in disarray, a little thing like appreciation might have seemed rather immaterial. But tears flooded Millie's eyes nonetheless. Oh, she knew tension still existed between her and John. It hovered beneath the surface, a labyrinth that would doubtless cause its confusion again sometime—preferably when they had the energy to venture into such a maze.

For now, they had more pressing matters to attend to.

Chapter Fifteen

illie stood with the gathering of mourners in the snowy, windswept cemetery on Jasper Mountain. Reverend Warren's voice echoed over the valley below.

"Jesus said unto her, 'I am the resurrection, and the life: he that believeth in me, though he were dead, yet shall he live.'"

He went on to speak of heaven, but despite his comforting words, Millie shivered beneath her cape and muff. She glanced beside her at Katherine, who was little more than a narrow wisp of black crepe waving side to side in the wind. Millie moved closer, should the woman need a sturdy arm to grasp for support. *It's good that she's wearing a weeping veil.* Even the thin, gauzy material was better than nothing between her and this bitter breeze.

But it would seem that Katherine's mind wasn't on the weather. She stood on tiptoe to whisper in Millie's ear.

"Look at them." Her birdlike gaze darted from one onlooker to the next. "Just waiting to get to the bottom of why Stephen isn't with us."

Millie blinked. She followed Katherine's stare to the group of attendees, Ann and Dr. Murphy among them. It hadn't occurred to her that some of them might be agog with curiosity. From what she could see, most eyes held only sympathy. *Why must she always assume the worst?* But of course, Stephen's absence was bound to be marked. Wondered at.

And his mother is bound to be humiliated by it.

Millie pressed Katherine's gloved hand. "You've nothing to be ashamed of. Just look how nicely the children are behaving."

Lucy stood next to Beatrice, meekly holding the maid's hand, her small face stoic. Charlie was wide-eyed and silent in his uncle's arms. He and John were dressed identically in high-buttoned black suits. It was Charlie they'd decided should throw the ceremonial first handful of dirt onto the coffin, when the time came. Young as he was, he was the only man of his house available at the moment. Still, Millie didn't envy the child his task, nor John his duty of coaxing the boy to perform it.

At least John didn't have to dig the grave.

Yesterday, he'd gone to the mercantile, where the men often gathered to play checkers. His intent was to hire help with the unpleasant chore, but when he arrived, he found that Dr. Murphy and an assortment of townsmen had already done the job for him. Millie knew that even the sharpest pickaxes and shovels were little match for the frozen earth. *It must have taken them hours.* But they'd refused payment. Millie was accustomed to such kindness but suspected that the Drexels were not. *Kindnesses are not bought out here in the West.*

Reverend Warren's voice, filled with quiet assurance, called Millie back to the present.

"Now unto Him who is able to present this dear one 'faultless before the presence of His glory with exceeding joy, to the only wise God our Saviour, be glory and majesty, dominion and power, both now and ever. Amen.'"

He let the final words, taken from the book of Jude, settle into the listeners' hearts. Then he nodded at John, who in turn murmured something in Charlie's ear.

Thankfully, the boy obeyed without a fuss. His plump hand scooped a fistful of dirt from the pile and released it onto the coffin. It fell with a pelting sound. Lucy followed suit, then Katherine and John.

Reverend Warren cleared his throat. "Let us sing together, 'Rock of Ages.'"

After the closing hymn, Millie remained at Katherine's side. The first to come express sympathy to the family was Maude Parkison, the pharmacist's wife, her smartly dressed little son Walter perched on her hip. She held out a tiny glass bottle to Katherine.

"This is a mixture of special oils, a recipe of my husband's." She gave Lucy and Charlie a look filled with pure motherly pity. "Put a drop of it on their chests at night when they're feeling anxious or upset, and it might help calm them, the poor darlings."

Next to come forward was the town scavenger, Milt Crosby, who'd plainly made an effort to look presentable. Only the dirt under his fingernails told of the hours he spent removing garbage from the streets. He held his hat in his hands, his focus on the movement of his thumbs as he toyed with the brim. "I'm real sorry for your loss, ma'am—all of you."

Many more followed, and though Katherine seemed near the end of her endurance, a soft light of gratitude appeared in her eyes.

Dr. Murphy and Ann approached at the end, and Millie was able to feel their reassuring presence, if only for a moment.

Ann's words were for Katherine, but her gentle, stricken gaze was on the children, just as Maude Parkison's had been. "Please let us know if there is anything we can do for you."

Dr. Murphy nodded his agreement with his daughter's offer. As he left, he gave Millie's shoulder a squeeze.

Soon afterward, the ring of shovels resounded. Florence's funeral had come and gone, in the same blink of an eye everything else had.

❤

Millie paced the Oriental rug in the drawing room with the crying baby that evening, uneasiness gnawing at her. *What's wrong with her?*

Mercifully, Katherine's afternoon nap had begun late today, and she was still asleep. Millie wasn't sure she could manage both of her patients at once.

The door opened, and a hot breeze wafted into the already sweltering room. The maids had been instructed to keep all the hearth fires lit for the baby's sake.

John entered and shut the door behind him. He leaned heavily against it, both palms pressed flat.

"How're the children?" Millie bounced the baby gently in her arms and continued pacing back and forth.

It took him awhile to answer. *Perhaps he doesn't understand the question.* "Asleep, I think," he said finally.

It was difficult to blame him for his befuddlement. Lucy and Charlie, after their one moment of compliance at the funeral, had turned into veritable dragons. The last time Millie had seen John, he was hurrying to the kitchen, where Mrs. Winters was reportedly on the verge of a conniption. Apparently Lucy had taken advantage of the cook's absorption with her work and went into the nearby scullery with a bottle of molasses, which she poured on the floor. Mrs. Winters found her there, skidding in the molasses from stocking feet onto her side, like a baseball player sliding into home. The result was a sticky coating on one side of her body, including her hair.

Thus began the miserable afternoon.

Charlie climbed out of his bed during his nap and tipped over Lucy's "treasure box," which was perched on a dresser. It fell on his head and he cried, but other than a small bump, he wasn't really hurt.

Lucy, thought to be happily painting in her room—and only left to herself for a minute—sneaked downstairs and hid in the wine cellar, where she promptly dozed off. They couldn't find her for hours.

Charlie escaped Sally's clutches in the washroom and jumped into the basin with the dirty laundry, murky water and all.

As for the children's baby sister, she'd been crying all day.

Millie stopped pacing and looked across the room at John. He returned her gaze without a word, two soldiers gathering their wits after a battle.

But this battle isn't finished. There was still the wailing baby to see to.

John pushed himself off the door and came to stand beside Millie. *We've had to work together in order to emerge triumphant.* Of course, triumph wasn't the sensation she felt just now. Drowning seemed a better description.

"Has she eaten?" John asked.

"A little this morning, and again at midday. But nothing since."

"Perhaps we should speak with that wet nurse—"

"It isn't Josie's fault. She tried for nearly an hour, and gave up right before I brought the baby in here. I thought the quiet might do her good." Millie shrugged. "But as you can see. . ."

As if to emphasize her words, the infant's wails turned into piercing shrieks.

Millie glanced down at the swaddled bundle in her arms, at the red—no, purple—face. Veins bulged out on the baby's forehead and protruded beneath the downy fuzz on her head that passed for hair. *Won't such cries split her tiny body in two?* Each shriek was followed by a terrible moment in which the baby's breath seemed utterly stolen from her. *Oh, I wish Dr. Murphy was here.*

John's voice rose above the ruckus. "Have you tried changing her—"

"Josie saw to that before turning her over to me." Millie looked helplessly down at the infant again. *What can I do?* Florence's children were in distress, and she was unable to help them. Especially this poor baby. And Millie's prayers seemed to be of no avail. Didn't God care?

"I'm going to go fetch her nurse." John's tone was grim.

Millie shook her head, and he paused. She brushed a finger along the baby's cheek and considered the outraged little face. *Even if I sent for Dr. Murphy, what would he do?* Indeed, what would she herself do, if not so frantic over this particular case? She'd been called to the home of more than one hysterical new mother whose infant wouldn't cease crying. What had she said to those women?

But then, this baby was premature, which made the situation more frightening. *Still. . .*

Upon reflection, Millie decided the baby would not, after all, split in two from crying. She'd never known an infant to do so. *She's worked herself up, that's all.* Likely she hadn't wanted to eat, and was annoyed at being cajoled. *She just needs to go to sleep.*

As for John, he resembled a caged animal. "I don't think I can listen to her cry anymore."

Millie put a finger to her mouth and began humming quietly. Without thought, she'd chosen the hymn sung at Florence's funeral. A slow smile turned her lips upward as she hummed the calming melody. *"Rock of ages, cleft for me, let me hide myself in Thee. . . ."*

John stared at her as if she'd gone mad. But when she beckoned him to join her, he looked at the bawling baby, whose screams had, in fact, lessened, and began to hum too.

Slowly, ever so slowly, the wee eyelids started to droop. The babe jerked herself awake and commenced shrieking again, but there seemed to be less rage in the sound. What felt like hours later, but was in reality only minutes, her crying diminished to a shuddering whimper. Then little by little, she nodded off to sleep.

"I'll be back," Millie whispered to John.

She tiptoed upstairs with her slumbering charge and carefully laid her in the cradle.

♥

John collapsed onto the sofa, head back against the cushion, eyes half-shut. The days had been a haze since he'd arrived home, each chaotic moment melding into the next.

It's a good thing Millie is adept at managing crises. Left to himself—or worse, his mother—their lives would be a wreckage.

Something had to be done about the children. And what of that pitiful babe upstairs? Was it just two days ago he'd interviewed her wet nurse? The woman was rough-hewn indeed...to be charitable. In no way was she an appropriate companion for his niece.

But what could he do? With Millie worn so thin, he couldn't very well ask her to go in search of another wet nurse. *Not when I'm about to abandon her too.* He grimaced. He hated to leave again, particularly during so trying a time. When he'd first arrived home, he'd vowed to see

Millie properly cared for. Now he was about to break that promise.

Millie reentered the room. "She's sleeping, snug in her cradle." She walked over and sank into the armchair across from him. Her hands went limp in her lap. Her hair, once again loose from its pins, slid to the side, giving him a glimpse of her lovely neck. She appeared oblivious to her surroundings, practically asleep already.

Silence prevailed.

Ah, silence.

After a while, she glanced up at him. "I remember a time—I couldn't have been more than seven years old—when a neighbor woman fell ill, and Mama, who wasn't well herself, sent Papa to look in on the family. When he came home, he reported that all six of the children were running amok, untended and unwashed. The next morning, he went off to sea, to fish, and Mama sent me to the neighbor woman with a pot of broth. Her baby was crying, the toddler clinging to my skirts as I tried to light a fire in the stove. The rest of the children were all but climbing the walls." Millie chuckled. "This is worse."

John gave her a tired smile. His lips moved with the news he didn't want to give her. No sound emerged. Finally he said, "I must leave in the morning to look for Stephen. I think I know where he might be."

She nodded before he even finished speaking. "I understand." But the life seemed to ebb from her eyes.

He knew his departure was the cause. "My brother cannot just abandon his family, even in his bereavement."

She nodded again. "I'm sure we'll manage without you, somehow. The baby, being premature, will require extra care of course. I could give it to her, but I'd need to be less attentive to your mother." Her voice turned wry. "I do not foresee that being an option."

No, probably not.

"The next most pressing concern is the children," she continued. "With my time wholly consumed, someone must see to them."

He looked at her curiously. "Where is Nettie?"

"She went home to care for her father. He suffers from a weak heart, and her mother sent word two weeks ago that he was completely bedridden."

John rubbed his aching forehead. "Wasn't she the only one of Stephen's servants who was a whit of help with the children?"

"She and Tansy. But your brother's staff must eat, and Tansy is busy cooking their meals."

"What of Sally and Beatrice?"

"They have their own chores to do. Sally looks after the children when she can, but today she showed me the laundry. Heaps of bedding and clothes overflowed the washroom. And Beatrice must assist Mrs. Winters in your mother's kitchen." Millie started to say more then stopped.

"Yes?" he asked.

"You may have noticed that—" she hesitated. "Well, it's difficult, for the servants. They're ill-equipped to provide the special care the children seem to require."

"Are you referring to the fact that my niece and nephew behave like frenzied wild animals?"

Millie gaped at him, and he smiled.

"Florence didn't seem a very firm mother," Millie mused. "I don't mean she wasn't a good mother," she added quickly. "She was kind and understanding, so very gentle. Just not. . .firm." Her voice grew choked. "The children must miss her terribly."

John nodded. "Yesterday, while Lucy was crying over something, I heard her say, 'I want Mama.'"

Millie's eyes dampened, and she didn't speak for a time.

"I didn't mean to upset you," he said.

She shook her head. "I just wish we could do more for them. They need someone tender, like their mother, but more strict. Someone educated, who can teach Lucy to be genteel, and Charlie to mind his manners." She appeared deep in thought for a time. Then all at once, she brightened. "I know! I don't know why I didn't think of it before."

He waited.

"Ann!"

His brow furrowed. "The doctor's daughter?"

"Yes, she would be perfect for the children. Although—" Millie frowned. "It's a demanding task, one I hate to ask of a friend. If only I were free to give her assistance, even from time to time. But there's still the baby's care to oversee, and my first responsibility is to your mother."

He groaned. *Why must we keep encountering these hindrances?* Still, it was nice to talk things over with someone. His father used to discuss important matters with him, but since the man's death, John had relied on himself. Perhaps going it alone hadn't been the best way to live. Yet there wasn't time to develop intimacy with Millie, or with anyone, while they remained in so topsy-turvy a situation. *Anyway, she probably still resents me.*

Maybe it was best that he was leaving.

He rose from his chair, prepared to depart the room. "Hire your Ann. I'll speak with my mother about permitting you to divide your attention between her and the baby."

That, at least, was something he could do for her.

Chapter Sixteen

Millie entered Katherine's bedroom with her afternoon tea to find the woman dressed and seated in her rocking chair, a pink-blanketed bundle in her arms. An empty cradle stood on the floor beside her. Only an hour ago, Millie had left her lying abed, complaining of a headache. Now here she was, tenderly rocking her granddaughter, no trace of the former strain on her face.

To add to this surprise, the baby was silent.

Katherine lifted a warning finger to her lips. "Shhhh." Her gaze followed Millie's to the cradle. "I commissioned young Tom to build it a few days ago." Tom, a cheerful, down-to-earth farmer's son, was the new hired man John had employed just before his departure. He was a bit mischievous on occasion but proved able to make repairs, hoist things, and in general see to tasks not normally performed by women. His presence made John's absence less conspicuous, as did the addition of Ann. Like Tom, she'd arrived shortly before John left. She and Millie were continually exhausted from running after the children, and Millie often shuddered at the thought of tending to them on her own.

"It seemed sensible," Katherine said, "to have a place for the baby to sleep in my room, where we often find ourselves."

Yes, it did seem sensible. But it was the sort of solution usually thought of by a practical-minded servant, not the lady of the house.

At least, not this lady. Again, Katherine had surprised her. *She's been so very. . .useful lately.*

It occurred to Millie that she'd intruded on a special moment between grandmother and granddaughter. She set the tray on the tea table. "I'll leave you two to your rocking, Mrs. Drexel. Ring if you should need me."

Katherine shook her head. "Stay."

Millie sat on the edge of the chaise. The sway of the rocking chair was a calming sight, but it failed to soothe her nerves. She feared the recent truce between herself and her patient would prove all too temporary, and she wasn't sure when it would end.

"I've wondered," Katherine said, "about your mother."

Millie stared at her. She could do so without any awkwardness, for Katherine was looking down, wispy golden lashes just touching thin cheekbones.

"I regret that I never had the opportunity to meet her," she added.

"She—she passed on," Millie stammered. "Not long before you began summering in Nantucket."

"Yes, I know. Do you imagine I didn't have your history examined, young woman? The playmate of my own dear children?" Katherine drew herself up, as if arrogance were her first impulse. Then she sighed. "Your mother, regrettably, married beneath her—from all accounts."

Millie tried to ignore the slight upon her father and to instead fasten on the compliment meant for her mother. "She was a true lady, my mother. I was but eight when she died."

Katherine fell silent for a moment, eyes pooled with some deep emotion. "Such a terrible trial, for a girl to lose her mother." She looked at the babe in her arms, mouth drawn into a tight frown.

Like this poor baby. Millie knew those were the words Katherine had left unspoken. The troubling question, one Millie had asked herself before, stole into her mind once more. *Does she blame me for Florence's death?*

But when Katherine glanced up, there was no censure in her eyes.

"I've wondered how your mother died."

The rare pity in her voice kept Millie from resenting the question. Still, it was difficult to speak of her mother's death. *She succumbed to the same disease that robbed us of Florence.* "Typhoid fever."

The answer caused Katherine to grow visibly limp. "Oh! To leave one's daughter motherless in so agonizing a fashion."

The memory of a red rash upon a perspiring chest, once-beautiful black hair limp and brittle upon flaming forehead, flashed into Millie's mind. But she said only, "Her death was what made me want to be a nurse." Helping Dr. Murphy deliver the baby at the boardinghouse in Denver had only been part of it. "Even as a child, I always wished I could have done more for my mother." *And for Florence too. . . . How I wish I could have saved her.*

"Some things cannot be helped, my dear."

The softly spoken remark struck Millie deep within. Had Katherine Drexel just defended the fisherman's daughter?

Abruptly Katherine rose and laid the baby in the cradle. "See how peacefully she sleeps? It's as though she hasn't a care in the world."

After a brief hesitation, Millie joined her beside the cradle and gazed down at the baby.

"She reminds me of my own sweet Rena." Katherine smiled. "Oh, not her appearance, just. . ." A grandmotherly pride illuminated her face. "There's a real pluck about her, isn't there?"

Millie regarded the baby. She'd long since decided that the infant wasn't beautiful. Her body, clothed in a soft gown and swaddled in warm blankets, was still terribly skinny—although she'd begun to nurse more regularly, and with less turmoil. Her head, too large for the rest of her, was red, veins visible beneath scraggly wisps of hair. She looked fragile enough to break into two pieces.

And yet, she has fought to live.

A grin slowly spread across Millie's face. "She's a plucky one, all right."

They continued to gaze at the slumbering baby.

"I've thought about naming her Violet," Katherine said.

Millie considered that then nodded. "Florence's favorite flower—I remember." A hush enveloped the room. "It's a good name," she murmured finally.

And so, the baby was named at last.

♥

"Don't cry, little one." Millie tucked the bedcovers up over Lucy's trembling shoulders. "I'm here—I'm here."

Lucy tossed, twisted, and threw the covers off. "Mama!" she cried, eyes unseeing but terrified.

What must this poor girl be remembering? They'd kept Lucy from the sickroom when Florence was afflicted with the fever, but the child had undoubtedly heard her mother's groans from the hall. *Perhaps Lucy's vivid imagination filled in the rest.*

"I'm here," Millie repeated. "Go back to sleep." She groped for Lucy's hand beneath the blankets and held it.

A vague wakefulness filled the child's gaze, and though she didn't look at Millie, she tightened her grip. Clung, really. She glanced across the room at Charlie, who slept with his fist against his fat cheek. At the sight of her brother, Lucy's grip loosened, and her expression grew more peaceful. She lay slowly back onto her pillow.

Ever since Ann's arrival, Lucy had been difficult to manage. To be fair, both children had always balked at being given instructions—or rather, being expected to follow them. But while Charlie's fits of temper rarely lasted long, Lucy threw herself to the floor often, where she kicked her feet and shrieked in protest. In those moments, it had been hard to pity her. *But now. . .*

Millie released the child's hand and quietly retrieved a chair from the corner of the room. She sat down beside the bed and began to sing softly. By the end of the first verse of "Rock of Ages," Lucy had fallen back asleep. Millie lowered her voice and continued singing.

". . .Could my zeal no respite know, could my tears forever flow—"

She stopped. A shadow had fallen over the bed. *It's probably just one of the maids, looking in on us.* They'd no doubt heard the commotion and come to see what was the matter.

But when Millie looked up, it wasn't a maid who stood in the doorway. It was John.

She wasn't sure why a tingle of nerves seized her. Perhaps it was because he'd been away, and seemed a stranger tonight. The growth of stubble that shaded his jaw gave him a dangerous air, and his eyes were hooded beneath the brim of his hat.

"I hope nothing's the matter." He gestured toward Lucy. "The child isn't ill, or. . . ?"

"No, not at all. She merely had a nightmare."

He glanced at the door that led to Ann's adjoining room. "Where's Miss Murphy? I should think she'd be the one to tend to—"

"She usually does, but I sent her back to bed. Since I was awake anyway, I thought I'd care for Lucy myself."

He entered the room and removed his hat. His fingers drummed against the felt-covered brim. "I thought to spare you extra work, and here I find you fast at it again."

"No, it's been wonderful, having Ann's help."

His fingers ceased drumming abruptly. "I couldn't find Stephen."

She noted the heaviness of his voice. "I'm sorry, sir."

He looped his hat over the bedpost and stared hard at it. "Three weeks, I searched. I started in Denver and worked my way eastward, stopping in every place I could think of. I even went to Nantucket." He lifted his gaze to hers. "My brother has vanished. And I've failed his children."

She wanted to say, "No, *he* has failed them," but she stayed her tongue. Bitter remarks weren't likely to help the situation. For a time, she just sat mutely returning his gaze, hoping he'd see the sympathy in hers.

She looked away. In the darkness, his eyes had appeared jade-hued, so like Stephen's. *Only somehow more intense.* It made her aware of how late the hour was, how alone they were, save the presence of the children.

And here I am, wearing little but a flimsy dressing gown. She wondered if he'd noticed it too. But since she'd have to look at him again to find out, she'd assuredly never know.

She remembered another time when she'd worn her nightclothes in his presence. It was the night of his mother's dreadful attack. She recalled riding behind him on his horse. She'd felt the warmth of his back, her arm around his waist. In the urgency of the moment, he'd seemed oblivious to her state of undress.

But there's no urgency tonight.

She dared to glance up at him. She saw that he was still looking at her—and there was nothing oblivious in his expression. Belatedly, she wrapped her arms around herself.

He jerked his gaze to the wall, his throat working. "You're cold, Miss Cooper. Perhaps you should return to bed."

"No, I'm fine." She searched for something to say, anything, but what proceeded came without thought. "Mr. Drexel, maybe it would be best to simply let your brother be, for a time."

His faint grin didn't reach his eyes. "It doesn't appear that I have a choice."

"No," she agreed. "In spite of what some might assume, and whatever his faults, Stephen isn't dim-witted. If he doesn't want you to find him, you probably won't."

John's brows rose, high. "A veritable mastermind, is he?"

"No, I just—"

"It seems I should have engaged your services. You might be a better investigator than I, as you'd be sure not to underestimate him."

She bit her lip, stung.

He sighed and rubbed both hands down the sides of his face. "Forgive me. My travels have left me overwrought. I'm hardly fit company for anyone." There was so very little pause, then, so very little warning, before he spoke again.

"You love Stephen, don't you?"

Never had he put it so bluntly—no careful hinting, no hedging or circling the matter. *Just asking the question.* For this reason, she knew she must answer him honestly. The trouble was, she didn't know the honest answer.

Thankfully, she was saved from replying by a knock on the door. This time it really was a maid. Sally had come to ask whether everything was all right with the children.

Chapter Seventeen

*J*ohn's morning ritual, coffee and reading the *Glenwood Echo*, was interrupted by the sound of stomping boots in the entrance hall, followed by laughter and a general ruckus. Quickly he raised the newspaper to cover his face. *I'm hiding in my own home, from a woman.*

But it was Ann, not Millie, whose voice came from the doorway.

"Sir, the children have something they'd like to show you, if it would be convenient."

He lowered the paper.

Lucy and Charlie approached, eyes alight. Lucy's hair was wet as a kitchen mop, and Charlie's trousers were muddy up to his knees.

John feigned interest. "What could it be, I wonder?"

The children lifted their mitted hands to display two sharp, pointed objects.

"Icicles!" he exclaimed. "How very exciting." His puzzled gaze sought Ann's. There'd been icicles on the porch eaves for months now.

"The icicles were melting this morning," she explained. "Spring has arrived."

John looked again and saw that Lucy's and Charlie's mittens were soaked with puddled water beneath the translucent spears. He grinned. "That's very good news indeed."

It truly was. He'd begun to wonder if another futile search for Stephen might be preferable to spending his days snowbound with a gaggle of women and children—and Tom, the hired man. *At least the children are better behaved than they used to be.* Ann had proved an unobtrusive and useful member of the household. Lucy's fits of temper had been reduced, if not fully cured. On occasion, in fact, she and Charlie were a delight.

What are they chattering about now? If he was interpreting Charlie correctly, it had something to do with finding "Miss Miwwie." The boy had trouble with his *L*s.

At the mere mention of her name, John groaned inwardly. Ever since that night in the children's bedroom, Millie had scarcely spoken to him. Of course, she was rather busy tending to his mother and Violet. The baby, though still homely, was gaining weight, to the relief of everyone in the house. She held her head erect for seconds at a time, and had mastered the unusual feat of sucking on her fingers backward, palm facing up.

But John sensed that Millie's preoccupation with Violet wasn't the only reason he rarely saw her. He could only blame himself. He'd caused the awkwardness between them with his unanswerable question. What woman in possession of her senses would admit to harboring feelings for a man who'd broken her heart by marrying another woman? Not to mention running off in the night and leaving her to care for his ill-behaved children.

No, she would never admit it. *True as it may be.* The thought tightened painfully around his chest.

He turned and saw Ann looking at him intently.

"Is everything all right, sir?"

"Yes, I just. . .I'm as restless as the children, I'm afraid, being confined to the indoors these past weeks."

"We all are. It's been difficult, keeping them cooped up for so long. I probably shouldn't have let them go out today, it still being cold, but decided it was worth the risk."

If only childish restiveness was all that plagued me.

"Perhaps," Ann said, "a walk in the fresh air would do you good."

A wry smile touched his lips. "As a matter of fact, there is something I've been putting off, something that would require venturing outdoors."

"Oh?"

"It's a miserable hovel, but the Drexel name is on the deed, so I might as well see what can be done with it."

"Is it a store, or—"

"A hotel. Formerly a. . .place of ill repute."

Ann flushed. "Perhaps it might be put to some use, nonetheless."

"Perhaps." But he doubted it.

❤

Fancy Leona's was, unfortunately, just as John remembered it. The hotel his brother had bought was a sagging structure in need of repair, with several broken windows and missing shingles, among other unsightly shortcomings.

John departed the front steps and began exploring the grounds. To his surprise, he found a small spark of interest igniting within him. He rubbed his chin. Rickety fence, strewn glass, and overgrown shrubs aside, there might be actual promise here.

In front of the building, the property sloped down to meet the mighty Grand River. The front lawns, though likely still brittle and brown beneath the snow, were quite extensive. To the east was a large, untamed field, bordered by a patch of aspens that separated the hotel grounds from the houses of town. The north end provided a breathtaking view of evergreen-covered mountains in the distance, topped by the majestic Sopris Peak.

The place was bound to be a money-draining enterprise, yes. It would also require a lot of work, most of which he'd want to oversee personally. That meant not returning to the East anytime soon. *Perhaps I could hire Hampton to manage the estate there for a time.* While back home in Philadelphia, John had been reacquainted with Florence's cousin, Roger Hampton, a first-rate businessman looking for a respite from Wall Street.

John glanced around. Could this place be worth renovating? Most locals couldn't afford lavish vacations. Nor would they be awestricken by the beauty of the shining river, the vast splendor and diversity of the mountain ranges. Inhabitants of Glenwood Springs beheld such grand vistas every day. But prosperous easterners were a different matter. To those who were weary of the pace of the big city, the bustle and noise, the hotel might seem a refuge.

John looked down at the months-old letter in his hand, written in Stephen's bold script. *"I think with some renovations, the place would really come into its own."*

A sudden vision arose in John's mind. He saw a new, gleaming wrought iron gate, open to reveal an imposing, poplar-lined drive. Manicured lawns on either side were dotted with guests clothed in absurdly proper swimwear. Though covered from straw hat to high-topped bathing slippers, they appeared relaxed and happy.

Much as I hate to agree with you, dear brother, I think you might just be brilliant.

♥

John wondered that he'd ever considered Ann Murphy's presence unobtrusive. The meek woman had somehow convinced his family to host the annual harvest dance, a fundraiser put on by members of her Women's Relief Corp.

It wasn't the first time Ann had persuaded his family to participate in her good deeds. Throughout the spring and summer, there'd been maypoles to decorate, barns to raise, picnic basket auctions to organize. The flurry of charitable events, combined with a cantankerous, teething baby at home, made John glad he'd been spending every spare moment at the hotel.

The work there was progressing well. The front drive and lawns had taken shape just as he'd envisioned them. A handsome brick structure was being built in the same location as the shabby hotel they'd torn down. Only the field beside it remained an eyesore. John didn't have any idea what to do with that field. His investors back east had suggested several options, some of them almost tolerable. But he had yet to act on them.

He looked around his mother's entrance hall, bedecked with floral garlands, the archways and railings a bower of late-blooming flowers and satin bows. Maids scurried past him carrying silver platters of food. All was in readiness for the horde of guests that would soon walk through the door, arrayed in their finery. They'd expect him to make engaging conversation, the one task that had always fallen to Stephen. *He performed it with such ease too.* But John wasn't adept at these things. In vain, he attempted to loosen his collar and still the nervous drumming in his ears.

"Enjoying yourself, sir?"

He tore his gaze from the garlands and saw Tom standing beside him. The curly-haired servant was dressed in a stiff-looking tailcoat. He would serve as footman for the night.

Are you? John wanted to retort. *Would anyone be?*

He was still searching for a civil reply when a swishing noise drew his attention upward. The swish was evidently caused by layers of petticoats that created a bell shape in the shimmering dress. A soft shade of pink, the garment was studded with sparkling beadwork, illuminated by candlelight.

All the breath left John's lungs as he beheld Millie Cooper at the top of the stairs. *Close your mouth,* he told himself sternly. *People will see you.*

The reprimand did little good. He'd grown accustomed to seeing her in practical dresses, durable fabrics in dark blues or grays. This ravishing creature with proudly held head and perfectly coiled hair was a stranger to him. *Shoulders bare, throat exposed, skin flawless. . .* He found it impossible to look away.

But he did. Eventually. Too late, as it happened.

He'd lost the war, a war he'd fought since first seeing her in Dr. Murphy's office. Plain, shapeless dress and all, she'd made a stammering dolt of him back then. And now, even as he cursed himself for his weakness, he knew it was useless to struggle any longer. *Might as well just have it done with.* Lift his eyes to hers and let them proclaim his true feelings like a trumpet's blast.

But he couldn't. He was stopped by a memory.

He recalled the night Stephen came searching for her, when Florence was worried about the baby. It was the first time Millie had seen him since Nantucket. John envisioned her face when his brother appeared in the study doorway. She looked like she'd seen a ghost—a handsome, wholly engaging ghost, judging by her expression.

A ghost she couldn't seem to forget. *Even though he's hurt her, I know he has.* The evidence was in her eyes every time Stephen's name was mentioned.

"Shall I answer the doorbell, sir?"

John recalled Tom's presence with a start. He turned to see the young man looking at him with an impudent grin.

"Funny thing about doorbells, Mr. Drexel—they're almost impossible to hear when they're blaring that loud."

"Just let our guests in," John growled.

Tom did as instructed. He opened the door and admitted a gust of cold air, along with a throng of visitors.

John forced himself to walk over and greet them, very aware of Millie joining him. Her dress skimmed the floor, the soft pink of her bodice a match for the delicate flush of her cheeks. He noticed that the gentlemen guests, from the second they entered the room, couldn't keep their eyes off her. He longed to take her by the hand and steal her away to the dance floor. His keen attentions toward her as they danced into the night would declare, "She's spoken for."

She wasn't, of course. *At least, not by me.* So, John stepped aside and surrendered to the inevitable. He let the men swarm around her.

Chapter Eighteen

illie glided across the dance floor in Dr. Murphy's arms. She inclined her head toward Katherine, who was talking to Mrs. B. T. Napier on the other side of the room. "It's gratifying to see Mrs. Drexel welcoming the townspeople so warmly. Isn't Mrs. Napier's husband one of the men who helped dig Florence's grave?"

Dr. Murphy nodded. "I saw Mr. Drexel talking to him earlier. Asking how things in the dry goods business are, and all that."

Yes, Mr. Drexel has talked to many people tonight. In fact, it seemed he'd greeted just about everyone but Millie. He'd barely glanced at her all evening.

Dr. Murphy studied her. "Not such a bad chap, Mr. Drexel."

"No, he isn't."

"He appears in sore need of a dance." Dr. Murphy winked.

She felt her hackles rise. "He could always ask."

The doctor regarded her once more. "It's intimidating for a man, vying for a dance with the belle of the ball."

"I'm no such thing, but thank you."

He smiled gently. "You and my daughter share the honor tonight. I had to worm my way in with you, so to speak. But I'm an old codger who doesn't scare easily."

"I assure you, Mr. Drexel doesn't want to dance with me."

He looked pointedly to his right, where John was weaving his way across the crowded room toward them. "Oh, doesn't he?"

At that moment, the music slowed to a halt.

John gave Millie a little bow. "May I have the next dance?"

Dr. Murphy answered before she could find her voice. "You may. I was just telling Miss Cooper that she's the belle of the ball. Wouldn't you agree?"

John's smooth expression revealed nothing. "Certainly."

Dr. Murphy gave Millie a bracing squeeze on the shoulder and departed.

John stepped forward and held out his hand. She slid hers into it and felt his other arm encircle her. He pulled her to his chest, where she'd often longed to lay her head. But now she stood erect, mouth dry and pulse throbbing. He wore a black evening coat over a blue silk vest, and looked every bit the dashing aristocrat—lean, pressed, and tailored.

As they moved through the first steps of the waltz, he gave her an even look. "You are, you know."

"Pardon?"

"The belle of the ball."

She shook her head. "Thank you, but flattery won't—"

"You've not been without a partner all evening."

She lowered her gaze. "I didn't think you'd noticed."

He laughed, a hollow sound. "Perhaps I didn't wish to look goggle-eyed, like the other men who've stared ceaselessly at you all night."

There's absolutely no danger of that.

He stopped, right there on the dance floor, and peered closely at her. "Let me amend my mistake—since a mistake it evidently was."

She couldn't help smiling, but said only, "You needn't go to the trouble."

His blue eyes flickered. "Oh, it's no trouble. I've grown accustomed to being unable to breathe ever since you appeared at the top of those stairs."

She felt suddenly afflicted by a similar emotion but made herself say lightly, "So you like my dress."

He grinned. "Suffice it to say, little Millie Cooper from Nantucket has grown up."

"And you, sir, were born grown up."

He tilted his head. "Was I?"

"Yes. Or at least, I remember thinking so as a child. You were always so serious." *And never more so than when you came to tell me that your brother needed to make a better match.* The thought dampened her spirits, encroaching on her enjoyment of the dance. "Nothing I did back then could sway you, you know."

He shrugged. His focus somewhere beyond her, he spoke over her head. "You've no way of knowing the effect you had on me."

"A gangly girl in a patched dress? I can imagine." Her throat constricted painfully. "Though I scarcely need to, given the way you informed me I wasn't good enough for your brother."

"I never said that."

You implied it. And his mother had confirmed it.

There was frustration in his voice. "Tell me, Miss Cooper, did you ever, just once, imagine you saw me looking indifferent? Or can you possibly think I enjoyed that wretched mission—one I had little choice but to embark upon?"

Her lips tightened. "You had a choice."

He fell silent. Now that the past had risen to the surface, it was plain to see it hadn't been forgotten. No, those memories had been there all along, burrowed deep within them both like bristly burrs. *Why, why does it matter so much?* her heart cried. She only knew that it did.

As if to punctuate her misery, the dance chose that exact moment to end.

John released her slowly and stood looking at her. "I've no reply," he said finally.

"You could tell me that you should have left things as they were." She was near to tears.

A shadow darkened his eyes. "I can't do that."

"Then you're not sorry." It wasn't a question.

He shook his head, gaze regretful. "If given the chance, I'd do it all again."

Not only had he deemed her unfit all those years ago, his opinion of her hadn't changed. Millie couldn't have continued dancing another instant but would have fled the room regardless of whether the dance was finished. Her body taut with suppressed sobs, she hurried across the dance floor and escaped to the drawing room.

♥

Millie wiped the trickle of tears from her cheeks and leaned back against the sofa. *You're being a child,* she told herself sternly. But restrained cries all but choked her. She gulped them down and brushed at her damp face again.

She heard a noise in the doorway and looked up to see Katherine swing open the door without ceremony. "One moment you and my son were dancing, my dear, and the next you were departing in haste."

If you think I'm going to tell you why, you're sorely mistaken. Millie answered without inflection. "The dance was finished."

Katherine gave her a long look then crossed the room and seated herself regally in her favorite armchair.

Sure the prying woman was eager for the chance to defend her son, Millie waited in wary silence.

But when Katherine spoke, it was in a reminiscent tone. "When John was very small, perhaps no more than eight or nine years of age, we lived in a country house just outside Philadelphia. During that time, we owned a dog, or rather, the dog owned *us.* She had simply appeared on our doorstep one rainy afternoon, and the children begged to keep her. Princess was a mangy creature, mottled in color and possessing a thin, pointy face. But the children loved her as if she'd been a gift from the Queen of England. Sadly, the day came when we had to move back to the city, and we were obliged to explain to the children that Princess must be given to a family who had plenty of room for her to run and play." Katherine smiled wryly. "Oh, the howls of anguish that arose at that dire announcement."

Why is she telling me this? Millie braced herself for the blow that was sure to fall.

"Do you know which of my three children suffered the most over that dog?"

Millie shook her head.

"Well, I knew." Katherine chuckled. "A mother always knows. Stephen stormed and fumed, and Rena had to be pried away from Princess finger by wee finger. But John, my manly little John, behaved with stoic acceptance—while his father was present. After my husband went to bed that night, I passed John's room and heard the sound of quiet sobs. I went in and sat by him. Held his hand until he fell asleep." A faraway look entered Katherine's eyes. "That was the last time I saw my son cry."

Maybe that's because his heart fled his stony rib cage and hadn't the courage to return.

They sat in silence for a time before Katherine broke it. "Goodness knows I'm not excusing him. John is a grown man, and ought to have the gumption to apologize to a body when need be."

Millie thought her ears must be deceiving her. *Is she truly on my side?* "Then you—you know we've quarreled," she said in a low voice.

Katherine's eyes turned pitying. "I wanted you to understand that John hasn't owned his deepest feelings, even to me, since he was a boy."

Just tell her the truth. "Unfortunately, I already know his deepest feelings toward me." *They're the same as his mother's, and they pain me daily.*

"If you do know, that's probably more than he does." Katherine emitted a dry laugh. "Men are so blind when it comes to these things. Honestly, sometimes I think John puts a wall around his heart that even he cannot penetrate." She hesitated. "You see, he's had to be strong for the family." She took a deep breath, shoulders rigid. "And now I shall tell you why."

Something in that last pronouncement made Millie sit forward, ears pricked up.

"From a very young age, my husband placed on John, as his firstborn, a weighty mantle of responsibility. He often said that if anything should happen to him, John must be ready to assume leadership of the family." She gazed out the window and stroked her taffeta overskirt absently. "And then it happened—our beloved Dr. Philips closed my husband's eyes for the last time. Charles succumbed to winter fever, you know. In that instant, John became head of the household." She sighed. "That alone wouldn't have been so bad. But things weren't as they appeared. After the funeral, John discovered that his father had made several ill-advised investments and acquired a great deal of debt as a result." She continued in an odd, throaty whisper. "There were other reasons he was in debt as well."

What is so distressing her? Whatever it was, Millie didn't wish to make it worse. "You needn't tell me the rest, Mrs. Drexel."

Katherine lifted her chin. "Yes. I must. My husband had been keeping a secret for years, even before he wed me. He'd had a dalliance, at eighteen years of age, one he never got over. He proceeded to buy a beautiful cottage off the coast of Maine and frequented it during our marriage, when I thought he was away on business." Katherine let out a shaky breath. "He fathered a son and daughter not my own. This second family became a drain on his pocketbook."

Say something. But Millie's mind was frozen. Somewhere within it was a deep empathy for Katherine, and. . .nothing else.

"I hardly need tell you that if news of this scandal ever reached the ears of polite society, my family would be ruined."

I understand. "I will never breathe a word about any of this." And she wouldn't. After a moment, she asked, "None of you ever knew?"

Katherine shook her head. "Only my husband's lawyer, who'd been in his confidence. Charles must have been a mastermind, keeping the affair hidden for decades like that. He'd met the girl while summering in Maine as a boy, and grew enamored with her a few years later, after he'd already promised himself to me. He didn't seem to notice she was practically destitute, daughter of a poor logger. But his family certainly did, and forbade the match."

How familiar it sounds. Millie was suddenly burdened by the pressing knowledge that to Katherine, she'd been no different than the logger's daughter, a thoughtless girl capable of ruining a family. *We're not the same.*

"At any rate, you can see the predicament John found himself in. When Florence Hampton, who was wealthy as Midas, showed interest in Stephen, John saw his opportunity and encouraged the match." Katherine's posture sagged. "Please understand, upon my eldest son's shoulders was a shameful secret that could destroy his family, not to mention the very real threat of becoming impoverished, with no way to support his mother and sister. Thus, in desperation, he did the only thing he knew to do—tell Stephen the truth and call upon his brother's sense of duty to respond aright."

A bitter taste filled Millie's mouth. "Still, he should have told me."

"Stephen?" Katherine's brow creased. "He didn't see you after he'd made the decision, did he?"

"No. I meant John."

Katherine shook her head. "It wasn't John's fault. I forbade him from ever speaking of his father's shortcomings, both about the debts and the ...indiscretion."

A fray of emotions filled Millie, not the least of which was a sudden desire to shake the woman across from her. *How could you? I'd never have told a soul, and at least then I might have understood.* Might not have railed at John. Yet part of her wondered if he could have tried harder, could have refused to surrender until he'd found a kinder solution. *If he didn't care about my feelings, he might at least have considered Stephen's.*

And then, Katherine unknowingly delivered the blow that, strangely enough, freed Millie from a deep, long-festering wound.

"Stephen is so like his father," Katherine mused. "Already engaged to Florence that summer when he began his entanglement with you."

Chapter Nineteen

$\mathcal{T}$he day after the dance, Millie wandered into the kitchen to enjoy a bit of conversation with the servants while Katherine was busy rocking Violet to sleep.

The moment Mrs. Winters saw her, Millie realized her mistake.

"Oh Millie," the cook wailed, wringing her hands, "I'm in such a fix. I remembered today that payment for our monthly grocery bill is past due."

"How late is it?"

"A week."

"Who usually pays the balance?"

"I do, but I've been so busy, racing to and fro, cooking up that fancy dinner for the harvest dance."

And now she's elbow-deep in bread dough for tonight's dinner. Millie glanced into the scullery and saw that Beatrice wasn't a likely candidate either. She was scrubbing dishes, the drainboard buried under the heaping mounds of pots and pans. "What about Sally?"

Mrs. Winters shook her head. "Sally doesn't know how to do figures, and Mr. Kamm at the mercantile likes to review the bill with us."

Millie sighed. She knew very well who would be taking the payment to Mr. Kamm.

♥

Millie walked down the quiet lane toward town, the paper bills tucked in her apron pocket. She hadn't gone far before the beauty of the fall afternoon began to seep into her. She tugged up her sleeves to let her skin feel the fresh air. *How blue those faraway mountains are against the vibrant colors of the trees.* A playful breeze seemed to blow the cobwebs from her mind.

The need to put the house back in order after the dance, while still performing her usual duties, had left her little time to think. *I've hardly even had a moment to wonder about what Katherine said.* There were so many revelations to ponder. So many bits and pieces of the past had been exposed. Among them, the most difficult to face was the knowledge that Stephen had been engaged to Florence while he was courting her. A summer once cherished, now sullied.

And yet, that same revelation, so difficult when she thought of Stephen, created an altogether different sensation when she thought of John. A niggling voice inside her whispered, *You feel many sensations when you think of John.* She tried to dismiss it, but she was never entirely successful.

Nothing Millie learned from Katherine, shocking as it was—Charles Drexel's secret affair, the illegitimate children born to his mistress, his surplus of debts—could change her view of the past quite the way Stephen's engagement did. It lifted a burden she'd carried far too long. She knew now that a sweet and worthy girl had counted on marrying him. If he'd ended his engagement to Florence, it would have been a breach of promise, would have shamed her before family and friends. *As well as broken her heart.*

And John, compelled not only to save his family from poverty, but driven by a sense of duty toward Florence, had made his brother live up to his obligations. In doing so, John had taken it upon his shoulders to clean up Stephen's mess, to go and break the news to the disconsolate fisherman's daughter. Or so Millie assumed. *If only he'd told me that Stephen was engaged.*

She could ask him why he hadn't. But somehow, the idea of even talking to him made an inexplicable bashfulness well up inside her.

At that very moment, Millie heard footsteps approaching along the lane. She looked up and saw John walking toward her. Thankfully, his head was down, which gave her some time to gather her composure.

He glanced up and blinked twice, as if to be sure he was seeing properly, and then gave her a feeble smile. "I was just at the hotel."

"I'm on my way to pay the grocer," she said at the same time.

He furrowed his fingers through his hair, only to drop his arm agitatedly to his side an instant later. "It's a beautiful day, is it not?"

"Oh yes! Quite a lovely afternoon for a walk."

Silence.

Everything that remained unspoken between them filled that dreadful silence. But Millie was determined not to be the first to speak.

"I've been busy at the hotel," he said at last. "This morning the foreman wanted me to approve another lumber purchase, and it became a rather lengthy ordeal."

Say something. Millie opened her mouth but was mortified when only nonsense emerged. "I hear the grounds are beautiful, that the hotel is also becoming—that it's being built very—that things are—" She stopped. *He must think I'm an imbecile.* "I'd love to see it," she finished lamely.

His expression, puzzled during her speech, brightened at the end. "The construction is far from completed, but I find it a pleasure to explore nonetheless." He hesitated. "I could take you there someday."

How about today? "Your mother is being well tended."

He looked confused. "I'm sure she is."

She tried again. "She told me she'd lie down a bit, once Violet fell asleep, which the babe almost was when I left. And Sally promised to look in on your mother often during her nap." *Just ask him.* "Perhaps we could go and see the hotel now?"

His expression finally cleared. "Ah. But I must warn you that it's a good distance from here."

She shrugged. "It's a beautiful day for a walk." *I already said that.* She really *was* an imbecile.

♥

John walked alongside her toward the hotel, his mind racing. No matter how civil she was being at this moment, he'd watched her flee his presence in near tears at the dance. She couldn't possibly be happy with him. *"Why don't you tell her how you feel about her?"*

He was convinced that the question came from somewhere other than his own mind. Perhaps it had been brought to him from the heavens, borne on the autumn breeze. Though he dared not contradict the Almighty, he was sure Millie Cooper didn't wish to hear such a declaration. Not from him, anyway. In fact, he was sure she wished the opposite.

He made desperate, trivial conversation with her, talking about how the children were getting along, and how Violet was growing altogether too fast. Thankfully, the time passed quickly, and they soon arrived at the hotel.

Instead of leading her up the front porch steps, he led her around to the side. He gestured with a grand sweep of his hand toward the weedy, waving expanse of nothingness before them.

A justifiably puzzled look appeared on Millie's face.

"I finally know what to do with it," he explained. "What would you say to the idea of turning this field into stables?"

"Well," she answered slowly, "I'd say that first you need horses."

He chuckled. "A worthy observation. I plan to have my best stock brought out from Pennsylvania by rail." The words themselves were a thrill. He was eager to see one horse in particular. It had taken some convincing to persuade Night Hawk's owner to even consider selling. Unsure how the venture would end, John nearly whooped when his clerk wrote him that the final papers had been signed.

Millie didn't quite meet his gaze. "But I thought you were returning to Philadelphia. Won't you want your horses to be there with you?"

He longed to lift her chin and bid her look at him. *Do you want me to stay, Millie?* "I decided to remain here for a while. From all accounts, the estate back home is flourishing under Roger Hampton's supervision—that's Florence's cousin. He's proving an astute manager, so there's no pressing need for me to return yet. Work at the hotel consumes my time. The crew has come to depend on my direct involvement." *But the biggest reason I can't leave now, woman, is you.*

She glanced around the field again. "I like the idea of stables. And this is an ideal place for them. Wouldn't that be quite an undertaking?"

"It would." If he looked at her much longer, he feared he'd act on his errant impulse to tuck that silky strand of hair behind her ear. And watch her pull away from him.

How he wished he could explain the past to her. But his hands were tied. His mother had seen to that. She'd made him vow not to speak of their family's turbulent history. Instead he said, "There's enough space here to build stables equal to any I've seen in the East. Of course, they would rather cut into the gardens, fountains, and man-made pond suggested by my investors."

Her brows drew together. "Can't wealthy guests stroll through lavish gardens whenever they like, without leaving the city?"

He grinned. "That's precisely what I thought." He believed that the hotel's true appeal lay in the feral river and expansive wilderness it flowed through, the freedom of being far from the pressures of everyday life. He'd hoped that stables, horses. . .adventure. . .might be an additional draw.

Millie gave him an encouraging smile. "I'm sure the stables will be beautiful. And it'll be such fun when the horses arrive."

He nodded. "Back home, there was nothing I loved more than smelling the sawdust in the stalls, hearing the snorts and restless pawing of the horses. It's why I thought the vacationers would enjoy such things too. Seems to me they couldn't help it. And they're sure to appreciate a soak in the hot springs more if they first experience the exertion of working a horse in the paddock." He rubbed his palms together. "I tell you, every man ought to feel pounding hooves beneath him at least once, feel the wind against his face—" He stopped and looked sheepishly at her. "Apparently, it's a topic I can become quite eloquent about."

"Please, don't apologize. I find it all quite fascinating."

There was a sweetness in her voice that made him long to abandon his reserve and reach for intimacy with her. *But she never answered my question that night in Lucy and Charlie's bedroom.* Probably because he'd never had the courage to repeat it since. He told himself he'd just been avoiding an awkward topic. But deep within, he knew the truth: He was afraid of hearing that she still loved his brother.

She inclined her head toward the hotel. "May I see the inside?"

❤

Millie had little space to stand in the unfinished guest room. It was tucked into the far corner of the fourth floor, an extremely cramped area of the hotel due to the crates of nails and piles of boards stacked in every possible niche. The floor beneath her feet was made of rugged chipboard. The walls were comprised of skeletal beams, no siding. Tiny particles of sawdust filled the air. The dusty smell mingled with the scent of the man beside her. *He smells like a rain-soaked forest.* That fact alone made it difficult to concentrate on anything else.

John circumvented a sawhorse and went to the window. "See, the mountains are beautiful from up here. I thought you'd like to have a look." He pointed at the distant hills. "Sopris Peak is visible off to the south, and of course you can see Red Mountain right there, just across the river."

She joined him at the window and looked out. The view was indeed glorious, a myriad of colors before her eyes like a watercolor painting, one hue overlapping another until it was difficult to tell where one left off and the other began. The steep rock hills of Red Mountain were sometimes pink, sometimes coral, sometimes rose-hued, while the southward hills melted from shades of green to shades of blue.

John was standing so close. She could feel his sleeve brushing against hers. "How lovely!" she managed to say.

"The rooms on the east side overlook the field. An unpleasant view at present, so I prefer this side of the hotel. Sometimes I come up here just to look at the mountains and think."

He probably wasn't aware that their hands were now touching. Nothing separated him from her. *Nothing physical, that is.* A silence arose and came between them.

It lengthened.

Suddenly John leaned forward, expelled his breath, and gripped the windowsill. "I'm sorry for my behavior the other night."

Which behavior is he referring to, exactly?

A muscle leaped in his jaw, which was covered with a hint of coppery stubble. His gaze went to some point beyond the window. "I acted harshly. I should never have said that I'd do it over again—keep you and my brother apart, I mean."

Aha. Even though Millie knew the truth of that misty eve, understood his reasons for coming and buying her off, she didn't tell him so. She wanted to hear what he would say.

"The truth is, I simply meant that I'm glad you didn't marry Stephen." He paused for a moment before hurrying on. "Not for his sake. For yours. Look what he's done to his family. He's just like our father."

She stiffened. "Florence's death is hardly Stephen's fault." *Why am I defending him?*

John gave her a stony look but said only, "No. It wasn't."

This man all but announces that he considers me too good for his brother, and I go and ruin it. She hesitated then reached out and boldly touched his arm. "Thank you for wishing only the best for me."

He glanced down at her hand on his arm and turned toward her. He spoke in a halting voice. "There are things I've wanted to tell you, Millie—about—about the events leading up to that night. You know, when I came to meet you and told you Stephen wasn't coming. But I couldn't, not then. . .or now. I just hope you'll believe me when I say it was a very difficult decision, one that I—"

Millie lifted her fingers to his lips before she could think better of it. "Shhhh. Your mother told me about your father's. . .indiscretion. About the debts. About Stephen being engaged already when he and I were making our plans."

His eyes widened. He removed her fingers from his lips but didn't release them. "She did?"

Millie nodded.

An expression of disbelief clothed his face. "My mother hasn't told those things to anyone."

Yes, I was rather amazed by it myself. "I don't know why she would confide in me, only that she did."

He seemed to ponder that for a moment, his thumb stroking her index finger almost absently. But there was the slightest flicker in his eyes that indicated awareness of the motion, of the intimate contact. *She* was certainly aware of it.

"She trusts you, apparently," he said.

His touch was undoing her. "Why didn't you tell me that Stephen was engaged that summer?" Her voice shook.

He must have heard it. He looked down at their clasped hands. His thumb ceased its stroking. His Adam's apple bobbed. "I don't know, I suppose I just couldn't cast such a stain upon my brother, not in the eyes of someone he truly cared about."

Did Stephen truly care? Millie felt dizzy. She didn't need the answer so much as she needed to be in John's arms. She slipped her hand free, but instead of lowering it to her side, she slid it onto his sleeve. She toyed with his cuff without meeting his gaze, without even breathing.

He stopped her, wove his fingers through hers. "You're wrong, you know."

"About what?"

"If I wanted the best for you, Millie Cooper, I wouldn't be about to kiss you."

"Why?"

"Why?" He laughed raggedly. "Because if I were to kiss you now, and someone happened upon us, your reputation could be irreparably damaged."

No, I mean why do you want to kiss me? She didn't speak the words, merely stepped closer to him.

For the second time, he let out a lengthy breath. Then slowly, agonizingly so, he touched the curl that lay alongside her cheek. His fingertips soon departed the curl and drew a featherlight line along her jaw to her lips.

"John. . ."

His eyes deepened, midnight instead of blue. His head lowered. "I told myself that if you ever called me that, I would do this." And then he kissed her.

She scarcely had time to fully realize that his lips were on hers, that the warmth of his breath mingled with her own, when he withdrew abruptly. She could only stare straight ahead and attempt to regain her balance.

He backed away, his hands up like they were pleading for distance.

She stepped away too, felt behind her, and realized she'd backed into the corner of the room. Propped against the supporting beams, she tried to understand what had just happened. *Did I do something wrong?* She had little experience with such things. Or perhaps she'd only imagined his interest. Perhaps he'd never meant to be anything more than her oh-so-formal employer. If so, she'd sorely misplaced her hopes. *It can't be.* But the more she thought about it, the more convinced she became.

A sob arose to choke her. It kept swelling, and she kept suppressing it. "I promise I'll keep to formalities from now on, *Mr.* Drexel," she managed to say.

He groaned. "Please, don't."

Her chin trembled. "Then I'm afraid I don't understand."

"I can't do this *here.*" He swept the room with a wave of his hand. "It's too great a risk to your reputation." His smile was lopsided. "You see, I'm trying with Sampson's own strength to be a gentleman."

Ohhhhh.

Courage restored, Millie spoke softly. "Perhaps small allowances may be made, at times, even for a gentleman. . .John."

He shook his head, gaze reproachful. But he crossed the floor to her in two strides.

Chapter Twenty

*H*elpless, John kissed Millie again, thoroughly this time. He let his mouth tell her everything he'd been afraid to say. *I love you; I've always loved you, even when I was too blind to see it.* He was hardly aware that he was clasping the front of her apron, clutching the fabric to hold her closer to him, like a drowning man clutching a lifeboat.

Then his senses returned to him. Only, instead of heeding the voice inside that warned him he was losing his heart, with no assurance that he possessed hers, he trailed kisses from her mouth to her jaw.

That's when he heard footsteps approaching from the servants' staircase. And because he loved her, he lifted his head quickly at the sound.

She must have heard it too, for she jerked away from him.

He placed a palm flat against the beam behind her and turned sideways so she could move past him.

The footsteps grew louder. Within seconds, John's foreman, Denny Hayward, entered the room. He stopped short when he saw them. His gaze darted between them, and comprehension dawned on his face. He folded his arms over his coverall-clad chest and gave John a wide, unrepentant grin.

John knew he needed to find a way to save the situation, but he couldn't think. Everything within him longed to pull Millie back into his arms. He glanced at her and was gratified to see just how erratic her breathing had become.

He returned his attention to Denny and tried to appear casual. "I've been showing Miss Cooper here your magic, Hayward. She wanted to see the hotel, and there's nothing prettier than the view from up here."

"Nothing, sir?" Denny's dark eyes gleamed.

John wanted to kick the man, especially when he saw how Millie's cheeks flamed. He decided to employ another tactic. Allowing sternness to enter his tone, he said, "Tell the men I want them working until the last shingle is in place on that lobby roof. Shouldn't take them more than a few hours."

Denny shrugged. "You're the boss." Then, with another grin and a wave, he ambled toward the door, whistling as he went.

Without pause, Millie scurried after him.

John let her go. He needed time to recover his wits anyway. And he wasn't too worried about Denny. The man might be a rogue, but he rarely strung three words together at once. He wouldn't mention the matter.

As John stood in the dusty room waiting for his pulse to slow, all he could think was, *I kissed Millie.*

But remembering the incident wouldn't help him remove this ridiculous smile from his face. With effort, he turned his mind toward the hotel, to the work that still needed to be done.

After a while, he departed the room and went in search of the crew. He wanted to make sure the roof was progressing as planned.

Once he'd assured himself that the men were working with due diligence, he started for home. When he reached his mother's front porch and strode through the door, he noted the return of his absurd smile. He hoped no one would ask him anything that required a lucid answer.

His mother stopped him in the entrance hall, glancing at him. . . twice. Her eyes narrowed.

"Whatever is the matter with you, John?"

He willed himself to appear blank. "Mother. I thought you were napping."

"I was, until I awakened. And now it seems I've misplaced my nurse."

Millie isn't back yet?

"She went to the mercantile to pay the grocer, and never returned."

"I wouldn't worry," he said smoothly. "She's probably just enjoying this beautiful fall weather." *Or wandering the streets, waiting for her flushed cheeks to cool.* The thought made him want to pound on his chest like an exultant wild gorilla.

His mother peered at him a long moment, and then shrugged. She pointed to her left, where an enormous crate stood against the far wall. "The new mirror for the upstairs hall arrived today. Tom has been waiting for you to come home and help him carry it upstairs."

"Well, I'm here now. Where is he?"

"In Millie's room. I asked him to repaper her walls."

His brows rose. "Oh?"

His mother's gaze faltered under his stare. "That wallpaper is an eyesore, I assure you. The poor girl can hardly be expected to keep in bright spirits for the children if she's forced to look at those horrid walls all the time."

John only laughed.

His mother threw up her arms. "Oh, mock me if you will. Perhaps it's merely the batty whim of an old woman. But that doesn't change the fact that I want that mirror moved out of my entrance hall. Preferably before the judgment."

John walked off, shaking his head. He knew very well that his mother's decision to improve her nurse's living quarters wasn't a mere whim. *She's been softening toward Millie for weeks now.*

He soon saw that Millie's room was littered with bottles of glue, measuring sticks, and rolls of blossom-covered wallpaper. Tom stood on a stool, head craned to one side, tongue visible out the side of his mouth. He held a vast section of wallpaper flat against the wall. The sloped ceiling was flush against his curly, dust-covered hair. One corner of the paper seemed to be causing him particular consternation as it kept furling backward.

"Would you hand me that bottle of glue, sir? The one closest to the bed?"

John picked up the bottle and noted how light it felt. He opened the lid and looked inside. "It's empty."

Tom frowned.

"Why don't you just use one of the other bottles?" John asked.

"They're all empty. I'll have to go to the workshop and fetch some more."

"Can't you just tell me where they are?"

"Could, but you probably wouldn't find them. My workshop isn't what you'd call real neat." So saying, Tom clambered down from the stool and strode from the room.

John glanced over at the little mirror on the dresser. He envisioned Millie sitting before it, sandy-brown masses of hair loose about her shoulders. He gulped at the knowledge that this room was where she brushed her hair at night. . .where she lay down to sleep. In spite of its unsightly paisley spread, he envied the bed its nightly proximity to her.

He looked again at the dresser. There was a hairbrush with a spray of pink roses on the handle, a little turquoise bottle of perfume, and a cream-colored hat. To the right was some sort of treasure box. Or so he assumed by the tiny golden lock on the front. On one side of the box was a row of worn books, and on the other, a leather-bound Bible with an envelope tucked inside it.

Without thinking, John lifted the Bible up. He tested the solid weight of it in his hands and furled the delicate pages, careful not to drop the envelope. The book's worn appearance marked it as old, but its fine quality shone through the years. Was it a cherished keepsake, passed down from generations of Coopers?

Curious, John opened the cover and glanced at the first page.

My darling girl, began a message written in a flowing script. *This Bible was given to me by my father, a minister. He taught me many things, but none so vital as the importance of calling*

on the Lord, especially amid life's many storms. I long to pass
this on to you, Millie, before I am called home to heaven. It
won't be long now.

My cherished daughter, you are my joy and my delight.

"Call unto me, and I will answer thee, and shew thee great
and mighty things, which thou knowest not." Jeremiah 33:3

My prayer for you is that you will continue to call upon
the Lord, for great and mighty things await you.

> *Your loving mother,*
> *Nora Gallagher Cooper*

Feeling as though he'd just eavesdropped on an intimate conversation, John closed the Bible. He started to set it back on the dresser,
but at that moment, a bird flew against the window. The rapid flutter
of wings, the thump against glass, startled John, and his grip loosened.
His hand opened, just enough for the Bible to slip from his fingers.

The bird flew off unharmed, but the Bible wasn't so fortunate. It fell
to the floorboards, thin pages splayed out in all directions. With a muffled groan, John knelt to survey the damage.

He thumbed through the book and inspected it on all sides, relieved
to find nothing amiss. He returned it to its place beside the box on the
dresser.

Then he noticed the envelope lying on the floorboards. It must have
fallen out when he dropped the Bible.

But it wasn't the envelope that caused his heart to thud to a halt in
his chest.

It was the locket that protruded from the envelope's top fold. The
second he saw it, a bitter cold spread through his limbs.

He'd immediately recognized that precious piece of jewelry. He knew
its perfect pearl and engraved rosebuds well. If those familiar details
weren't enough, the elegant *D* certainly was. The Drexel family heirloom
had gone missing. . .about the time Stephen had fallen in love with Millie. *Remarkable, that I've never noticed that blatant coincidence before.*

John didn't blame Millie for accepting the locket. Nor did he want it returned to his family. He didn't even care overmuch that Stephen had given away something of such value.

But oh, he cared that Millie had kept it all these years. *Or, really, it's not even that.* The soul-crushing discovery was that she'd kept it *here.* Enshrined next to her treasure box, nestled safely within the pages of her beloved Bible, alongside her last message from her mother.

John didn't want to think about it, didn't want to admit the truth. But it crept into his spirit, coiled around his soul nonetheless.

She never stopped loving Stephen. I have to face that.

With the thought, a heavy slump bowed John's shoulders low, and an unbearable bleakness entered his heart.

❤

The quiet lane just past downtown was awash in dwindling sunlight. The rays warmed Millie all over, as did the daze that had followed her since she left the hotel. She scarcely remembered her visit to the mercantile to settle the grocery account, and hoped Mr. Kamm hadn't noticed her addled state.

She knew she should be getting home. There was no real reason to linger, yet she'd been wandering aimlessly for what seemed like hours.

It was no dream. She could still feel the pressure of John's lips against hers. Could still remember how safe she'd felt in his arms. *Oddly so, since he certainly wasn't holding anything back.*

Several times before, Millie had glimpsed an intensity in John, particularly in the dead of night, when little Violet was in the habit of awakening the household. His tired eyes would kindle to life, and he'd give Millie a look that conveyed a world of meaning.

Later, she'd be sure she imagined that look. And anyway, glimpses were very different from what she'd experienced at the hotel.

Strangely, it wasn't only his kiss that was responsible for her besotted state. She recalled the boyish excitement in his voice when he'd told her about his idea for the stables, about his hopes and plans for the hotel.

He'd shared a bit of himself with her. Could it be that he actually considered her a friend?

The wind whispered over the rooftops and caused front porches to creak. With it came the fragrance of the hot springs, a mineral-infused steam that contrasted with the clean, cold scent of the two rivers flowing through the valley. Millie breathed deeply of the heady air around her.

Perhaps blessings are meant for this lifetime after all. She remembered thinking they weren't, in church, when they'd sung about the firm foundation.

"I will be with thee, thy troubles to bless."

She hadn't really believed it then. But now, as she recounted the past several months, she wondered.

Baby Violet had improved. She grew stronger every day, and Millie believed she was out of danger.

Lucy and Charlie were thriving. They seemed content with Ann, and Ann with them.

Even Katherine appeared less disagreeable of late. She'd been kinder to Millie, arranging for her bedroom walls to be repapered and asking Beatrice to make a new quilt for her bed. *She even told me an amusing little anecdote this morning, as though we were friends.*

Millie's own turmoil, the trauma over losing Florence and being blamed for it by Stephen, had started to lessen.

Was the storm truly passing?

For the first time since that terrible night, she thought maybe, just maybe, she might be ready to forgive Stephen. Especially since there was an awareness, deep within, of another. That awareness crowded out feelings of animosity, replacing them with something far better.

Millie's pulse began to speed, along with her footsteps. The sooner she arrived home, the sooner she'd see John.

Chapter Twenty-One

Why tonight must be Ann's night off, John didn't know. Neither did he know why every servant in the household had more pressing tasks to do than overseeing the children. It wasn't that he minded spending the evening with his nieces and nephew, but his proximity to them meant proximity to Millie, the woman he loved. . .who still loved his brother. Every time he doubted it, he remembered the locket he'd discovered in her bedroom. And every time he thought about that terrible moment, he grew more determined to avoid her.

Which he now realized would be impossible.

The drawing room was bursting with chaos. Lucy and Charlie circled John's legs, chanting something about a rosie and a pocket filled with posies. In an elegant wire cage in the corner, the children's new pet cockatoo squawked, his screeches even louder than the cries of Violet. *There's no explanation for that baby's ill temper tonight.* Her diaper was dry, her stomach full, and every effort was being made to see to her comfort. Such was often the case with the finicky Violet, John had learned.

Millie hummed a lullaby and paced the floor with the fussy baby. John's mother, complacently seated on her Venetian throne, seemed as unaffected by the chaos as did Millie. *How can they behave as though nothing is amiss?*

Perhaps because their world hadn't just crumbled around them. The bedlam didn't usually bother him either. Tonight, everything did.

Whenever Millie brushed past him, he sensed her unspoken remembrance of their kiss, a kiss he'd rather not acknowledge by word or deed. *With any luck, she'll think I make a habit of kissing women in empty hotel rooms.* Maybe she'd surmise that it meant little to him. Of course, the opposite was true. Holding her in his arms had shaken him to his very core.

Her soft voice jarred him from his thoughts.

"Perhaps we might find something quieter to do." Her eyes indicated Lucy and Charlie, who still circled his legs. "Now that bedtime is nearly upon us."

Before he could answer, Charlie interjected, "I'm not sleepy." His words were accompanied by a fierce scowl, followed by a yawn.

"No, you never are," Millie countered with a smile. "Never the least bit tired, are we?"

She turned quizzical eyes on John. "But your uncle appears to be."

"I'm fine." In truth, he *was* tired. Tired of loving her and resenting Stephen.

The hurt that covered her face at his terse words made him regret them. Still, he didn't wish to discuss things. Especially not here, with an audience. He was very aware of his mother glancing between them, a keenly observant light in her eyes. *How very irksome she is.*

"Let's find a picture book for you to look at," Millie told Charlie. With Violet held capably in one arm, she knelt gracefully beside the bookcase and perused the bottom shelf. Why, oh why, did she have to be so lovely?

She rose and extended a book to him. He accepted it, taking pains not to graze her fingers with his.

She was about to turn away again. He had a contradictory impulse to lead her into the entrance hall. *"We need to talk,"* he longed to say.

But did they? Hadn't the locket said everything already?

Stephen possessed her heart. *How can a woman possibly kiss me like that when she's in love with someone else?* Perhaps she'd been thinking about Stephen the whole time. The thought sickened him. He called on God in a desperate prayer.

At that precise moment, the drawing room door opened. John felt the draft, heard the sound of dogged footsteps crossing the threshold, and became conscious of Millie's muffled gasp.

His mother rose partway out of her chair, hand pressed to her heart.

Lucy emitted a high-pitched squeal. "Daddy!"

John reflected humorlessly that God had an odd way of answering his prayers. He watched, frozen, as Lucy raced toward the door, Charlie close behind her.

Time seemed suspended as Stephen stooped to welcome his children into his embrace. Eyes closed, and with a visible lump in his throat, he clasped them to him. *I'm sorry,* he mouthed silently. *So sorry.*

Millie stood motionless.

Baby Violet stopped crying, for no knowable reason.

John's mother groped behind her for her chair. She sank down onto the cushion with a weak exhale.

Stephen straightened and looked across the room at Millie. *Or is his focus on the babe in her arms?* John admitted that Stephen's gaze was fixed on his baby daughter. *Has he ever seen her before?*

The question caused John to regard Violet with new eyes. She'd grown into a pretty baby in the months since her infancy. She didn't have a bit of pudginess, but her skin was properly soft, baby-like. Her round face was white as porcelain, her lips rosy. Her wispy hair was fair. She resembled the flower that had inspired her name, delicate but with an underlying heartiness that couldn't be denied. *She's very like her mother.* More so than the other two children were.

John returned his attention to Stephen. Slowly, an unexpected emotion grew within him—gladness, he realized, as if someone had rung an invisible bell inside him. Seeing his brother standing in the doorway, whole and unharmed, lifted a weight he hadn't known he carried. *Perhaps I don't hate him after all.* Oh, but he wanted to. Especially when he saw Millie's stricken face.

Stephen lifted Charlie into his arms and took Lucy's hand in his. He started across the room, pausing beside his mother's chair to give her a contrite look. He began to say something, but she shook her head firmly. "You're home, that's all that matters."

He simply nodded.

Millie, though appearing to be in a wakeful dream, must have had some presence of mind, for she approached Stephen with the baby.

"What's her name?" he asked.

"Violet," Lucy and Charlie hurried to say at the same time.

Stephen ruffled Charlie's chestnut mop, set him down, then carefully took Violet from Millie. He stared down at the baby, speechless. "Well Violet," he murmured at last, "aren't you just the sweetest thing." She graced him with a coy little grin, and his expression turned doting. "Yes, yes you are." He touched his nose to hers. "Oh yes, you are."

He went on talking to her as though there was no one else in the room; then, after a few moments, he lifted his gaze and looked straight at Millie.

Never, in John's life, had he seen his brother look so resolute. It filled him with a glacial dread.

❤

Stephen's home.

Those two words swam about in the muddle of Millie's mind, mingled with a growing concern for Katherine. *She must be so overwrought by all of this.* Would the excitement prove too much for her?

In the short time that it took for Stephen to speak, Millie noticed that he seemed to have aged since he left. He had more lines about his mouth and a new maturity in his blue eyes, which glowed green in the light shining through the stained glass lampshade. Somehow, he'd also grown taller. Or maybe he just appeared towering. The last words he'd spoken to her arose to haunt her. *"How dare you come into my family's home and decide whose life should be traded for whose."*

Now he stroked a finger along Violet's smooth cheek. "I've wronged you, Millie Cooper," he said without preamble. "Twice. The first time, I made promises that a man in my position, a man betrothed to anoth—" He stopped and glanced at Lucy and Charlie as though recalling their tender ears. He looked at John, a silent plea for help.

John straightened from the wall where he'd been leaning. "Come, children, it's your bedtime." At their noisy protests, he raised a hand. "Your father will still be here in the morning." He looked at Stephen dourly over their heads. "I hope."

"Yes of course." Stephen smiled at his children. "I shall eagerly await seeing you both tomorrow."

A shadow fell over the doorway, and Sally appeared as if from nowhere. "I'll tend to the children, Mr. Stephen." She bobbed a curtsy. "And welcome home, sir."

"Thank you, Sally."

Without further ado, the maid ushered the protesting children through the door and closed it behind them.

Millie watched John go sit on the sofa near his mother, his back as rigid as a soldier standing at attention. *At least Stephen isn't going to rail at me.* Her numb thoughts could venture no further.

Stephen's eyes were on his baby daughter's face, rather than on Millie. "It was a long time ago. You've probably quite forgotten that summer that we—that we—" He halted abruptly. "I was engaged to another woman while I was pursuing you. Only a rake would do that."

In the uncomfortable silence that followed, Millie couldn't find her voice.

Stephen continued. "And the second time I behaved badly was the night we lost. . ." He couldn't seem to finish the sentence. "Lost. . .my wife. I said some very hateful—and wholly untrue—things to you, when you'd been nothing but a friend to my family." He finally looked at Millie. "I very much hope you'll forgive me."

Will I? Though she still wasn't entirely sure, she heard herself say, "Yes of course."

Some of the tension drained from his face. "That means more than you know. You see, I had a good deal of time to think while I was away. There wasn't much in the barren plains of Nebraska to excite a man, or to distract him from remembering what a cad he'd been." He glanced at John. "Yes, I stayed in Grandfather Rush's trading outpost on the Missouri River. I knew you wouldn't think of it." He returned his gaze to Millie. "But as I said, I had plenty of time to ponder my behavior, and it made me realize something—I might be able to make amends."

Millie was reluctant to ask how, fearful of the answer.

But he answered anyway. "I want to marry you, Millie."

His words floated to her as if he'd spoken them from the other end of a hollow log. She thought she saw Katherine's jaw go slack. She couldn't bring herself to look at John.

"Stephen, no!" His mother's eyes were wide.

He faced her head-on. "I know, Mother, it's too soon. I haven't observed the proper period of mourning for Florence yet. But at least listen to my reasoning. I'm sure you'll feel differently if you do."

I very much doubt it.

He turned back to Millie. "I have another motive for wanting to marry you, a compelling one. I wish to make no mistake about this, but to be straightforward from the beginning this time. The truth is, I'm anxious to secure a mother for my children. As soon as possible." His expression was as determined as she'd ever seen it. "I abandoned them when they needed me most. Thought only of myself in my grief. There's nothing I can do to change that now, and it pains me deeply, thinking of all the time I lost. But I can give them what they lack now—a mother. And there's no one I'd rather entrust them to than you, Millie."

She remained without words.

"I've taken the liberty of finding another nurse for Mother, in the event that you accept my proposal. I traveled to Chicago before coming here and searched until I met a capable old battle-ax who'd do the job." He smiled wryly. "It took a little time to assure myself that there was a good heart under all that bluster, but there most certainly was. And she said she's always wanted to see the West."

Somehow, Millie was aware that Katherine and John were staring at Stephen, mouths agape.

"Marry me, Millie," he said. "Let me prove myself a changed man. The only thing I'll ever ask in return is that you love my children."

Strangely, at that astonishing moment, all Millie could think was that it was past Violet's bedtime. *She usually goes to bed before Lucy and Charlie. How very tired she must be.*

Hands shaking uncontrollably, Millie reached out and took Violet from Stephen. But instead of taking the baby upstairs to the nursery, she handed her to Katherine.

Think, Millie, you must think. Rational thoughts eluded her. She looked, not at Stephen, but at John. He was the man she'd worked alongside these past months. She knew him, knew she could depend on him.

Only, he hadn't spoken a word during this entire mad exchange. Now he stood and met her eyes, and to her dismay, his were utterly impassive. She could read nothing—nothing—in that cloaked expression.

"I need to think," she said. After a bewildered glance around the room, she departed on unsteady legs.

Chapter Twenty-Two

*T*he kitchen had long been a place where John could depend on a welcome reception, on plainspoken, everyday conversations with Mrs. Winters, the reigning monarch of her brick-and-mortar domain.

But today, when he entered the room, he stopped abruptly.

Millie stood at the stove, alone, her attention fixed on the firebox grate. She slid it forward, presumably to cut off the fire's supply of air. Judging by the scorched smell in the room, it was too late to save whatever she'd been cooking.

Last night, after Stephen's return—and shocking proposal—John had somehow succeeded in avoiding Millie. It was better this way, he reasoned. Until he could face her without losing his tenuous control, he needed to keep away from her. His self-possession had been reduced to a frayed thread, dangerously close to snapping in two. The same words kept circling around in his brain and wouldn't leave. *Stephen is home. He's the one she's always loved. Stephen is home. He's the one...*

And on it went.

Millie glanced up. Her hand stiffened on the grate.

He backed toward the door. "I was just looking for—for—Mrs. Winters." *We've had the same cook for a year, how is it that I couldn't remember her name?* He turned and fumbled for the door handle, casting a harried explanation over his shoulder. "Mother asked me to tell Mrs. Winters to prepare roast duck for dinner. But she's not here." *Well, that's obvious.* He yanked the handle downward, desperate to escape.

"Wait."

He held fast to the handle and stared intently straight ahead.

"I'd hoped that we might. . .talk."

He raised his gaze upward, an appeal to the Almighty. With effort, he plastered a neutral expression on his face and turned.

She'd moved away from the oven and now set slices of bread in a skillet on the worktable. Beside the skillet was his mother's tea tray, complete with a little glass dish of strawberry preserves. Beyond the tray were the blackened remains of what had started out as bread.

"You've been busy, I see." He nodded toward the burnt toast.

Millie followed his gaze and sighed. "I don't know what's the matter with me today. I've burned your mother's toast twice."

He didn't comment.

She drew in a deep breath. "Or rather, I do know what's the matter." She toyed with the corner of her apron but said nothing. Nor did she look at him.

She wants me to broach the subject of Stephen for her.

When he didn't, she lifted her eyes to his.

He struggled against the potent force of her gaze and felt himself losing the battle. Her eyes reminded him of the multicolored bark on that pretty tree behind the house—or would, if bark possessed the ability to bewitch him. *No, don't relent.*

"We haven't spoken of what happened last night." She fidgeted once more with her apron. "You never said much when we were in the drawing room, just let Stephen go on, and. . ." She looked away. "The truth is, we never had the chance to talk about what happened yesterday afternoon at the hotel either."

If she'd poured icy water over his head, it couldn't have had a more shocking effect. *I cannot talk about kissing you, not when you're planning to marry my brother.* He made himself glance at her and saw that her cheeks were flaming. For both their sakes, he must put an end to this terribly uncomfortable conversation. "If you're feeling upset about. . . that, I'll tell Stephen, and you won't have to." *He'll be greatly annoyed, but I'll still tell him.*

"No. This doesn't concern him." She sounded like she was trying to convince herself.

"Doesn't it?"

"John, please. . ."

He yearned to cover his ears, to block out the sweet sound of his name on her lips.

The silence between them grew.

Her focus was on her apron once more. "If we're to discuss Stephen, I must ask—what do you think about what he said last night? Regarding his proposal, I mean."

Must I endure this? "That's for you to decide."

"Won't you tell me what you think?"

If you'll tell me why you kept that locket from him for seven confounded years. But his pride kept him quiet.

Smoke started billowing up from the oven, and she hastened to open it. She jerked out the skillet and set it on the worktable. "I value your opinion, you know."

"I think," he said evenly, "that you would make my brother happy."

She stared hard at the skillet. "You said that you were glad Stephen hadn't married me. You told me his family has suffered." She selected the few unburned slices of toast from the skillet and set them on the tray. "That he's too much like your father, that—"

"Well, he isn't." *So that's what this is all about.* She'd sought his advice because she wasn't sure she could depend on Stephen. Oh, how easy it would be to tell her that he doubted his brother's reliability. *And don't I?* Certainly. But he knew if he were to live with himself after this, he couldn't sully his brother's reputation or impede their marriage again. Though his reasons had been valid the first time, he'd always felt badly for their sakes. For her sake. *This is what she's always wanted.*

"I've reconsidered," he said slowly. "It was unfair of me to assume that Stephen is like Father. My brother has made mistakes, yes, but never without remorse, never without considering the welfare of others in the end." He realized that it was true. "And he's proved himself by returning home and showing his willingness to right his past wrongs."

After a brief silence, Millie whispered, "Is there anything else?"

Yes, just nothing I'll permit myself to say.

She drew herself up, face pale. "John, can you give me any reason not to marry Stephen?"

This is your opportunity, his mind screamed. But an inexorable pain filled his heart as he replied. "No, I can't."

♥

A sweeping tide of emotions deluged over Millie in encompassing waves. Blindly she lifted Katherine's tea tray, heedless of the toast toppling into the jam, and hurried toward the kitchen door. "Your mother is waiting for me."

John made no attempt to stop her.

In the servants' hall, she encountered Beatrice, who peered at her— and peered again. The maid blocked her path.

"Are you ill, Miss Cooper?"

"No, I'm fine." Millie felt the tray being lifted from her grasp.

"I'm taking this to the missus for you," Beatrice insisted. "You go on to your room and lie down for a while."

Millie shook her head. "I think maybe—maybe I could use a little air." Without waiting for a response, she moved quickly toward the front door. Not fully realizing where she was going, she dashed from the house and down the porch steps.

She sped all the way to the banks of the Roaring Fork. Heedless of the sharp brambles, she fought the underbrush along the water's edge until she came to the trail that led to the little clearing she'd discovered the previous autumn. She collapsed onto the fallen log and sank her head into her hands.

Many moments passed. Time stretched on until she grew aware

that she was cold. She lifted her head. The gray sky cast a pallor over the boulder-covered hillside that towered over her across the river. The ground, wet from a recent rain, drenched her skirt. The coolness that rose from the rushing current, so pleasantly reminiscent of an ocean spray before, now merely chilled her. She shivered and hugged her knees to her chest.

Like the mist that emanated from the water, like the clouds that blotted out the golden glow of the sun, a question plagued her once hopeful heart. How could a man who'd kissed her with such ardor become so indifferent? *He was so detached last night after Stephen returned.* And today in the kitchen, he'd seemed more wary than a hunted deer. *What changed him?* Mere hours before his brother walked through that drawing room door, he'd given her reason to hope. Perhaps even reason to believe he loved her. Certainly reason to think he desired her.

She fought a fresh surge of tears. Maybe that was all he'd felt for her—desire. *No, surely not.* But as Millie sat there and listened to the tumbling roar of the river, her doubts multiplied. After all, she'd just given John the chance to claim her, and he hadn't taken it. *He must not care for me.* Her tears poured down now, unstoppable.

Her dear, newfound dream, so vivid and real only yesterday, lay at her feet in ruins. The storm hadn't passed on, not at all. She'd been wrong about that, childish in her belief that the future held promise. *Life is not a wonderland filled with rainbows.*

How odd it was then that she should notice a shimmer of lovely colors dancing on the surface of the water at that very moment. She raised her eyes and beheld not one, but two, beautiful rainbows in the clouds. They were radiant, neither the slightest bit faint. No name appeared in bold letters across them, but Millie knew those rainbows were for her. As if God Himself was saying to her, *"Millie, remember My promises."*

The trouble was, not one promise came to mind. All the sermons she'd heard, prayers she'd memorized as a child, passages lovingly marked in her Bible, had fled. She couldn't think of a single line of scripture, though of late, she and Ann had helped Lucy commit many to memory.

The reflection of the rainbows, a splendor of shifting colors on the sparkling water, reminded her of how crystal looked in the sunlight.

It's all so beautiful, dear Lord. But she had yet to recall any promises. And then she remembered it—the song.

"I will be with thee, thy troubles to bless."

The words echoed over and over in Millie's mind, until there came a moment when peace flooded her. An assurance that was difficult to explain. Oh, troubles still abounded. God hadn't promised to remove them. But the rainbows in the sky, the simple words of a song, assured her of her Savior's presence. The Master of the crashing sea was with her. He was Lord. . .even of this storm.

The question was, did she trust Him? What would she say, if asked, *"Where is your faith?"*

She recalled hearing those words before, when she was considering John's offer to be his mother's nurse. Millie had summoned her strength and answered her Lord with obedience, but little faith.

Now, in the midst of this storm, would she trust Him?

She thought again of John and, with a nearly physical pain, knew she was bruised, wounded. Her confidence in him, in everything, had been shattered. But then, a softly breathed realization wended its way into her spirit.

This is a choice.

No, she argued. *A choice is different.* Deciding to care for Mrs. Drexel and Florence had been a choice. Responding to Stephen's proposal with yes or no would be a choice.

But then, she reasoned, *the disciple Peter sank into the stormy sea because of a choice. Didn't he?* When he started to sink, couldn't he have fixed his gaze on his Lord instead of on the raging waters?

Couldn't she do the same?

Millie knew it might be necessary to reaffirm her choice day by day. But at this moment, she was resolved. By God's grace, she would choose to trust Him.

♥

Millie was in the nursery when Stephen found her. By the purposeful-ness in his eyes, she knew he'd been looking for her.

"You're a difficult girl to track down."

She formed her mouth into a smile and gestured to the crib, where Violet sat blinking up at her, wide awake as could be. "I've been busy with Violet."

He crossed the room and joined Millie beside the crib. His brow furrowed as he gazed down at his daughter. "She isn't ill, is she?"

"No, just unhappy. She's teething again."

"I thought my brother hired a wet nurse—I presumed that meant you and Miss Murphy could have a moment to yourselves on occasion."

She shrugged. "It's been awhile since Violet truly needed to eat at night. She merely likes to be sure her sufferings don't go unnoticed, whether it's sore teeth or a pea-sized lump in her bed that's causing a discomfort not to be borne."

At the wry words, Stephen grinned. He glanced around the room. "It looks different in here."

"Yes, we'd hoped to make her feel at home." The formerly spartan decor in the trunk room had been softened to accommodate the baby. Lavender-hued gingham curtains hung at the window, and a little white dresser with heart-shaped knobs stood opposite the crib. Above the dresser was a painting of an angel watching over a baby in a lacy bassinet.

"It's lovely," Stephen stated.

Millie knew what he'd left unsaid. The room would soon be empty. He'd be taking his children home with him, now that he'd returned. She couldn't imagine daily life without baby Violet, ill temper and all, or without Lucy and Charlie.

Violet, plainly not the least bit tired, drew one dimpled knee up and tried to climb out of her wooden prison. *Of course, life will be easier when she leaves.* But easier didn't necessarily mean better.

To Millie's surprise, Stephen gently pushed the baby back down and drew her soft pink blankets over her shoulders. "It's time to sleep, sweetheart."

Violet slumped onto her mattress in a dramatic fashion and proceeded to sob into her wee palms, the very image of despondency. But Stephen remained unmoved. *Just when did he decide his children shouldn't do exactly as they pleased?*

As if he'd heard her, he said, "Miss Murphy suggested I should be firmer with her—with all my children. She's quite good with them." He hesitated then motioned toward the hall. "Can we talk a moment?"

Millie nodded, and he waited for her to precede him. Violet's sobs increased as they left the room.

Stephen closed the door behind him and turned to face Millie. "I've scarcely seen you since I arrived home." A guarded look appeared in his eyes. "You do recall me asking you to marry me?"

She wished she weren't too numb to fully realize that the man she'd once loved wanted her to be his wife. "Yes."

He rubbed his jaw. "Is it how I acted toward you when Florence. . . when we lost her?"

Millie hardly knew how to answer. There were so many reasons she hadn't sought him out since his proposal. Was his tirade on that terrible day Florence died one of them? Or did her reluctance stem from something else?

She avoided his gaze. "I was hurt by what you said of course. It was difficult, being blamed for her death."

"I was out of my mind with grief—surely you know that. It's not an excuse, only. . .I hope you won't believe I meant any of it."

He was silent so long that she raised her gaze to his.

"Millie?" he prodded.

"It's understandable," she said finally. "Saying things in the throes of grief that you don't mean. That day was difficult for all of us, but especially for you."

"I know I should never have left like that. It was a selfish, cowardly thing to do, putting a burden on you and poor Mother, who had her own grief to contend with."

Millie didn't argue; she only said, "I'd come to care for Florence too." She wasn't sure why she'd said that. In fact, she hadn't really known she felt that way until the words were out of her mouth. *But she was easy to love.* "A kinder, gentler woman never existed."

He rubbed the back of his head, which made his short dark hair stand on end. "Yes. Well."

Upon reflection, Millie supposed it might be discomfiting for a man, to discuss his first wife with the woman he'd recently proposed to.

He set his jaw as though determined to have the worst over with. "I've owned that I was engaged to her while at the same time giving you every reason to believe I loved you. I didn't intend for any of it to happen. Deep inside, I knew it was unfair to both of you, but the more time I spent with you, the more I ignored my conscience." He smiled and tilted his head to the side. "In my own blundering way, I think I'm trying to tell you that my affection for you was sincere."

He was confessing that he'd cared for her, before. She'd often wondered about that, even agonized over it. Now she knew. *Then why do I feel so empty?*

"John told me you've always considered what's best for others, Stephen, when all's said and done." *It seems he might be right.*

For some reason he appeared less than pleased by the compliment. "My brother has had plenty of time, I think, to say many things to you."

What an odd thing to say. "We've spoken of the past, but only rarely."

He folded his arms over his chest. "Well, I'm here now. If there's anything you want to know, you can just ask me."

She thought a moment. *Actually, there is something I want to know.* "Did you send John to meet me in the clearing, that night we'd planned to elope?"

"No." He shot her a rueful look. "I told him that if he insisted on making my decisions for me, he could jolly well tell you so himself. Only I didn't use the word *jolly.*"

I'm sure you didn't.

195

"I'd agreed to break things off between us for the sake of Florence and my family, but I can't say I was glad about it." He hesitated. "How much do you know of my family's situation at that time?"

"Your mother told me about your financial difficulties. About the...scandal."

He lifted his brows. "Mother? Truly?" He shook his head again. "I couldn't understand John at first, thinking he had the right to dictate who I should or shouldn't marry. But then I realized it was partly my fault. You see, he was always the one to swoop in and manage our family crises. I never put my oar in. I was content to let him do what he thought best." His voice took on an edge. "That is, until his best involved me."

"I'm sorry."

He laughed flatly. "Don't be. The miserable affair made a man of me. I'm better off for facing up to my duties and going through with marrying Florence. John was right to insist on that." He rubbed his face, eyes weary. "It seemed harsh at the time though. I thought surely there must be a way out of our money troubles without separating two people who. . ." He gazed unseeingly ahead for a moment then looked at her. "But I can fix all that now, Millie, if only you'll give me the chance."

They were talking, really talking. He'd told her things she'd never known, couldn't have known, since he'd all but ignored her while she was Florence's midwife. And he'd repeated his offer of marriage, though not in so many words. *This is my second chance at happiness.*

And yet. . .

"I need more time, Stephen."

He studied her, the silence lingering for several seconds. "Give me your answer whenever you're ready then. I can be patient."

She hoped so.

Chapter Twenty-Three

Miraculously, there were no patients in the waiting room at Dr. Murphy's office when Millie arrived. The pleasantries she'd planned to say died on her lips the moment the doctor appeared in the doorway, with that patient air about him. He always had a way of putting ailing visitors at ease. *There's no hurry,* his gray-blue eyes seemed to assure. *Just take your time and tell the doctor all about it.*

If Millie were a child, she'd have thrown herself into his comforting arms. As it was, she stood stock-still and wordless, the pummeling uncertainty of the past week raining down upon her.

The awareness that something was wrong flooded his face. He glanced toward the empty waiting room then steered her back toward it. "As you might recall, there's a perfect place for a chat right over. . . here."

She sank gratefully onto the worn red armchair.

He sat on the bench across from her. "Now, tell me what's the trouble." He frowned. "Mrs. Drexel's condition isn't worsening, is it?"

"No, she's doing well." Millie gazed past him, out the window at the town, so small against the steep mountains that surrounded it. "She'll always have asthma, I think, but her attacks have been mild and far between this fall." She knotted her fingers together in her lap.

"It's a more personal matter, I'm afraid."

His expression didn't show too much dismay, so she continued.

"I'm in need of advice from someone I can trust, someone older and wiser than myself. Mrs. Winters, our cook, might have done nicely, but she and the other servants still treat me as a superior. Mrs. Drexel is intelligent of course, and much kinder than I thought at first. But she's the last person who'd be objective about this."

"And what is 'this'?"

"Her sons."

"Ah." He leaned back on the bench, a knowing look on his face. "The topic was bound to emerge sometime."

She sighed. "Stephen came home last week."

"Yes, Ann told me." He gestured with twinkling eyes toward the table beneath the window. "See the flowers?"

Millie smiled at their private little joke. Ann always insisted on fresh flowers for the waiting room. She argued that a bouquet of daisies or primroses could cheer an ailing patient better than any medicine. Her father and Millie were of a more practical bent, not inclined to trouble themselves with needless trimmings. *Yes, if there are flowers, Ann's been to visit.* "Did she tell you that Stephen asked me to marry him?"

Dr. Murphy's eyes widened. "No, she did not."

Perhaps she didn't know, when she was here. It had taken a few days after Stephen's return for Millie to find a moment truly alone with Ann. News of such magnitude must be shared in strictest confidence, with plenty of time to mull it over together. "Well, he did."

Dr. Murphy steepled his hands together. "Hmmm. What does his brother think of all this?"

A painful tightness squeezed Millie's heart. "John says I would make Stephen happy."

The doctor gave her a searching look. "And would a man who abandoned his family make *you* happy?"

Her gaze faltered. "Perhaps Stephen proved himself by coming home and attempting to make things right."

He studied her yet again. "Is that what you think?"

I don't know! she wanted to shout. "I think that Stephen is handsome, wealthy. Pleasant as can be. I'd be foolish not to at least consider his proposal."

"I see."

But his brother kissed me in a hotel guest room, and I haven't been able to think rationally since.

Dr. Murphy hesitated. "I thought I saw something between you and John at the harvest dance. Was I mistaken?"

She made herself tell the truth. "John's had his chance with me."

There was silence.

"Do you care for him, Millie?"

"It doesn't matter." Everything within her seemed to wilt at the words. "Not anymore."

A look akin to pity stole into Dr. Murphy's eyes. "What brought about this change in Stephen?"

She shrugged. "He said he had a lot of time to think while he was away—that he realized he could make things right by coming home and proposing to me. I'd be a mother to his children, which he desperately needs, and he could mend his past behavior by marrying me now."

Once again, the room was silent.

Dr. Murphy cleared his throat. "I suppose that's as good an explanation as any. But what about your feelings for him? Do you regard him as someone you'd wish to spend your life with?"

In spite of asking herself that very question, Millie's primary emotion regarding Stephen was still confusion. She shrugged once more. "I don't know."

"Well, that's a bit of a fix." The doctor's voice lowered to a murmur. "And I suspect there's still more to be told, about you and your John."

"He isn't my John," she all but snapped. She exhaled slowly. "I'm sorry. Honestly, I don't know what to say. John and I had been growing—closer.

But we talked after Stephen's proposal, and he didn't. . .that is, things between us, in essence. . .came to an end." With trembling fingers, she wiped away her tears. "I must give Stephen an answer. He'll expect a reply."

Dr. Murphy shook his head. "No need to rush. If he truly wants to marry you, he'll wait."

"Yes, he said he would."

"Good man."

She was quiet for a time then looked imploringly up at him. "What should I do?"

His eyes were kind, fatherly. "No one can decide for you whether or not to marry a man, Millie. You must determine on your own whether you trust him. You must pray, and seek the will of God."

There didn't seem to be anything more to say.

Which was just as well, for at that moment, the door opened and a weary-looking woman crossed the threshold, leading an elderly man by the hand. Dr. Murphy rose to greet his patients. Just before he ushered them into his office, he gave Millie a gentle smile.

She knew he'd be doing some praying himself—and that she would be unfailingly included in those prayers.

❤

Over the next weeks, which stretched to a month, Millie contemplated Stephen's proposal. True to his word, he waited patiently. With servants to oversee and preparations to make for the children's arrival, he mostly kept to his own house. He'd decided to reconstruct his upstairs, knock out walls and make three bedrooms for the children instead of two.

Millie saw little of John. Whenever she passed him in the hall or met him in the servants' quarters, he nodded curtly and continued on his way. If they were forced to speak, the exchange was all business, usually with several other people present. The ease that had grown between them while Stephen was away had vanished. It pained her to find that, romantic disappointments aside, she missed him. Of course, there were moments when she longed to feel his lips on hers, to be the recipient of his intense gaze. But mainly she just. . .missed him.

As often as she could, she slipped away to her special spot by the river, where she'd plead with God for answers. He seemed oddly silent.

One night, she lay awake in her room, again vacillating between acceptance of Stephen's proposal and refusal. If she said yes, she'd have the life she'd hardly dared dream of as a poverty-stricken girl in Nantucket. She'd be the wife of a wealthy man, the proud mother of his three darling children. She'd occupy a beautiful home, this time as the woman of the house, not the nurse. Yet lately, she'd found herself thinking about her old position as Dr. Murphy's assistant. Nursing had taken on a whole new meaning when she'd become Katherine Drexel's personal attendant, and at times she looked wistfully back at her former life.

But tonight, as darkness gave way to the light of dawn, only one thought began to reign in Millie's mind. *I'd be a fool not to marry Stephen.*

She'd loved him once. Why couldn't she do it again? She ignored the niggling doubts that arose at this logic. God hadn't given her a clear reply, but maybe the rainbows were His way of saying Stephen was His choice for her. Maybe Stephen was God's way of blessing her trials, of delivering her from the storm.

When the sun had risen above the mountaintops, Millie dressed quickly, washed her face, and combed her hair. After stopping to look in on Katherine, she went in search of Stephen.

A knot formed in her stomach as she descended the stairs. She reached the entrance hall and started toward the front door, her steps muted on the immense Oriental rug. She hoped the knot in her middle would ease once she'd given Stephen her answer, and all was settled between them.

She passed John's study and felt his blue gaze upon her through the open door. Her knot tightened. She bemoaned the stillness of the morning. Despite the softness of her footsteps, she'd disturbed the silence and inevitably drew his attention.

Well, since he sees me, I might as well go in and get this dreaded conversation over with. He was her employer, and deserved to know that there would be a change ahead for his household. She hesitated. "May I come in?"

He nodded curtly, as he'd been known to do lately. But this time he couldn't escape her. She saw that awareness in his wary eyes. Nonetheless, he rose politely and remained standing until she was seated.

With him sitting across from her, it was difficult to avoid looking at him. She pretended fascination with the bookshelves so he wouldn't see the pain in her expression. The gold-stamped books were arranged in alphabetical order by author. *How like him, to keep his world neatly arranged, no matter what is happening around him.*

She glanced at him. His hands were folded on the desk in front of him, his dark blue sleeves rolled up, strong forearms covered in reddish hair. *He is so. . .mannish.*

"How may I help you?" he asked.

She forced an even tone. "As my employer, I thought you should know that I've decided to accept your brother's offer of marriage."

"As your employer?"

The incredulous question hung in the air like a hovering fog. After several moments passed, John's face flushed, as though he'd spoken without thinking and was mortified.

"Of course," he said. "Things are bound to change when you wed, especially concerning my mother." He paused. "I appreciate you telling me."

The quiet descended and grew burdensome.

"Have you told Stephen yet?"

"No. I planned to talk to him first, but I saw you on my way to do so and decided I should let you know."

"Are you giving your notice then?"

"I'm not exactly sure." She stared at her lap. "I'll have to discuss it with Stephen, determine the length of our engagement, and whether or not I'll continue my employment with you during that time." She realized she'd be discussing many things with Stephen in the coming days, perhaps even intimate things. The thought should have caused her cheeks to redden, the blush of the jittery bride-to-be. Instead she felt a lump, solid as clay, settle in her chest. She lifted her head to find John's eyes on her. Something in his gaze made her heart ache. *Ask me, John. . .ask me if I love him.*

But he didn't.

There seemed nothing else to say then. With unsteady hands, Millie gathered up her skirt and took her leave.

♥

Millie didn't go to Stephen's house right away—she was prevented by Beatrice, who informed her that Katherine was awake and asking for her.

The woman's demands kept Millie occupied until nightfall.

In the starlight, she walked up to Stephen's house and unlatched the white picket gate. She glanced up and saw that he was sitting on the porch swing, a long-barreled gun in his lap and an oil-stained rod in his hands. Even in the shadows, she could see the gem-like, blue-green hue of his eyes as he watched her climb the steps.

He scooted over to make room for her on the swing. "Come to help me clean my rifle?"

She shook her head and sat down beside him.

The stillness of the night was broken only by a wolf howling in the distance.

Abruptly she took in a long gulp of air and met his gaze. "Yes," she said, her voice shaky.

He raised his brows.

"Yes," she repeated. "I will marry you."

He covered the tip of the rod with a rag and slid it into the barrel. "Are you sure?"

"Yes," she said yet again. And yet again, she fought the heavy-as-clay lump in her chest.

"I'm glad." He pulled the rod out and pushed it back in, busying himself with cleaning the gun. He made no move to touch her, for which she was thankful.

They sat quietly for a time, not talking, just sharing the starry night with the wolves.

Everything will be all right, she told herself. She rehearsed the words until she was nearer to believing them.

Chapter Twenty-Four

A carpet of damp leaves muffled the sound of hoofbeats in the paddock. John leaned against the rail and watched Night Hawk canter fluidly in a circle at the trainer's commands. The stallion had arrived last week by rail, along with John's other horses from Pennsylvania. Their presence made it almost impossible for him to stay away from the newly constructed stables. He loved hearing the snorts rising from delicate flared nostrils in the coldest hours of dawn. He loved the scent of hay in the cribs, the honeyed grain in the wooden troughs.

For days, John had carefully observed the trainer at work. So far, the man seemed competent. He didn't spook the horses with sharp tones or bewilder them with conflicting commands.

"Well, you think he'll do?"

John stiffened at the familiar-sounding voice. He glanced over and saw Stephen approach up the narrow path. John moved over so his brother could join him at the rail. He was sure Stephen hadn't come to discuss horses or their trainers. *He's here to announce his engagement to Millie.* Oh, but John was already aware of it. His mother had told him last night, after it was made official. And he'd realized that as long as he resided in her house, he couldn't escape Millie's presence. Being with her, but not being *with* her. Last night, he'd thrown a jumble of clothes and other necessities into a trunk and moved into his skeletal hotel.

Now he wondered if he might have been just as eager to distance himself from Stephen as Millie. His brother's very presence irritated him. *What is it he wanted to know, anyway? Oh yes, the trainer.* "The man seems capable enough. He has a soft voice and light touch. A good horse can be ruined by rough handling."

Stephen nodded and rested his arms on the rail. Together they watched as the trainer slowed the stallion to a walk and led him toward the stables, beyond which were a cluster of slender white aspens. Farther still loomed the rooftops of town, smoke drifting up from chimneys and birds darting about from gables to front porch eaves. The town made a charming backdrop to John's new white outbuildings and matching fences. He couldn't help feeling his chest expand as he surveyed it all.

Stephen, who'd been looking about too, gave a low whistle. "Worth every bit of the pittance we paid for it. Didn't I tell you?"

Yes, you're brilliant, Stephen. John worked to remain pleasant. "You were right. So far, the hotel is proving to be quite a venture."

"Of course, it's impossible to know for sure if it'll be a success before the grand opening. But I just knew there was something here." Stephen winked. "It's fortunate that I know how to recognize a good thing when I see it, eh?"

John suspected that his brother wasn't talking only about investments. But he refused to be goaded into a conversation about Millie. "I thought perhaps you might be about to say, 'I admire what you've accomplished here, John.' Or perhaps, 'My, what excellent progress you've made in my absence.'" He couldn't help emphasizing the last word a little.

Stephen's manner was deceptively casual. "Oh, but I did come to thank you. At least, I presume it's you I must thank for the change I noticed in a certain young woman. When I arrived home last month, Millie seemed. . .different. And based on our history, I'd supposed she might be keener to wed me."

John felt his control slipping away. "She *is* keen. That's why she's marrying you, you imbecile."

Stephen shrugged. "I gather you've heard the joyful news then. Last week I telegrammed the nurse I found for Mother, and she agreed to come in the spring, once she completes her term of service in her current position. The wedding is set to take place soon after that."

A bitter gall rose in John's mouth. "Congratulations."

Stephen gazed out at the paddock. Finally he spoke in a musing tone. "It almost seems as if something might have been said—something to make Millie reluctant to marry the same fellow she was once eager to elope with."

John nearly exploded. "Oh, something was said, all right, Stephen. Something rather like, 'My brother has changed, Miss Cooper. He's not the same man who walked out on his children. He's proved that by coming home, taking responsibility for his actions.'" His knuckles were white on the rail. "And I sincerely hope he won't make a liar of me." He paused. "I didn't say that last part to her."

Stephen held up both hands. "I believe you—I believe you. I just needed to know for sure." He looked at John strangely.

John realized he was practically panting and took a calming breath. When his composure returned, he felt his whole body sag. "You really thought I would derail your chance at happiness, didn't you?"

Stephen hesitated. "Well, you must admit, the past being my only indicator. . ."

John willed himself not to retort.

"But you do seem a bit overly agitated." Stephen gave him a long look. "Are you sure there's nothing more you'd like to tell me?"

"I don't know what you mean," John lied. *If I tell him, it's bound to end badly.*

"What's eating at you?" Stephen's question was met with silence. He began plucking at a loose splinter on the rail. "Did something happen between you and Millie? You know, while I was away?"

John didn't answer.

Stephen spoke again, his voice deadly quiet. "If there's something I should know, brother, I'd be grateful if you'd come out and say it."

But John hedged. "You came looking for me, not the other way around."

"Yes, I did—to tell you personally of a change ahead for our family. I was trying to be fair to you."

Suddenly John could endure no more. "Fair? You think it fair to leave in the middle of the night, saddling me with the family you abandoned?"

"A family you forced on me." Stephen clamped his mouth shut and said no more. His jaw worked, clenching and unclenching.

The two brothers stared at each other in bitter silence.

"I didn't mean that," Stephen said at last.

"Didn't you though?"

"Not about Florence and the children. *You*, on the other hand, I still think are a—"

"I wouldn't finish that sentence." But John wasn't so sure he could best his brother in a brawl, now that they were grown. Stephen stood two inches taller than him, his chest a bit thicker. And regardless, John didn't have the energy to go to battle with his brother. Nor did he wish to alienate the very person he'd often regretted not being close to. "I don't want to fight you." John leaned all the heavier on the rail and waited.

After a time, Stephen nodded. "I suppose I'll see you around then."

John watched him walk off, his temples pounding, his heart like lead inside him. The barrier between him and Stephen, always present, was more formidable than ever.

♥

Millie savored her bowl of steaming oyster soup and listened to the clink of Katherine's spoon across from her. The mistress of the house used to dine alone when John was away, the only human soul at the vast table, fifteen empty chairs around her. She'd share an occasional dinner with Stephen and Florence, but never the children, whom she regarded as too unruly for a formal meal. And she'd most certainly never dined with Millie.

Yet here I sit, at her table. It was one of several changes Katherine had instituted since learning of Millie and Stephen's engagement. She hadn't shirked her duty but displayed her acceptance of this soon-to-occur event. . .an event in which the fisherman's daughter became the wife of her second-born son. Though Millie still winced whenever she recalled those days of rejection as Katherine's new nurse, she also reminded herself that hurts—such as the one Katherine had endured from her unfaithful husband—sometimes created blindness.

"You're awfully quiet tonight, my dear."

Millie glanced up from her soup. "I'm sorry. It's been a tiring day."

Katherine made a disapproving sound. "That fiancé of yours has you at his beck and call, forever demanding your time."

Is she feeling neglected? Worse, did she have good reason to feel so? Millie looked Katherine up and down. A better than usual bloom of color filled the woman's thin cheeks, and her pale blue eyes contained a spark of health. *Or is it more a spark of curiosity—or even concern?* The latter, Millie decided. "It isn't Stephen's fault. We do have a wedding to plan, you know." She tilted her head. "Although, come to think of it, Ann is more of a help with that than he is." *And speaking of Ann. . .* Millie attempted to keep her voice casual. "Do you know, Stephen has asked Ann to remain in his employ after the wedding, as the children's nursemaid?"

"Oh?" Katherine reached for her wineglass and stared at Millie over the rim. "Sensible enough, isn't it? After all, Miss Murphy is very devoted to the children."

Is she hinting that I'm not devoted to the children too? Millie traced the leafy pattern of the tablecloth. Ann already lived at Stephen's house. She'd moved in when he brought the children back home to stay. *And he didn't even ask me what I thought about it.* Millie loved her friend, but she wasn't sure she would enjoy sharing her new home—the first home of her own—with another woman. She took pains in dolloping honey onto her roll, but Katherine wasn't fooled.

"You mustn't worry that Ann's presence will make the children love you less, my dear. You'll be a wonderful mother."

Will I? The task before her suddenly seemed mammoth in size. *I will be their mother.*

Katherine frowned at her suddenly. "Are you overexerting yourself lately?" When Millie didn't answer, the woman regarded her for several seconds. "How terribly alike you and my son are. Once you get it in your minds to see a task completed, you proceed doggedly to the end."

Millie tore off a bite-sized piece of her roll. "Yes, Stephen is determined to finish building a larger crib for Violet this week. She climbs out of the one she has with ease."

"You mistake me." Katherine dabbed at the corners of her mouth with her napkin. "I was referring to John. Never have I known a man so possessed over a project as he is over that hotel. I've not even glimpsed him in weeks." She tapped her chin in thought. "In fact, I think it must have been about the time of your engagement, or thereabouts, when he became so scarce."

Millie's roll lodged in her throat. "Oh?"

"Have a drink, my girl. You're choking."

Millie complied, cheeks hot.

"I couldn't help wondering." Katherine's gaze was shrewd. "He's been so unaccountably absorbed in that hotel. Do you happen to know why?"

If I did, I wouldn't care to discuss it with his mother. Nor did Millie care to think about it herself. It only brought an ache inside her, an unsuitable yearning to see him.

She grew aware of the utter silence in the room.

"Millie?" Katherine asked softly. "Are you. . .quite happy?"

Millie managed to nod.

After a prolonged, searching look, Katherine began speaking of other things. But a troubled crease remained between her eyes.

Chapter Twenty-Five

*D*istracted by the book Ann had lent her, Millie lost track of time. She realized with a start that over an hour had passed since she'd last looked in on Katherine, whom she'd left embroidering in the parlor. *Goodness, I hope she's all right.*

Millie hurried downstairs and nearly passed the dining room without noticing that the woman herself was standing in the doorway. But the movement of a bony beckoning hand brought Millie to a halt.

"Look who joined me for dinner today." Katherine's face was beaming.

Millie followed the woman's pointed finger and saw John rising from the table.

Her heart forgot to propel blood to the rest of her body. Or at least it seemed to. *Is he thinner than before?* She watched as he came forward to join his mother in the doorway. The scent of woods after a rain assailed Millie's senses.

"Miss Cooper." He nodded.

Katherine shot him a scolding look. "We've taken to addressing her as Millie, John, when we're at home."

"Forgive me."

Millie was unsure if his apology was for his mother or for her. She only knew that she longed to be elsewhere.

Katherine looked back and forth between them, an odd glint in her eyes. "I regret that I must excuse myself, but I have something important to see to."

Don't you dare leave me alone with him.

But Katherine had already turned away. "I must go and speak to Mrs. Winters about dinner. We've had entirely too much pork recently. It's time for a change."

John practically snatched up his mother's arm. "I'll go with you then."

She disengaged herself. "Nonsense. You'll stay and tell Millie all about your hotel, since she missed our dinner." She walked off toward the entrance hall without a backward glance.

John gazed after her. He shoved his fingers into his hair and kept them buried there, like a dismayed little boy. Then slowly, he faced Millie with a sheepish smile. "It would seem my mother is determined to prod us onto more friendly terms, Miss Cooper."

Warmed by his bashful manner, Millie no longer felt like leaving. It didn't matter that this promised to be an awkward exchange. Didn't matter that she feared having nothing to say to him. Didn't even matter that he'd taken three steps backward into the dining room, as if she were a wasp seeking to sting her nearest victim. "In truth, I have been wondering how your work at the hotel is progressing."

He leaned against the table behind him. "The crew is nearing completion of the interior—I'm especially thankful they've finished the floor my room is on." He grinned. "The sound of hammer and saw from dawn to dusk doesn't create an ideal atmosphere for transacting business."

If you're weary of your current situation, you have a perfectly good study here at home. Not wishing to form an even worse wedge between them, she merely said, "And when do you expect to be ready to receive guests?"

"Not before late spring, I'm afraid. The roof is still pretty rough, and I hate to ask the men to work in the snow."

"Did you ever build stables, like you'd hoped?"

He brightened. "I did, yes. The horses have all but taken over the place."

In addition to his forest-like scent, she detected a clean, starchy smell, doubtless emanating from his suit. She knew from Sally that he liked his suits freshly starched and pressed in the mornings. "You must have built the stables before the first snowfall."

He nodded. "The crew worked like an army of ants once I told them my plan. The stables were erected, though unpainted and without all their shingles, by the time the horses arrived. They're whitewashed and fully roofed now, with almost as many stalls as the stable I boarded my horses at back east." Again, that sheepish smile appeared. "Which is probably more than you cared to have answered."

"No," she said without thinking. "I'd love to see it. Perhaps you'd show me sometime?"

A shadow stole into his eyes.

With dismay, she recalled the last time he'd shown her around the hotel. That kiss they'd shared still stood between them like a stone wall, derailing what might have become a friendship. For her, it was also a stark and disquieting contrast to the times she'd spent alone with Stephen. It unearthed misgivings she'd done her best to ignore. He'd kissed her, but only the briefest of dutiful kisses. He never lingered. *Why not? Am I not alluring enough?* Was there something unappealing about her?

I could ask for John's opinion.

The thought came unbidden. It was unthinkable. Disquieting. But it remained and grew in potency, and she couldn't be rid of its clinging clutches no matter how hard she tried.

"Speaking of the hotel," she said casually, "I can't help remembering that day you took me there. It's a terribly discomfiting topic, I know, but—" She paused at the shuttered reserve that arose in his eyes, closing him off from her like a slammed door. She gathered her courage and stammered on. "I t–trust you haven't—haven't forgotten what passed between us that day."

His nod was barely visible.

She forced the words past her suddenly dry lips. "Didn't I. . .do it right?"

♥

John thought surely she could hear the rapid thudding of his heartbeat. With everything he had, he longed to escape this room. But Millie stood in the doorway, blocking his exit. And he found that her vulnerability affected him in a way that he couldn't disregard. He glanced at her face and softened. *Stephen, Stephen, what have you done to make this woman so unsure of herself?* John knew he couldn't withhold the answer she needed to hear.

He made himself meet her eyes, his grin crooked. "Perhaps, Miss Cooper, if you'd had time to observe my sorry state after that particular lapse in good judgment on my part—risking your reputation, I mean— you'd be assured that you did a thorough job of. . .things."

Cheeks crimson, she stepped farther into the room, all too near to him. "I'm afraid I'm not very experienced at deciphering these matters."

Ah, then let me teach you. He sternly reminded himself that this woman was his brother's fiancée. "Have you considered that Stephen may be—hesitating—simply because you are?" It was a guess, but he was fairly certain it was a good one.

She shook her head.

"Maybe if you were a bit more. . .forthcoming with him, things would be different." Oh, how bitter the words tasted. *My brother, the luckiest man alive, left me to straighten out his mess once again.* And Stephen had unwisely created a seed of doubt in his fiancée. *His utterly captivating fiancée, who is a mere step away from me. . .*

John's expression must have betrayed his struggle, for Millie's breath caught. Her pupils grew. She leaned toward him, barely discernibly, but the action chased every sound, levelheaded thought from his mind. At that moment, while desperately fighting for control, he heard a voice from the doorway.

"I trust I'm not interrupting anything?"

John looked past Millie and saw Stephen entering the room, his gaze shifting from John to Millie, then back again.

Say something, you fool.

John's voice nearly cracked in an effort to keep it even. "Mother insisted I give your fiancée a report on how our newest venture is coming along. The hotel seems to be a topic of interest for the ladies of the house." He didn't even glance at Millie as he spoke. If she wanted to give her fiancé a more thorough explanation, that was her affair. His part was to excuse himself from this dreadful situation as quickly as possible. Which was easier in theory than in practice—leaving her nearly killed him.

But she'd chosen his brother twice now. It was time to surrender to that cold, miserable fact. So John left the room. He felt Stephen's gaze on him as he strode across the entrance hall, but he didn't look back.

♥

Fancy electric streetlamps shone from one side of the pathway, while on the other, the surface of the water reflected the golden gleams. Snowbanks rose high between the path and the houses of town. Beyond the banks, moonlit rooftops were blanketed with feet of snow.

The peaceful sight was like a painting of Bethlehem but couldn't succeed in soothing Millie's inner turmoil as she crunched along the hard-packed pathway beside Stephen. She didn't fear that he would do something drastic, like break off their engagement—she possessed a curious numbness about that. What she dreaded was the inevitable confrontation about to take place.

They walked along the water's edge in silence, Millie searching her mind for something to say. Stephen saved her the trouble.

"Perhaps you might explain the scene I just stumbled upon between you and my brother."

Her eyes were carefully innocent, though she doubted he could see them in the sheltering darkness. "What do you mean?"

"I think you know. And Millie, I saw what I saw."

Don't answer him directly. "What did you see?"

He shoved his hands into the pockets of his wool overcoat. "Let me make this simple for you. I saw my brother making eyes at my fiancée—and it looked for all the world like she wasn't doing a thing to discourage him. Rather the opposite, I'm afraid."

She knew then how useless it was to play games. His voice was altogether too aware. There'd be no pretending with him. And anyway, that wouldn't be honest, or fair. Still, she didn't respond right away but sought the words to express herself. *How can I explain something I don't understand?*

"It's been difficult," she said finally. "Being the second woman in your life. Following in such perfectly charming footsteps. Sometimes I can't tell if you truly wish to be my husband, or—"

"Was John about to kiss you?"

"I don't know," she answered truthfully.

"Has he done it before?"

She hesitated. "Yes," she whispered.

"After you and I were engaged?"

"*No.*"

He looked at her for a few seconds, gaze assessing. Then he shrugged. "That's all I needed to know." He resumed walking, this time toward home.

She hurried after him and fell into step beside him. "I've wondered how long it took you to fall in love with Florence once you were married." If she expected him to deny his devotion to the woman, she was to be disappointed.

"About a month."

His answer should have stung. And to be sure, Millie's hackles rose. "You forgot the girl from Nantucket so quickly?"

"I didn't forget her. That would have been easier. I removed her from my heart with a wrenching extraction I barely recovered from." He paused to circumvent a fallen log then continued down the path. "But that doesn't mean I didn't love Florence."

She walked swiftly to catch up with him. "How could you love us both at the same time?"

He stopped so abruptly she almost bumped into him. "After what I happened upon only this afternoon, you can ask that?"

She thought it wise to abandon the subject.

They walked on in silence for a while.

"I didn't mean to sound so severe," he said at last.

"No, I'm glad you loved her." It was true.

They'd nearly reached Stephen's front gate when Millie suddenly chuckled. "I suppose that locket you gave me really is mine now."

"Of course it is. Though I'm not sure what made you think of it." He exhaled slowly then smiled and inclined his head toward his mother's house. "Shall I see you home, milady?"

"No, but thank you. The children will be waiting for you to tuck them in. I know my own way back."

He stepped forward to give her the usual brief kiss on the cheek, but before he could, her hands came up to grasp the lapels of his coat. She pulled him to her and lifted her lips to his.

And for the first time in over seven years, Stephen Drexel kissed her. Really kissed her.

This was no peck on the cheek after a long absence. This was a real kiss.

But though she could feel the accelerated beat of his heart, and though the pressure of his lips was warm against hers, he wasn't the same old Stephen. Of course, he was bound to have changed. He was no longer tentative. No longer a boy. He'd certainly claimed what was his. Yet something was missing. Perhaps he could sense it, that she wasn't quite offering herself to him wholeheartedly.

She only hoped she could rectify that state of affairs before it was too late.

Chapter Twenty-Six

*M*illie stood before the mirror in the trunk room while Ann fitted the veil over her hair. Her everyday shoes of dull brown leather peeked out beneath the elegant white gown.

"My hair will look better than this on my wedding day." Millie attempted to smooth the rumpled strands then looked down at her feet in dismay. "And I'll be wearing different shoes."

"Of course you will," Ann soothed, winking. "We must employ our imaginations and visualize you as the glowing bride you'll be on that grand day."

The seamstress had just finished Millie's wedding dress after the final fitting last week. This was the first time she'd donned the entire ensemble—gown, white gloves, veil, prized Drexel family locket. Surely any feminine heart would comprehend the importance of such a moment. Ann certainly seemed to. As soon as she'd heard of the gown's arrival, she'd promptly left the children in the care of Tansy and hurried over to be at Millie's side.

Late afternoon sunlight streamed through the single window, illuminating the thousands of particles of dust that filled the musty room. Outside, the arrival of spring and a recent snowmelt had created rivulets of water that ran down the hillsides. These small streams made everything appear alive, awakening.

Millie glanced at the lavender-colored curtains at the window, a remnant of Violet's time in this room. Another such remnant stood in the corner. Somehow, the sight of that little cradle caused a pang within Millie. She remembered well the day she'd first laid the baby in it. Taking charge of Stephen's children after his disappearance had been no easy task, to be sure. But at least she'd known what was expected of her then. More importantly, she hadn't had time to think about anything beyond immediate concerns. *Nor did I face the terrifying prospect of standing before God and a crowd of witnesses, making an eternal covenant with the children's father.*

The thought made her feel like restless hummingbirds were flitting about in her stomach. The sensation wasn't new. It had begun around the time her engagement to Stephen was announced in the *Glenwood Echo.* An unnecessary proclamation, since everyone in town already knew about the approaching wedding. But that was the way things were done in the Drexels' world. *And isn't this what I've always wanted?* The very man who'd once asked her to elope with him under the cover of darkness was now proclaiming his intent to marry her, to anyone who would listen. The hopes of a poor fisherman's daughter were being more fully realized than she could have ever imagined. *But why do things have to be so complicated? Am I doing something wrong?*

Ann's voice pulled Millie from her distracted thoughts.

"Lift your hair up, would you?"

Millie did as asked, and Ann fastened the locket around her neck. Her friend rearranged the veil and gestured toward the mirror with a smile. "There. Have a look."

Despite Millie's less than tidy hair and drab shoes, she nearly gasped at the sight of her reflection. From tulle-crowned head to the hem of Brussels lace at her feet, she looked like a princess. The pearl-and-emerald-studded locket nestled against her throat, a costly and precious treasure. Sheer organza sleeves rustled about her upper arms, while her hands were fashionable in white kid gloves. The gown itself, sewn in graceful lines, formed a lovely silhouette, snug at the waist and belling softly outward.

Millie's rapt moment of admiration was brought to a halt by the wistfulness she saw on Ann's face in the mirror.

"You're positively beautiful, Millie."

Here I am, preening like a peacock, while my dearest friend longs to be married too. Specifically, to Reverend Warren. It was a topic that might cause more harm than good. *Still...*

"Ann," Millie began hesitantly then stopped and tried again. "Are you—are you truly glad, about being the children's nursemaid?"

Slowly Ann turned her gaze from Millie's reflection to Millie herself. "Why do you ask?"

Millie paused before forging ahead. "It's just that you've been so attached, ever since I've known you, to Rev—"

Ann shook her head, cheeks growing pink. "That's done with. I've finally been able to accept that Reverend Warren doesn't care for me in that way. He didn't say as much, but..." She smiled with seeming effort. "I'm sure you're relieved to hear it."

"I am." But a lurking shadow remained within Millie. *She doesn't look happy.* Through the mirror, she could see Ann kneeling to busy herself with the flowing white train on the floorboards.

Finally, her friend's hands stilled on the fabric, and she looked up. "Some time ago, Mr. Drexel—Stephen, not John—approached me about Reverend Warren. It was in the beginning of winter, I believe." Her blush deepened. "Apparently, he'd noticed that I was lovestruck with the man, and thought he ought to mention the matter to me."

Millie nearly groaned. *Stephen, what did you do?*

"He confronted me after church one afternoon." Ann's eyes were stricken, her voice a whisper. "He said he couldn't understand why I was still pining over a man who didn't truly appreciate me." She toyed with the hem of Millie's dress. "I flared up at him, and I'm afraid we had a dreadful quarrel."

Millie could easily envision the moment, could imagine Stephen's passionate nature getting the better of him. *Just as it did when he was a boy*. Or a young man on the verge of adulthood—besotted with a girl from Nantucket. The trouble was, Millie hadn't seen a hint of such passion from him since, other than that one kiss in the moonlight, and of course his tirade the day Florence died. *But that was different.*

Millie looked carefully at Ann. Beneath her friend's downcast eyes were dark circles, and her thin lips trembled. *Giving up Reverend Warren must have been so hard for her.* Or was it something else?

Not knowing what to think, Millie kept silent. After a time, Ann continued.

"Stephen repented well enough a few days later. By then, I'd had time to think about what he'd said. It caused me to see the wisdom in surrendering my affection for Reverend Warren to God." She released the gown abruptly and stood. "So you see? Nothing to worry about."

Millie simply nodded. But somewhere deep inside her, she remained troubled. Strangely, her worries had nothing to do with Ann's feelings for Reverend Louis Warren. What, pray tell, did they have to do with?

❤

Something isn't right. John gazed at the opulent hotel lobby, from the carved mahogany reception desk to the mural of an Italian vineyard on the opposite wall. Stare as he might, he couldn't detect anything amiss. The room sparkled, not a speck of dust on the furniture or wrinkle in the expensive Persian rugs. Still, he wasn't quite content.

He heard his brother's voice behind him.

"It's too cold."

John turned. "If you've come to ensure that my hotel meets your standards, you're too late. The crew is already disbanded. And it'll be warmer in here when the fire in the hearth is lit."

Stephen leaned against the doorframe. "The construction is flawless, brother. Well done. But if you'll heed my advice for the first—no, second—time in your life, you'll alter this room."

John laughed without humor. "When was the first time?"

Stephen didn't even hesitate. "When I told you that Mother didn't need a coachman."

And she hasn't, not yet. John kept his praise to himself. Stephen was looking especially fine today. His well-cut waistcoat emphasized his strong physique in a way sure to capture the attention of women, including his lovely fiancée. *He needs no affirmation.*

John indicated the room with a sweep of his hand. "What's the matter with it?"

"Nothing, if this was a Boston manor house."

"In a way, it is. I've marked wealthy easterners as our most likely patrons, residents of Boston included."

Stephen nodded. "Yes, precisely. Well-to-do guests from the East, possibly many of them ill. Ailing visitors are bound to be drawn by Colorado's fresh mountain air and our fair town's 'healing' hot spring. They might wish to feel invigorated by their surroundings, not coddled or confined." He looked about the room with a lift of his brows. "*This* is where they come to be so enlivened?" He shook his head and gave John a reproving look. "Let's give them a compelling reason to get well and come again, shall we?"

John thought about that, wanting to dismiss it, but also curious. "Such as?"

A hint of eagerness filled Stephen's eyes. "Create a sense of adventure. Rather than a stylish Italian villa, fashion the lobby after a hunting lodge. Replace the mahogany furniture with rustic items made of hand-peeled logs. Toss out the Persian carpets and cover the floors with bearskin rugs instead. Rather than the marble hearth, build one made of locally quarried stones. Hang antlers over it and place stuffed animals, such as elk, deer, buffalo, and wolves, throughout the lobby. Consider arranging books about hunting and fishing on a table by the hearth." He shrugged. "Such a room would bring me to life if I were feeling poorly."

John stood speechless for a moment. *Invite the wilderness indoors. Foster an adventurous atmosphere.* It was a wonderful idea. He only wished it had been his, and not his younger brother's. He refused to show his enthusiasm. "I'll think about it," was all he said.

The eagerness in Stephen's gaze dimmed.

John realized he should—no, needed—to say more. After their failed attempt at civility that day in the horse pasture, he and Stephen had rarely spoken to each other. *He couldn't have been overjoyed about the prospect of coming here.* John's forehead suddenly creased. *Why did he then?* It couldn't have been mere interest in the hotel.

John cleared his throat. "In truth, Stephen, your idea was worthy. And I do hope you'll plan on being at my side once I open for business. I could use a man who understands the minds of our patrons, a man who foresees their needs and tends to them promptly." A pounding began in his head. Had he really just asked Stephen to become his business partner? Into his mind flashed an image of their father paying bail to a disgruntled jailer for Stephen's release. *How many times did he get himself into scrapes? Neglect his obligations?*

For months, John had immersed himself in the inner workings of the hotel. As owner and chief administrator, he'd been responsible for every decision, but for once hadn't found his work a strain. If ever he needed a moment to sort through his thoughts, he'd venture outside. The wind and rain, trees and hoofbeats, would wash their calming flow over him. The trouble was, he had no one to share these moments with. He'd long been accustomed to relying on himself, but Millie had changed that. No longer could he simply dismiss the lonely void he felt inside.

Yet was he truly ready to surrender old prejudices, give his brother a chance to show himself useful? Worse, was he ready to relinquish the hard feelings he'd harbored toward Stephen on account of Millie? Though John's mind told him to do just that, his heart wouldn't listen.

"You're asking for my help, John?" Stephen clarified. "In an important family enterprise?"

John released a heavy, drawn-out breath. "I am."

Like a faint beam of sunlight, barely visible behind a cloud, a light began to shine in Stephen's eyes. But he said only, "I might give it some thought."

Well, what did I expect?

"But I didn't come here to discuss the hotel." Stephen avoided John's gaze and swallowed. More than once. "After the last time I was here, I wouldn't blame you for declining. But I came to ask you to be my best man. There's no one I'd rather have."

John had difficulty answering. His brother was asking him to be. . .a brother. *Just say it, you coward.* Still he remained voiceless. He sent up a prayer for help.

"I'd be honored," he said finally.

Chapter Twenty-Seven

reathe, just breathe.

Millie tried without success to calm herself as she pinned on the headdress that completed her outfit. Soon she must leave for the church, where Stephen awaited her arrival in his immaculate tailcoat and white bow tie. In the driveway, a team of horses stood ready, hitched to a bell-strung carriage. She felt as though every one of those bells clanged and clamored in her mind.

She needed Ann, but her friend had gone to the church to help the servants prepare the meal for the reception. Tasked with unloading crates of crab soufflé, chilled cucumber soup, golden loaves of bread, and more, Ann would scarcely have time to change clothes before the ceremony.

What about Mrs. Drexel? Is she dressed yet? Won't this cold spring wind trouble her lungs?

But Katherine wasn't Millie's concern anymore. The new nurse saw to the woman's needs now. *I'm the daughter-in-law, not the nurse.* Or would be, after today.

The notion seemed suddenly laughable. Millie fought the wave of hysteria that welled within her. Was she really about to marry into this highborn family? *No. No! I'm a Cooper, not a Drexel.* To her core, she was a sun-browned Nantucket girl, the daughter of a humble fisherman and his wife.

Neither of whom were here now.

Her father's absence was less noticeable than her mother's. Dr. Murphy had agreed to fill a father's role, promising to walk her down the aisle.

Down the aisle to Stephen.

Millie forced herself to breathe again. She looked around her bedroom and tried to quiet her thoughts. Prolonged seconds passed. *Last night was my last night in this room.* She'd hated it at first, but her feelings had changed. A cream-colored patchwork quilt had replaced the red paisley bedspread, and pale pink blossoms graced the walls instead of garish posies. Both improvements had been made at Katherine's insistence.

Millie gazed at her reflection in the mirror. *Ann certainly did beautiful work on this headdress.* Her friend had surprised her yesterday by coming by with the veil, which she'd secretly taken to embellish it.

It crowned Millie's head now, a splendid creation of orange blossoms and pearls, pinned over her coiffed hair. The veil and gown flowed to the floor. Her wedding slippers, white kid with satin ribbons to match her gloves, were barely visible beneath the hem.

Millie stood poised and radiant, the glowing bride. But something wasn't quite right. She looked, she felt, incomplete.

A daughter should be with her mother on her wedding day.

Millie could no more stop the knot from forming in her throat than she could stop the wind from blowing. *If you can see me now, Mama, I hope you're happy.* But her thoughts were met by a cold silence that tightened the invisible cords around her heart.

A knock on the door was a welcome intrusion. She turned and saw Katherine stealing into the room, her blue velvet dress a perfect foil for her fair skin and titian curls. The woman took a few steps toward Millie, glanced up, and halted abruptly. Her hand went to her heart, her eyes enormous.

"My dear girl! You're lovely, simply lovely."

The weight in Millie's chest eased a little. She struck a cheeky pose, arms held gracefully outward, fingertips extended. "So you think I'll do?"

Katherine nodded, voice awestruck. "My son won't be able to find his wits when he sees you, nor his head if it weren't attached."

Won't he? Millie curbed her panic and focused on Katherine, whose tone turned soft.

"Your mother would be so proud."

Millie's eyes misted. She could hardly see.

"Oh, will you look at me?" Katherine wiped her damp cheeks impatiently and emitted a wobbly chuckle. "I truly didn't come to impede your progress." She held out a sparkling silver bracelet. "I came to give you this."

Millie opened her palm and caught her breath at the sight of dozens of tiny diamonds winking up at her.

"I wore it on my wedding day," Katherine said. "Rena wore it on hers. I'd be honored if you would wear it too, Millie Cooper."

Somehow Millie managed to see through her mist well enough to fasten the bracelet around her wrist. The task completed, she met Katherine's eyes. What she saw there vanquished the last of her hesitations—hesitations she'd known ever since meeting this wispy, indomitable, sharp-tongued woman.

"Thank you," Millie whispered. And she found herself enfolded in Katherine Drexel's arms. She stood frozen a few seconds then carefully returned the woman's embrace. In that moment, Millie realized that she wasn't entirely without a mother today, after all.

How she longed to revel in the comfort of the arms around her, to forget that there was a church filled with guests, eager for the bride to appear. A preacher ready to perform a ceremony. A groom awaiting her arrival. *Engaged women get married, that's what they must do.*

Slowly, reluctantly, Millie loosened her hold and straightened.

Katherine gave her a final, bracing squeeze.

Millie gathered her ethereal skirt into her gloved hand and glided out the door.

♥

When she saw John in the entrance hall, Millie stopped short. So did her entourage. She was now being trailed by Katherine, the new nurse, and a few straggling servants who hadn't left for the church yet.

"Hello, John," she said.

Was it her imagination, or did the look he gave her seem. . .defenseless? Witless? He gulped, as though trying to swallow an apple whole. His voice, when it finally emerged, sounded choked. "You look beautiful."

She thought she said thank you, but she wasn't sure.

Sally reached for her elbow and prodded her toward the door. Millie went along dazedly, unable to feel her legs or the floor beneath her.

♥

John sat alone beside the hearth in the drawing room, an orange blossom cradled in his hands. It had fallen from Millie's veil in the entrance hall, but he'd been too stupefied, struck numb by her beauty, to offer it back to her.

He stared down at the flower, but all he saw was Millie. It was impossible to dispel the image of her, clothed in the radiant sweetness of a thousand ages. He'd always loved her, even when she was a dirt-smudged child and he a painfully reticent teenager. He'd loved her later too, the faithful nurse of his demanding mother, the sacrificial caretaker of his nieces and nephew. But John couldn't—or rather shouldn't—love her now, his brother's glowing bride.

God help me.

He tried desperately to focus on the task before him. To force his limbs to bear him up. To stand to his feet. He knew he'd be late if he didn't hurry. He'd instructed Sally to ask Tom to return for him after driving Millie and the others to church. The young man was likely waiting for him outside even now. *And if I were Stephen, I wouldn't delay the ceremony for the best man.* For anything, for that matter.

He should go. He'd given his word. He was expected at the church, at his brother's side.

But his body would not obey his commands.

While he sat struggling, he heard a noise in the entrance hall. Someone was passing by.

That someone stopped in the doorway and glanced into the room.

It was Beatrice. He hardly recognized her without her maid's attire. She was dressed in wedding-day finery, some wine-colored frock and matching hat. She looked at the orange blossom he held, and an awareness slowly dawned on her face.

He imagined the pitiful sight he must make, shadowed by the cold marble hearth, head bowed, lone blossom cupped in his hands.

Beatrice regarded him with tilted head. "Do you know why I'm here, sir?"

He shook his head.

"I was at the church, lighting the last of the candles for the ceremony, when your mother rushed up and informed me that Miss Cooper was frantic. It would seem she'd forgotten her locket, left it on the dresser in her bedroom. I assured your mother I'd retrieve it."

This tale was not a consoling one. John could still picture the terrible moment when he'd found that locket, tucked in Millie's beloved Bible. *It's fitting, I suppose, that she'd wear Stephen's gift on the day she weds him.*

Beatrice continued. "Before I left, your mother told me that Miss Cooper had recently confided in her about the locket. Apparently, Miss Cooper had kept it for years, as a reminder of her own mother. Just before she came west, her father gave her a beautiful, raven lock of her mother's hair. She put it in the locket, where it fit perfectly. She's kept it there ever since. At least, that's what your mother told me."

John could feel his heartbeat quicken. Had he been wrong? Was it really possible that Millie had been treasuring her mother's memory, and not her romance with Stephen?

"Of course, I understood," Beatrice went on, "how a girl might wish to have that token of her mother's love with her on her wedding day." A timid sincerity shone from the maid's eyes. "I'm no expert at such things, but it seems to me there must be more to Miss Cooper's panic than a missing necklace."

John's heartbeat thumped rapidly now. He could hear Beatrice's voice, but distantly, as though it came from someplace far away.

"I've seen the way she looks at you, sir. And I know it isn't my place to say so. . .but I'd hate to see her marry the wrong man."

He was vaguely aware of the maid softly retreating and departing.

For a long while, he just sat there and gazed alternately at the empty hearth and the single blossom in his hands, but he saw neither.

Her mother died when she was a child. I remember, it happened sometime the year before we bought the cottage. She told Stephen, and he told me.

Stephen was a comfort to her, I'll wager.

Stephen deserves her.

That last thought brought a pang, but with a mighty effort, John swept it aside—along with every last remaining prick of conscience. For the first time since finding that infernal locket in Millie's bedroom, he dared to hope. If a kitchen maid's judgment could be trusted, he just might have a chance with the woman he loved. And he wasn't about to let his confounded, virtuous qualms stand in the way.

His mind centered on the locket again. He could take it to her. Not Beatrice, him.

Beatrice knew right where it was. She probably already fetched it and went out to the carriage. Was she even now alighting the conveyance that would whisk her and the locket off to the church?

John rose from his chair and hurried out to the entrance hall. He crossed to the front window and drew back the curtain.

Stephen's loyal coachman Jay, with Beatrice as his lone passenger, was driving the team at a fast clip away from the house. The carriage was about to disappear down the lane.

Tom was nowhere to be seen. *Sally must not have relayed my message.* Or Tom had misunderstood, or—

John flung open the front door and tore down the porch steps. He raced down the lane after the departing horses.

"Wait!" he cried.

But the churning of wheels, the jingle of the harness, and the *clip-clop* of hooves drowned out his voice, his racing footsteps. The carriage rumbled on and became a distant dot on the horizon.

John stopped in the middle of the lane and put his hands on his knees, panting. After a moment, he took out his pocket watch and glanced at it. He groaned. The wedding was supposed to have begun a full minute ago. His heart sank until he reminded himself that Millie was waiting for the locket. *And I happen to own a very fast horse.*

Without another moment's pause, he took off down the lane toward the hotel. If he stopped there first, he could saddle Night Hawk and speed to the church much more quickly. With any luck, he'd arrive before the ceremony started, intercept Beatrice at the door, and claim the locket. Beyond that, he had no ideas. Other than that he would give the locket to Millie. Tell her he loved her.

The distance between his mother's house and the hotel had never seemed so long. The roads, a series of humble dirt lanes, became clouds of dust beneath his pounding feet. The sun hid behind the clouds, reappeared, and then did so again. The wind blew hard enough to chill him.

He sped on.

He arrived at the hotel out of breath and burst through the double doors of the stable.

"Lenny, saddle my horse!" he called as he ran.

Lenny Cowen, the young groom, was bumbling in every respect but one. He knew how to saddle a horse faster than any man John had ever seen.

The instant Lenny finished knotting the cinch around Night Hawk's girth, John snatched the reins, flung them over the horse's neck, and mounted.

With a flick of the reins and an intently spoken command, he rode out the stable doors.

The houses of town blurred by. Clothes hanging on lines and cultivated rows of flowers danced in the wind. Night Hawk's breakneck pace made that chilly breeze come at John like an Arctic blast. Perspiration stung his eyes. Hoofbeats drummed in his ears. With every pulsation, he heard Beatrice's words. *"I'd hate to see her marry the wrong man. . .hate to see her marry the wrong man. . .hate to see her marry the wrong man. . ."* He leaned forward and urged Night Hawk on.

The bell tower was the first thing he saw when he approached the church. The pristine white steeple rose into the sky as though reaching toward God in heaven. Next he noticed the carriages, traps, and farm wagons crowded in the front drive. They spilled out into the churchyard and the field beyond. He craned his neck to try and see among them. He'd nearly given up hope when he spotted a wine-colored dress between two of the wagons. *Beatrice.*

John pulled Night Hawk to a halt at the last available hitching post, jumped to the ground, and tossed the reins over the post. He jogged across the lawn, weaving between carriages, calling out her name.

She glanced up and paused.

"I'll take it to her," he managed to say between pants.

Oddly, Beatrice didn't ask what he meant, simply pulled the locket from her reticule and gave it to him. She left him panting there, but just before she entered the church, she looked back with a conspiring little grin.

He clutched the locket and hastened forward.

He mounted the steps two at a time but stopped when the bells began to ring. The chimes pealed through the air, heralded the glorious linking of two lives. Marked the beginning of something altogether joyous and wonderful.

This is my brother's wedding. I'm his best man.

John stood there, utterly still on the stairs. Those bells had caused him to fully realize what he was about to do. He sunk his head into his hands. "What about Stephen?" he said, to no one. Beatrice had already gone inside. *How can I be about to do this to my own brother?*

He couldn't.

Could he?

Oh God, she's getting married today. Tell me what to do.

Miraculously, a thought stole into his mind and brought with it a measure of peace. Perhaps even a subtle shift in his plan might—just might—make a difference. *But it's risky. What if it doesn't work?*

Risky or not, it was right.

Yes, he'd do it. He'd change that one small detail.

He wouldn't give the locket to Millie—he'd give it to Stephen.

Chapter Twenty-Eight

The church, John saw with dismay, was filled to overflowing. The residents of Glenwood Springs had come by the droves to celebrate the blessed event, dressed in their Sunday best. Mothers sneaked sugary morsels to restless toddlers; fathers gave stern looks to whispering children. As a whole, the crowd beamed in anticipation. Their gazes centered on the front, where Stephen stood waiting for his bride to appear. *He's an Adonis in tails and a bow tie.* John's own suit was crumpled, damp with perspiration. Somewhere along the way, the buttons had flown off and his tie had come undone. He had no wish to know what the wind had done to his hair.

He'd missed his cue, rehearsed last night. When the organist struck the transitioning chord, he was supposed to have escorted Ann down the aisle.

Yet there she already stood on the platform, on the opposite side as Stephen, the minister between them. *Am I imagining things, or do the maid of honor and the groom look unnaturally pale today?*

But John had more urgent matters on his mind. Keenly feeling the presence of so many onlookers, yet knowing he would regret it for the rest of his life if he didn't act, he stepped out into the center aisle.

No. . .no.

He quickly retracted his step and changed his course. The side aisle would be better.

He hurried along beside the row of stained glass windows toward the front. Though he moved as quietly as possible, the crowd twisted toward him as one. He proceeded on until he'd reached Stephen's side. He summoned his courage and turned to face the curious onlookers, shoulders squared.

"You're late," Stephen whispered.

There wasn't any time to lose. "Is she still waiting for the locket?" John whispered back.

Stephen stared at him blankly then shook his head. "No, she decided to carry on without it."

There *really* wasn't time to lose. John slipped the golden piece of jewelry into Stephen's hand.

"I'm in love with Millie."

There. He'd said it. Fairly blurted it out.

Please, please dear God, let him truly hear me. Truly understand.

His confession seemed louder than the organ's strains, but based on Stephen's reaction—and the lack of any reaction at all from the crowd—the words had reached his brother's ears, and his alone. *Or perhaps Ann heard it too.* The maid of honor's gaze had jerked toward him, shock in her eyes. Reverend Warren looked pleasantly out at the crowd, as ministers were wont to look.

The silence probably lasted only a few seconds, but it was an eternity to John.

"Are you mad?" Stephen hissed. "I'm getting married, in a matter of minut—"

"Yes," John cut in, sure he might burst if he didn't admit it. "Yes, Stephen. I'm mad. Mad for her." He needed to communicate that truth. "I'm hers, if ever she could want me. Wholly hers." He felt worse than when he'd run the entire way to the hotel stables. His lungs cried for air, though he stood in perfect repose. It was doubtless due to the fact that there was something else he must say—something stealing all his air. "Only—only I can't ask you to step aside. Not in good conscience." He drew an unsteady breath, aware of the onlookers. Thankfully, they still seemed oblivious. "That is, unless—unless. . ." Another deep breath. "Stephen, if there's a part of you, even a small part, that knows you don't feel for her what I do, then I'm trusting you to give me back that locket. If you don't, well. . ." He looked in the opposite direction, unwilling for his brother to see the sheen in his eyes. It was no longer his decision to make. All he could do was pray, which he certainly did.

Especially when Dr. Murphy appeared at the back of the church, the bride on his arm.

♥

The crowd rose to its feet and turned to gaze in admiration at Millie. She couldn't distinguish one person from another. It was a sea of faceless figures, a swirl of color, women's springtime poplins mixed with the browns and grays of men's suits. The aisle seemed to stretch on and on. It narrowed, that long path she must tread, until it reached the minister, Ann, Stephen. . .John.

John stood out in sharp focus. She felt the force of his blue-eyed gaze across the length of the church.

Music from the pipes swelled. The prolonged strains signaled the beginning of Millie's march down the aisle. She heard it, must have stepped forward, but this reality was more a dream, one she'd fallen into and kept dreaming, though she tried to awaken. *I need my locket. I still don't have my locket.*

But she found herself walking slowly, steadily, beside Dr. Murphy toward the front of the church.

They arrived. The organ fell silent. The minister said something. A question. Something about who it was that was giving her to Stephen this day. Dr. Murphy answered it.

A tiny shiver of alarm coursed through Millie when her hand was transferred from the doctor's grasp into Stephen's.

Stephen led her up the steps. She noticed, without real awareness, that he looked ill. Like a white statue, with absolutely no blood in his face.

Oh God, awaken me. Or, if this isn't a dream, help me do whatever is expected of me.

They faced one another in preparation for their vows.

Vows are forever.

Suddenly, Millie awakened from her slumber. She knew, she knew, that she would be tied to this man forever, after today. And it was as if, at the very thought, she'd somehow lost herself. No more was she Millie Cooper—and no more did she truly know who Millie Cooper was.

Nearly giving herself whiplash, she looked in desperation toward the doors at the back of the church. How those doors beckoned her. *There's still time. I could still flee.* They hadn't spoken their vows yet.

But she was stuck, more surely than if the wooden floor beneath her were made of sinking sand. She couldn't move. She saw Katherine standing in the front row, fingers clutching her silken handkerchief in a death grip. *What does she have to be so nervous about?*

The minister asked the crowd to be seated, and they complied. "Marriage," he began, "is a sacred institution, a covenant ordained by our gracious Lord. In it we find that mystery, that unfathomable union between Christ and His Church." He opened his Bible. "In Ephesians chapter five, we read. . ." He went on. And on and on.

Somewhere in the lengthy oration, Stephen's grasp tightened on hers. *Is he hanging on to keep himself from falling?*

The minister arrived at a pause.

In that pause, Stephen turned—pale to his colorless lips—and looked at John.

John handed him something. *Or did Stephen give John something?* The exchange was made quickly, a blur.

Reverend Warren's pleasant smile faded. He leaned in close to Stephen and whispered, "We haven't gotten to the rings just yet."

"I know," Stephen answered.

The minister stared at him for an instant without blinking. Then he recovered and expanded his chest in a noteworthy manner, obviously the launch of something important. "Do you, Stephen Hammond Drexel, take this woman—"

"No."

But it wasn't Stephen who spoke.

It was John.

That single, intruding, wonderful, infuriating word came from John. He stepped forward and rubbed a shaking hand over his jaw. "He can't take her as his wife, Reverend Warren, because I can't let him."

Millie heard the gasps from the crowd above the roaring in her ears. She also heard a slow exhale and glanced back at Ann, whose eyes slid shut as though some constrained tension within her had taken flight. In the front row Katherine too appeared slowly liberated, her fingers easing their clutching hold on her handkerchief.

But preeminent in Millie's consciousness was one thought. It loomed larger than her misgivings, the doubts about who she was, who she'd become after wedding Stephen today. Even stronger than her impulse to flee was this one indignant thought: *Is John truly preventing Stephen from marrying me again?*

The temper of her Irish forefathers rose up in full measure. Millie temporarily forgot the crowd. She looked past Stephen and glared daggers at John. "You would keep your brother from marrying me a second time? On my wedding day?"

He flinched but said only, "This has nothing to do with him."

She laughed a brittle laugh. "Doesn't it?"

Stephen shifted his weight backward, a withdrawing from his bride, a pulling away. Though his retreat was subtle, it was enough to gain Millie's attention—and cause her dismay. *Don't you dare jilt me, Stephen Drexel. Not again. Not in front of all these people.* There were so many eyes on her. Tears threatened, and she longed to sink through the floorboards.

"Perhaps you'd better hear him out," Stephen suggested gently. "A man who makes a fool of himself in public—and looking worse than a derailed train—is surely in earnest."

Millie glanced at John. His face was haggard. His clothes might have been trampled by a herd of cattle, so rumpled they were. As for his hair, it was a russet-colored mess.

"I wanted to give you something, Millie." He opened his palm.

She saw her locket nestled there.

"I found this last autumn in your mother's Bible, after we. . ." His cheeks reddened. "Er, suffice it to say, I found it last autumn. Ever since then, I've wondered—" He broke off. His gaze darted toward the crowd, then back to her, pleading. "Couldn't we talk somewhere else?"

Reverend Warren shut his Bible. Plainly, this well-ordered ceremony was ruined. The crowd started murmuring, a buzzing sound that swept through the church and filled the air clear up to the rafters.

This cannot be happening.

But it was. Millie reached for the locket, and John readily surrendered it. Its solid gold weight in her hand couldn't have been more real. Nor could his gaze, warm upon her for an instant. But she felt powerless to think past the many murmuring voices, the many scandalized faces. Powerless to withstand the strain she felt, wrought during night after sleepless night that led to this day.

"I can't do this," she whispered. She turned blindly and swept past her too-silent groom, the limp minister, and the stricken best man.

When she reached the aisle, she began to run.

Chapter Twenty-Nine

John hurried after Millie, descending the platform so quickly he nearly stumbled and fell. He flung back what he hoped was an apology to Reverend Warren. . .and to Stephen. He'd brought his brother's wedding to a halt; the least he could do was say that he was sorry.

But what he was most sorry about was how he'd botched things with Millie.

He found her in the backyard of the church. She stood in the shade of a cottonwood tree, her face in her hands. The wind had stopped. The sun's rays brought out the scents of the bud-covered brambles that grew over the fence, and the earthy aromas of grass and wild plants mingled with the fragrance of orange blossoms in Millie's hair.

For a moment, he just stood there and watched her sob. *Dear Lord, does she want to marry Stephen so badly?* All his former optimism, ignited when Beatrice told him the truth about the locket, was being snuffed out. *She won't even look at me.* Yet he knew she must be aware of his presence. He stood no more than five feet from her.

"I can mend this," he told her softly. He pointed toward the front of the church. "I'll go right back in there and tell everyone I made a mistake. Tell Stephen that nothing occurred out here, that nothing ever really has occurred between us—"

She lowered her hands to her sides, fists clenched. "Don't you see that it doesn't matter?"

He was thankful she'd uncovered her face so he could see her, even if she would barely meet his eyes. "I'm not sure I understand."

She sniffed and didn't answer.

Again, he waved toward the church. "Aren't you crying because of what happened in there?"

She shook her head. "No. Well, not only that." A spark lit her eyes, turning them a dangerous golden shade. "Of course I was mortified. Who wouldn't be?" Fresh tears dampened her lashes. "Imagine being all but discarded, seen as unwanted, at the altar in front of everyone."

It isn't my fault that Stephen didn't fight for you. But wasn't it? Anyway, he couldn't probe those depths now. He had no desire to hurt her further. "I'm sorry."

Her posture grew rigid. "Was I so wrong for your brother—so ill-suited to your family, that you felt you had to interfere?" Her tears fell in earnest now. *"Again?"*

Please don't cry. He stepped forward, but she backed away from him. Helpless, he remained at a distance. "Hear me." How could he make her understand? "You are not wrong for any man. You couldn't possibly be. Be he the king of England or the noblest of paupers, any man would be lucky to have you at his side."

"Then why?" she cried. "Why did you stop the wedding?"

Does she really wish to know? "Millie, you'll remember that I kissed you once." *A frank beginning.*

"And yet you say that nothing has ever occurred between us."

Why would that be troubling her? A vague hope infused him. Yet he hesitated. "Does it upset you, my saying that?"

She shrugged, still rigid. "No girl likes her kisses to be forgettable."

"Do I look as though I've forgotten?" He punctuated the words with a telling look.

She blushed. Her chest rose and fell in sharp little jerks. Her satin gown shimmered in the sunlight, hugging her waist and flaring out in a way that accentuated her figure. Her hands, though clinging to the satin fabric of her skirt, nonetheless denoted strength. *She has the hands of a true caretaker.* Her eyes, sometimes brave, sometimes passionate, were now filled with. . .invitation?

He wondered how he continued to breathe. One thing was sure, he'd been a fool to think he could keep away from her. He narrowed the chasm between them, grateful that she had nowhere to go with the fence behind her. "I only meant that nothing occurred between us that would prevent you and Stephen from being happy together." He might as well finish the story he began in the church, though he wasn't certain she'd wish to hear it. He folded his arms over his chest and inhaled deeply. "After we kissed in the hotel that day, I went into your bedroom to speak to Tom, who was repapering your walls. While I was there, I found the locket in your mother's Bible." A muscle tightened in his jaw. "I thought it evidence that you still loved Stephen."

There was silence.

"Why didn't you just ask me?" she whispered.

He shrugged, avoiding her gaze.

"Didn't—didn't you want me, John?" Her voice trembled.

"Oh, thunder and blazes, yes."

❤

Millie gaped up at him. It was a moment of revelation for her. The over-wrought emotions she'd felt earlier, the humiliation caused by her disrupted wedding ceremony, had faded. Her mind was clear, awake.

She loved this man.

No longer was she a starry-eyed girl in Nantucket, infatuated with her dashing young sweetheart. She was a woman. And as a woman, she loved John Drexel. Unkempt suit, dirty shoes, hair in disarray, and all. Loved the way he'd worked willingly alongside her, shared his ideas and goals with her. She even loved his reserved nature, although at times like these, she rued that very reticence. It just might be keeping him from her. *Rest assured, I want you too, John.*

Her expression must have communicated her desires well. He searched her gaze once...twice. Then he cupped her face in both hands and kissed her, no further hesitation. His palms trailed down her shoulders and found her waist. He drew her against him. His warm, expressive mouth revealed a thousand unspoken emotions.

The fence was behind her, but only John was before her. She could gladly die in his arms, but longed for the moment to last forever.

Her soft sigh told him so.

But with a suddenness that made her reel, he drew away from her. He backed up until he stood several feet away. "Please, don't toy with me."

She did her best to sort through her befuddled thoughts. *Toy with him?* How could he possibly think such a thing? Then she realized that she hadn't actually told him how she felt about him. Smiling softly, she moved forward and boldly reached up to straighten his tie. "My, how haphazard this tie is—"

He grabbed her wrists gently. "It's hopeless," he muttered. "Truly. Don't bother. I'm a mess." He looked over the top of her head at the distant hills but didn't let her go. "Are you going to marry my brother?"

"No."

He murmured, "I've had eyes for you since Nantucket, you know."

The words fell upon her like liquid honey.

He continued to gaze over her head. "That night when you came to meet Stephen, it was all I could do to keep my jaw from dropping. I hadn't seen you in some time, you see, and it was plain as day that you were no longer a child. Your transformation nearly knocked the wits from me. But even that was nothing compared to those soulful, tearful eyes." He shuddered. "If I could have seen my way clear to do it, I'd have tossed my family to the fates and comforted you properly. The trouble was, I knew I had no ability to do so. You see, I'd seen the disappointment on your face when you realized I wasn't Stephen."

A look you'll never see again, I promise. She yearned to rest her head against his chest. It was home, his embrace, his heartbeat thudding against her cheek. She was safe there. Whole. Fully herself, while at the same time, fully his.

But he doesn't know that.

She spoke quietly. "When I first saw you in Dr. Murphy's office, that day you asked me to be your mother's nurse, I hated the way my pulse started to race. I wanted so badly to despise you, but my traitorous heart sped like a galloping horse just at the sight of you—the sight, John."

He swallowed but didn't meet her gaze.

"And then, when we spoke in your study, the night before you left for Leadville to visit the mines, I couldn't think. Couldn't breathe. Your irksome, heavenly scent—like the woods after a rain—was so. . ." Abashed, she couldn't go on.

A boyish grin fought its way into his eyes.

She called upon her flagging bravery. "You and I grew closer, after Stephen left, when you came home to help with the children. Being with you, talking and working together, seemed so right. I began heeding that instinct that had whispered to me all along, telling me I could trust you, that you wouldn't hurt me." Her lips trembled. "But I think I understand now, about the locket, and why you drew away from me." She was silent a moment then went on in a small voice, "Stephen did kiss me once, you know."

John just listened, his thumbs stroking her wrists.

"Well," she amended, "he kissed me once worth mentioning. And I hurt inside all the while, because John—" She choked on a sob. "He wasn't *you*."

At last he looked at her. She knew by the look in his eyes that he'd heard her, truly heard her. He spoke with a ghost of a smile.

"I believe you're trying to tell me that my ability to choose a tolerable cologne and have the good sense to kiss a woman as myself is superior to that of other men."

She emitted a half-cry, half-laugh. "Why, yes." She sniffed and wiped her tears. "That's exactly what I'm trying to say."

He reached up and touched her cheek. His mirth faded in the face of a tenderness that softened his every feature. "Well then, Millie Cooper,

I'll confess that I've lain awake nights, asking God to help me forget you." He slid his arms around her waist and cradled her close against him. "You've no idea how glad I am that the Almighty chose to ignore that particular request."

Oh, so am I. They stood there and held one another for an indiscernible length of time. Millie soaked in his nearness like a flower soaking up the sun's rays. The unmitigated joy of having arrived at this moment washed over her again and again. *Thank You, dear Father.*

After a while, she drew back, reluctantly enlarging the space between them. "I really should go and speak to the minister. To Stephen." She started to move toward the church but glanced back at him shyly. "What shall I tell them?"

He reached for her hand and pulled her back into his arms. "Nothing. If they have the wherewithal to recognize a man in love, they've surmised the truth by now." He focused on her mouth and slowly, slowly lowered his head. He paused, lips hovering over hers.

Millie caught her breath. Though he was smiling, that blue gaze of his left no doubt about his intentions, or the depth of his passion for her.

"If they come looking for us," he said huskily, "you can inform them that you're otherwise engaged."

And then he kissed her. Quite thoroughly.

Epilogue

Six months later

*T*he whole family, minus the one person Millie most wished was present, gathered in Katherine's dining room on the eve of another wedding.

The table was laid with fine china and polished silver cutlery. Flaming candelabras and cream-colored bouquets of roses served as centerpieces. Gilt-edged menus stood on elegant golden stands beside each plate. Despite the formality of the occasion, the mood in the room was jovial. *It couldn't help but be, with the children present.* Millie hid her amusement as she watched Katherine look suspiciously at her grandchildren yet again, as though she was sure disaster was forthcoming. *I'm surprised she permitted them at the table, even for such a special occasion.*

Millie joined in the laughter around her, but moments later, stared down at her plate to hide her eyes. How she missed John! She sipped her rich wine, nibbled the crispy edges of her glazed duck, and tried to think of something besides her new husband.

It would seem that the Drexel family has fared well here in Colorado. She glanced at each face in the room, softened by the flickering light of so many candles. With the hotel booked solid all week, Stephen appeared to be on top of the world. He'd proved to have a knack for managing the guests, even the most difficult to please among them. According to John, scowls were soon transformed into smiles under his brother's charming supervision. The grand opening three months ago had been a success, and the steady stream of business ever since had convinced John to sell the estate in Philadelphia and take his chances here in the West. He'd been in Philadelphia for three weeks now, making arrangements for the sale of the estate and shipment of family heirlooms back to Glenwood Springs. He was due home tomorrow.

It's good that Dr. Murphy and I have been so busy lately. Millie was once again a fixture at her mentor's side. It was an odd role for a married woman to take, but Millie wasn't afraid to be odd. Not when there were needful tasks to be done. It fulfilled something deep inside her, being out among her neighbors and friends again, nursing them through their trials and rejoicing over their triumphs. John had approved of her return to her former position, his pride in her work obvious. He'd even bought a house near the doctor's office so she could be close by in case of emergencies. With its potbellied stove and yellow gingham curtains, it reminded her of a storybook cottage. Katherine considered it a "primitive, backward hovel," and nearly had a conniption when she learned that her son and his bride planned to live there. But Millie, armed with all her old zeal once more, had refused to relent. Her tenacity was rewarded. She felt more at home there, tucked snugly with John in the heart of this valiant little mountain town, than any place she'd ever been.

Katherine's health was faring well, or as near to it as could be expected. More often than not, she appeared rosy-cheeked and alert. She occasionally employed the sharper edge of her tongue when addressing her new nurse, but the no-nonsense, broad-bosomed Chicago native seemed to carry on her duties as staunchly and good-naturedly as ever.

The children were minding their manners at long last, as evidenced today by even young Charlie's "please pass" when he wanted a particular dish. Lucy, eyes shining, sat as close as possible to Ann, who held the thriving Violet in her lap. . .and who would become their new mother tomorrow.

Which, undoubtedly, is the real reason Stephen cannot stop smiling.

He sat with his arm across the back of his fiancée's chair, conversing easily with his soon-to-be father-in-law, seated across from him. As solicitous as Stephen was of the good Dr. Murphy, his fair-haired betrothed scarcely had to murmur a soft remark in his direction, and he was all attention. He seemed ever aware of her nearness, always sending heated little glances at her.

Millie sighed. Stephen's glances bore a keen resemblance to those of his brother. *Come home soon, darling.*

She well remembered the day Ann had told her the news. Biting her nails in a most uncharacteristic fashion, her friend announced that Stephen had asked her father's permission to court her.

Why am I surprised? Millie remembered thinking. The pieces fit seamlessly. She couldn't imagine how she'd failed to put them together before.

When Millie had assured Ann that she was delighted for them both, her friend erupted into tears.

"I was so worried," she sobbed. "So sure you'd think that Stephen and I were carrying on, somehow acting improperly during your engagement—so afraid you'd think I'd behaved as the worst of friends."

Millie had shaken her head firmly. "Not when I know you, Ann Murphy."

Ann bit her nail one final time. "I must confess that I—that I cared for him, even then."

Millie acknowledged the words with a look she hoped was reassuring. "And he cared for you in return." It wasn't a question.

Ann's tears reemerged. "We never said anything, but somehow we both knew. Millie, I'm so sorry."

"You've nothing to be sorry for."

That resolved, Ann dried her tears and told the story of how Stephen came to her one night, two months after his and Millie's almost-wedding.

He threw pebbles up at Ann's window like a schoolboy, careful not to awaken her father. She opened the window and saw him standing there in the moonlight, clearly fatigued, his wrinkled nightshirt untucked and hanging out over his belt. With his head craned upward at an awkward angle to see her through the tree branches, he told her that he hadn't eaten or slept in days. That he didn't see how he could go on living without her, and would she please come down so he didn't give his neck a permanent injury?

Of course, Ann had complied.

Never, never had Millie seen her friend so happy as she'd been since courting Stephen. Their engagement was brief due to his eagerness to marry her. *She'll be the perfect mother to the children and the ideal wife for Stephen.*

Millie heaved another sigh. She'd had such a short time to practice being the ideal wife to her own husband. She'd been tempted to accompany him to Philadelphia, and was certainly invited to. Just before he'd left, he kissed her no less than five times and repeated his invitation over and over. But she'd felt obligated to stay and help Ann with wedding preparations. *After all, she assisted me with not one, but two weddings.*

The day Millie and John were married, it rained. This was especially troublesome since they'd chosen to be wed on the hotel grounds, their sanctuary the fragrant glory of the outdoors. Buckets and buckets of rain sheeted down from stormy clouds all around the canvas canopy, hastily erected by the hotel's former building crew and several helpful townspeople. Then, just when the bride and groom began speaking their vows, a shimmer of color appeared in the clouds. John never saw it, he said, but for a fleeting moment, Millie was certain she beheld the faintest of rainbows in the sky.

Oh, it was definitely still raining. The sun wasn't shining in the least. But it was as if God Himself was assuring her that He would remain at her side throughout all of life's storms. . .and that sometimes, He'd even bid the wind and waves be still. She'd known that if she had it to do over again—and doubtless she would, as storms had a purpose of their own that sunshine couldn't hope to accomplish—she'd choose to trust her Lord. He'd taken her on a choppy, blustery voyage that ended, not with sunshine, but with a rainbow. A promise. One she'd heard before, but hadn't dared to believe.

"I will be with you, your troubles to bless."

Standing in the pouring rain under that canopy, Millie had finally believed it.

Tears invaded her eyes at the memory. *How gracious You have been to me, dear Father.*

Her prayer of thanksgiving was interrupted by a noise in the doorway, followed by a quiet "Ahem."

It was *his* voice.

They came flooding back to her, another deluge of memories, accompanied by a kaleidoscope of vivid sensations. She was taken to that moment, over two years ago, when she'd stood in the stairwell at Dr. Murphy's office and heard the rich timbre of that very voice. She'd grappled with confusion, uncertain where she'd heard it before, but at the same time, certain she had. Her current emotions were so similar to those she'd experienced then, she wondered how she hadn't known. Hadn't understood that John had always been the man for her. A beautiful truth her mind refused to recognize, but her heart couldn't deny.

Just as it had before, Millie's pulse leaped at the sound of his voice. Her breath came to a halt in her throat. She twisted around, her entire focus on the man in the doorway. Only this time, the sight of John Drexel didn't shatter her confidence or cause a brick-like weight in her chest. This time, she felt like the most treasured woman in the world.

You came home early, she mouthed.

He nodded.

The knowledge that he'd missed her as much as she missed him filled Millie with gladness. She was vaguely conscious that the bantering conversation and clinking of silverware had stilled as the others noticed John standing there too. He, however, didn't seem the least aware of them.

Katherine turned and addressed Tom, who'd been serving the meal. "Please do set my son a place at the table, Tom."

The servant hurried to obey, and John wasted no time in claiming his seat next to Millie. As he sat down beside her, she inhaled his scent of dampened forests.

"Hello," he greeted her in a low voice. Without pause, he reached for her hand under the table and threaded his fingers through hers.

She glanced at him, nerves tingling. *Why does that coppery stubble on his jaw always make him seem so dangerously handsome?*

He winked at her.

She flushed hotly, still unaccustomed to being married. She'd marveled at the freedom of knowing someone so fully, of being wholly known in return. All barriers removed, her imperfections laid bare, and yet he was in awe of her. But it was still so new.

With obvious effort, John turned his attention to Ann and Stephen. "You're to be congratulated, both of you." He spoke to Ann specifically, his tone teasing. "You, Miss Murphy, are a kind and generous-hearted woman for taking pity on this poor, bedraggled brother of mine. And saying yes to his equally poor proposal—or so I hear."

The bride-to-be smiled and murmured something demure, and the hum of voices continued around Millie. She didn't hear a word of it. Her every sense was trained on the movement of John's fingers, lightly stroking her palm.

He leaned close to her. "I never knew three weeks could be an eternity." He took a bite of duck and nodded at something Dr. Murphy said. "If my wife will speak to me," he whispered in her ear, "I might admit to sleeping bolt upright on the train rather than stopping at hotels at night, so I could get here faster."

Millie's tongue finally loosened. "You seem a stranger tonight, for some reason."

His eyes kindled, two lit flames. "I'd love nothing more than to remind you that I'm not."

Before she had a chance to respond, Stephen interrupted them, grinning at John like the rogue he was. "Do you intend to sit there gawking at your bride all evening, brother, or will you kindly help the rest of us plan tomorrow's grand event?"

John looked momentarily confused. "Um, yes. . ." His expression cleared, and he returned Stephen's grin, his own broad as a barn. "That is, yes to the first part."

And to Millie's delight, her husband kept his promise.

Rebecca Jepson is a homebody who loves a good book, a cup of freshly ground coffee, and all things autumn. She is the author of *A Highbrow Hoodwink*, a novella included in the ECPA bestseller *The Lassoed by Marriage Romance Collection*. In addition to writing, she works as a paralegal and volunteers in various ministries at her church. She lives in Reno, Nevada, with her husband, Mike.

Read the series! How many have you read?

My Heart Belongs

My Heart Belongs in Fort Bliss, Texas

My Heart Belongs in the Superstition Mountains

My Heart Belongs in Ruby City, Idaho

My Heart Belongs on Mackinac Island

My Heart Belongs in the Shenandoah Valley

My Heart Belongs in Castle Gate, Utah

My Heart Belongs in Niagara Falls, New York

My Heart Belongs in San Francisco, California

☑ My Heart Belongs in Glenwood Springs, Colorado

My Heart Belongs in Galveston, Texas (July 2018)

My Heart Belongs in Gettysburg, Pennsylvania (November 2018)

Read More about the Series at
MyHeartBelongs.com

BARBOUR
PUBLISHING

Coming Next in the Series. . .

My Heart Belongs in Galveston, Texas
(July 2018)
Dodging bullets takes a simple missing person case to a new level as Jonah Cahill, a Pinkerton agent, and Madeline Latour, an investigative reporter, form a tentative truce in Galveston, Texas, 1880. Are they on to a much bigger story when their key witness is suddenly kidnapped?

Paperback / 978-1-68322-500-3 / $12.99

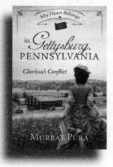

My Heart Belongs in Gettysburg, Pennsylvania
(November 2018)
Clarissa Avery Ross has everything a young woman could dream of including the undying devotion of the handsome Kyle Forrester. But she never dreamed a war would take the love of her life away from her. And she never dared hope the war would bring him back again in the summer of 1863.

Paperback / 978-1-68322-740-3 / $12.99